T0365667

THE UNTOLD STORY OF MANY A HEIWULEI CHILD

THE UNTOLD STORY OF MANY A HEIWULEI CHILD

XIAOMEI SUN

Archway Publishing books may be ordered through booksellers or by contacting:

Archway Publishing
1663 Liberty Drive
Bloomington, IN 47403
www.archwaypublishing.com
844-669-3957

ISBN: 978-1-6657-6840-5 (sc)
ISBN: 978-1-6657-6841-2 (hc)
ISBN: 978-1-6657-6839-9 (e)

Library of Congress Control Number: 2024924415

Print information available on the last page.

Archway Publishing rev. date: 04/02/2025

To the young man who was executed in Beijing on the 5th of March 1970 for writing an article against the *heiwulei* policy.

Heiwulei means five black categories, referring initially to the five groups of so-called class enemies (landlords, wealthy farmers, counterrevolutionaries, bad elements, and rightists) and later exclusively to their children.

AUTHOR'S NOTE

About six years ago I called the university I had attended back in China. Upon hearing I wanted an explanation for the way my 1982 graduation was handled, the male voice at the other end cleared his throat and told me I sounded angry. "Angry? I'm not, just need an explanation," groaned I. "Happened long time ago, let it go," said he before hanging up.

I have long tried to let it go, well aware of possible mental and physical harms caused by holding onto a grievance. But the truth of the matter is that it won't go. After so many years of trying hard, I have sort of concluded that my time as a *heiwulei* cannot be just left behind or moved on from, especially when it started so early in my life and lasted so well beyond my childhood. I have to tell it first, so I started to write.

While writing, I couldn't help but notice just how easy it had been to become an enemy in those days. In my case, I was just a second grader when I first learned I was an enemy because my father was a counterrevolutionary. At the time, even though I had no idea what my father had done to be an enemy, I knew counterrevolutionaries were the worst of all enemies because they often got executed. The moment I was being dragged out my elementary classroom for not answering a question about my father, I really wished I had been dead! Once the Cultural Revolution started, I couldn't go anywhere without being identified as a *heiwulei*. At the age of 12, I thought about hanging myself since so many *heiwulei* adults had done just that. I lived only because my mother kept telling me she needed me.

It wasn't hard for my mother to become an enemy either. All my mother did was to fall in love with a fellow college student who always had the best grades and marry him after graduation. When my father was arrested as a counterrevolutionary, my mother was urged by some to get a divorce. As far as I know, my mother never contemplated it. Some 14 years later, it was me who asked my mother to divorce my father and then marry a proletarian worker or a revolutionary soldier, not once but many times. Every time my mother just turned her head away and ignored me. My mother thought about drowning herself on the day she was brutally assaulted by a group of Red Guards. She didn't because I, her youngest child, still needed her as she later told me. For sure my mother and I saved each other's lives.

It wasn't any harder at all for my father to become an enemy. To be specific, my father was a historical counterrevolutionary, meaning he did something counterrevolutionary only before the 1949 liberation. What he actually did was that he joined the Quomindang or the Chinese Nationalist Party after graduating from college. "Why did he? So stupid," screamed I upon learning why he was a historical counterrevolutionary. "Well, your father admired the founding father of the Guomindang," explained my mother as if it was no big deal.

What really made me mad at my father was his total abandonment of not only himself but also his family. My father never said anything about his years in prison, but he was more dead than alive after being released. Then he simply left us; he simply went back to his hometown along the Yangzi River, where he taught small kids who knew just his last name. He did return some 18 years later, an old man who seldom spoke a word.

Also while writing, I came to realize the wounds from my *hei-wulei* days were still raw even after so many years. I found myself hesitant to get near where they were, which explains why I chose to write a fiction in the first place. I wrote a fiction also because I couldn't be accurate or specific about actual events and didn't feel comfortable with revealing names or locations.

Nevertheless, being as truthful or real as possible was the standard I strove for in writing *The Untold Story* of *Many a Heiwulei Child*. Based on what I had experienced or witnessed as a child, the story doesn't just go into great details about how a *heiwulei* child grew up but also places a lengthy focus on a school system that carried out policies against *heiwulei* children through concrete measures, specific programs, and routine school or classroom activities.

English is my second language. I didn't start to learn the English alphabet until I was almost 15 years old during the Cultural Revolution. Even though I have studied as much as I can, read as much as I can, memorized as much as I can, and practiced as much as I can, I simply cannot write in English the way a native English writer does. Being a grammarian in the English language can only help write correctly but doesn't really help write like a native. I have to come to grips with the fact that I will always speak with a foreign accent and write non-natively. So, forgive me for any awkward use of the English language in *The Untold Story of Many* a *Heiwulei Child*.

Today I'm done with writing *the Untold Story of Many a*

Heiwulei Child, and I'm also done with trying to get an explanation for anything that happened to me as a *heiwulei*. But I'm not done with hoping. If I still hoped a little back then, I have no reason not to continue to hope a little now. Since 1988, my little hope has always been: What happened then won't happen again.

CHAPTER 1

I toddled along a river that didn't seem to flow. Mama, not far behind, swayed to catch up with me. When she did, she turned me around to look westward. Where the sun was setting, what resembled a firebird had formed with its orange plumage fluttering upward like flames. For a moment I felt like a bird too, for Mama had propped my chin up and stretched my arms out, creating a silhouette. I giggled, my eyes sparkling with two birds, one in each.

As suddenly as the firebird appeared, it vanished with all its splendor. As if having lost my other self, I cried and cried like never before.

"Don't cry, it's there, always there," assured Mama, wiping off my tears.

"Always there?" asked I.

"Always even when you don't see it," reassured Mama.

On the way home, Mama and I passed by a man playing an *erhu* that didn't have a head and one of the two pegs. Was that really music? It sounded more like deep wounds. I shuddered, covering this ear and that ear with this hand and that hand. It wouldn't go away, though. It lingered, and it lingered on. But so did what I saw in the western sky that evening. It was there, and it was always there.

CHAPTER 2

On the backwall was a wooden board. Whenever I looked at it, it looked back blankly as if not in a mood. Never did it seem to be anything more until one day I noticed its uneven surface. Getting on my small stool, I groped, touching off a cascade of dust only to reveal a blossom that had large petals. The curvier a petal, the dustier it was, I concluded while stepping off the stool.

One morning when Mama couldn't open the front window, she came to the backwall and began to slide the wooden board. Right there a window appeared, through which a cloudy sky looked so far and so wide. Before Mama could leave, an excited me carrying my small stool had arrived, eager to see what was out there.

Out there was an alley quietly winding its way from one direction to the other. Also out there was a man sweeping. The broom he was using was like the one I used when I was sweeping. No wonder he had to bend so much, and no wonder he seemed of my height. He was sweeping toward me, he was sweeping past me, and he was sweeping away from me. As he was passing me, I sang something, but he kept sweeping as if not hearing me at all. Looking neither as young as my older brother nor as old as the grandpa living two gates away, he was an uncle. And he wore eyeglasses.

"Eyeglasses, the sweeping uncle wears eyeglasses," gushed I.

"He does, he used to teach," said Mama, seeming to know who he was.

That day on, I changed what I did in the morning. After some thin porridge, I would step on my small stool and slide open the back window to catch a glimpse of the uncle who was sweeping. He was always out there unless it was raining. Not once was he not. He was sweeping toward me, past me, and away from me. The sound of his sweeping was like that of the northern wind blowing autumn leaves off trees.

One time I stayed a little longer than the sweeping uncle to count what I could see. To my right, leaning against a low wall were two trees knocking each other's head. As I was trying to count clouds above, they quickly sailed into gigantic three. Further down to my left loomed just one city gate shrouded in a haze.

"Come down to get some paste for me," said Mama, who was making *gebei* at her *gebei* board. Within her hands' reach were some rags next to a bowl of paste. Once Mama pasted out a spot on the board, she would press a rag right there. The same step was repeated over and over again until the entire board was covered with two layers of rags. Then Mama would peel the sheet off, take it outside, and slap it on a wall to dry.

Stored under my older sister's bed were lots of rags, which were not picked up from street corners but bought from a junkman. Whenever he came, he would tell the same story that his rags belonged to a time when only emperors wore clothes. While Mama just grinned, I was the one who would pore over a rag, trying to figure out who was its original supreme wearer even though I couldn't name any.

"Did you hear me? Get some paste for me," said Mama again.

But the first thing I did after getting off my small stool was to open the door. As soon as a slant of daylight shot in, a fly was heard buzzing. Having circled around Mama several times, it landed on her back.

"Don't move," yelled I, holding the shoe removed from my right foot as a swatter. The fly obviously had sensed what was coming. Before I struck down, it took off with a you-cannot-catch-me groan.

"Told you to get some paste from the wok," said Mama。

"Where is the wok?" asked I, looking around.

"Behind the door, I put it there," replied Mama.

"Not there," said I.

"Not there? Aiya, must have left it on the stove," murmured Mama, patting her forehead with her sticky right hand. "Let me get it. Don't want you to get near that stove!"

Getting up, Mama first put her hands on her lower back before standing straight. She limped to the stove outside the door and limped back carrying the wok.

For a reason I didn't know, Mama wouldn't let me help with making *gebei*. Only once a month did I get to sort rags: bigger ones for vamp *gebei* and smaller ones for sole *gebei*. Also once a month Mama would take all the *gebei* she had made to a shoe factory. As far as I was concerned, it was the day I would get a candy. The size of my thumb, it often lasted for days.

CHAPTER 3

Across the yard lived Xiaoxiao, the girl I played with. Even though she was one year older, we were often mistaken as twin sisters, which I completely understood since we looked so much alike. Once together we would either chase around or dig dirt in a corner to the great displeasure of our mamas. Not once but many times did they say to each other we two didn't behave like girls. To be honest, neither Xiaoxiao nor I knew what that really meant.

"Let's go to play," said Xiaoxiao, popping her head through the door as I was eating my lunch, a steamed potato.

"Windy outside, play here," said Mama. But I was already on the other side of the threshold.

Once we reached the gate, Xiaoxiao pulled up my right sleeve and took a bite off the potato in my hand. Before I had time to say anything, what was left of my potato was gone.

"Sour mustard, salty turnip," hollered a man selling pickles. As he came near us, he stared, perhaps wondering if we were sent out to buy from him.

Xiaoxiao tilted her head and smiled. Charmed, the man curled up the corners of his mouth to smile back. At that moment Xiaoxiao held out a hand and said, "Give me a pickle."

The man was taken back, scratching his head as if to let loose an idea. Determined to get a free pickle, Xiaoxiao wouldn't withdraw her hand. With a sigh, the man poked in one of the two jars on his cart before handing over a tiny one.

Xiaoxiao snatched it and fled, leaving me to stand there by myself. "Come here," Xiaoxiao called behind a tree. When both of us squatted down, she gave me a wink and unfolded her right hand. She didn't take a bite. She just sucked several times before holding the pickle to me. "Ate your potato, it's yours," said she. I licked, nipped, and then pushed it back to her, not feeling very good about how she got it. "Aiya, worry too much," said Xiaoxiao, giving me a haughty look and thrusting the whole thing into her mouth.

We hobbled to our usual playground, an empty lot at the far end of the alley. Half hidden in a bank of dry weeds and drifted debris was a shallow cave where the land grandpa was said to have been residing. Neither Xiaoxiao nor I had any idea why the land grandpa didn't get a larger place for himself. It was Mama who, when asked, told me that he didn't need to, always out and about inspecting his real estate. He even turned cross-eyed for doing his job. The place was also where Xiaoxiao and I would say to each other what we would never say to anyone else.

I crawled in first, followed by Xiaoxiao. Side by side with dirt all around and falling, we talked.

"I'm him," said Xiaoxiao, referring to the land grandpa.

"… ok," agreed I, not sure what that meant.

"You're my woman," continued Xiaoxiao.

"… ok," agreed I again, not sure what that meant either.

"We have a baby, I'm baba," went on Xiaoxiao, peeking into her overshirt pocket. "Your baba, where is your baba?"

"My baba? Don't have baba," stammered I, having never heard about such a *ren* or person in my life.

"Here, my baba," said Xiaoxiao, showing me a photo that had only the face of a man wearing eyeglasses.

"Used to teach," said I.

"You know?" asked a surprised Xiaoxiao.

"Eyeglasses, his eyeglasses," said I.

"My mama told me about my baba. He and my mama made two babies, he used to teach, now is in a labor camp," mumbled Xiaoxiao, giving the photo a long lick before returning it to her overshirt pocket.

"Everyone has a baba?" asked I.

"Of course, everyone has a baba and a mama," said Xiaoxiao with her usual confidence. Well, she was older and always knew more.

We rolled out and went where an elevated ground sloped to a plain that extended further down to a creek. With a twig held between my legs, I charged like a warrior on a horse, and so did Xiaoxiao. By the time we halted our loose feet, we were looking at the creek.

Had its water come from the sky, we would have dipped our hands in to wash off dirt. It came from a concrete pipe out of the wall of a factory. Its sleek surface glistened, and there was that acid smell. Xiaoxiao and I held our breath and retreated, glancing backward in fright.

"I see its back," Xiaoxiao whispered, referring to a dark creature said to be living at the bottom.

A boy from a neighboring alley had told a terrifying tale after losing his footing while playing with a friend along the water. Dragged underwater by the dark creature, he was tortured with fire.

He would have been eaten up had he not managed to grab the long stick his friend was holding out to him.

We were back on the slope again only to see two women on their knees scraping the ground. With sharp screeches, dirt splashed up out of their hands.

"Aunties, why you need dirt?" asked Xiaoxiao.

"Not dirt, it's salt soil," replied one woman.

"Salt? Don't see any," said I, thinking about crystals in a little jar at home.

"White stuff," said the same woman impatiently.

All of sudden I saw salt, a layer of fuzzy white shimmering like frost on the entire slope. Why didn't I bring some home? Mama wouldn't need to buy salt with money. I told Xiaoxiao my idea, and she was thinking the same. Each with a shard in hand, we kneeled behind the two women and scraped, the same way they were doing it.

It wasn't long before one of the two women took a glance at us and mumbled something to the other woman. Then both of them turned around to a sitting position to face us.

"Leave, this is our place. We have to fill up that handcart today," yelled one, pulling down the cloth over her face to her chin and pointing to a handcart nearby.

"How dare you! We have mouths to feed at home, go away," snarled the other. Then both glowered at us as if we were their archenemies.

Scared, we gathered our buttocks and left. We didn't go home, though. We moved to another side of the slope, where the two aunties couldn't see us, to continue to scrape.

When we got a small heap of salt soil, the sun was already sitting on distant roofs. It was time to go home, we said to each other.

Xiaoxiao got up, stepped out of her shoes, and filled them up. Two shoefuls weren't enough for me. I took off my overshirt, made it into a bag, and scooped in all the rest.

The moment I stumbled inside the door, Mama's mouth popped open. You looked a dirt devil, she scolded. I just had time to put down my overshirt before Mama pulled me over and started to whip a cloth at me.

"Where have you been? Told you not to go out, didn't listen. Look at you," muttered Mama through her teeth. She was clearly upset.

While I squeezed my eyes shut, Mama yanked the cloth in rhythm with dirt shooting off me like rays. I sniveled in pain whenever my hair was caught. Heart-hardened, Mama didn't stop until her arms were probably sore with exhaustion.

Mama then stuck a finger into the cloth and made a swab, which was thrust into this nostril and that nostril of mine, coming out a dirty smudge. Mama wasn't finished. She poured some water in the washbasin and pushed my head in. The water turned muddy instantly. Dabbing my hair, Mama noticed I didn't have my overshirt on.

"Where is it?" she asked.

"There, have brought salt," said I, pointing at the overshirt at the door. I was sure I had done a good deed.

"Salt? Where you got it?" asked Mama in disbelief.

I was more than eager to tell her the two aunties who scraped on the slope.

"Not salt," concluded Mama after hearing my story. The next thing I knew she took my overshirt and went outside. When she returned, she flapped it again and again before throwing it in the corner for dirty clothes.

Sitting on my small stool, I cried. Every speck of that soil had come from my hard work. Even though my hands hurt, I endured because I thought I was doing something good.

While I sighed my sighs, Xiaoxiao's shoes tumbled out of her door and landed in the middle of the yard, scattering white stuff along the way.

CHAPTER 4

A man wearing an octagonal hat had started to visit. Every time he came, Mama would let him sit in the only chair we had and serve him tea. If my old sister was home, she would pull me to the side, whispering to my ear something like "the cadre from the residential committee." The last time the cadre from the residential committee showed up was an early evening. Seeing him through the open door, Mama got up from her *gebei* board to greet him.

"Move out, must move out. We don't want *diren* to live here," yelled he as Mama invited him to have tea inside.

"What's *diren*?" asked I, turning to my sister. "Enemy, we're not *diren*," said my sister in a low voice, looking upset. "We're not *diren*," repeated I in an even lower voice, looking more upset than my sister. I had heard *huairen* or a bad person many times, but it was the first time I heard *diren*. As my sister told me, a *diren* often didn't get to live every long.

"*Diren*, you are *diren*, *diren* cannot live here," continued the cadre from the residential committee. Only when his voice started to sound hoarse, did he adjust his octagonal hat and swagger his way toward the gate.

Back in the room my brother and sister tried to prepare supper, which they usually wouldn't do. Mama was at her *gebei* board again. Although shaken, she was making another sheet of *gebei* while tears dribbling down the sides of her nose. I had never seen Mama crying like that. I held up the front of my overshirt, leaned over, and dabbed.

Xiaoxiao's mother glided in like a fairy. Her slightly rouged cheeks made her always look cheerful. She walked over to Mama and pulled her up from the *gebei* board. Together they went to sit at the table.

"I know you don't want to divorce. Tell you, life is easier after I did and moved here with my two girls to live with my own mother. Here is an idea, pay a visit to the Housing Management Bureau," she suggested, patting Mama's hands like an older sister.

"Have been there many times. They always say no place for someone like me," Mama said, shaking her head.

"Go there every day if you can. When you go there, bring your youngest child. They can't let a small child sleep on the street," continued Xiaoxiao's mother as Mama listened.

It started to rain before I went to bed, and it kept on raining. I knew when Mama got up and opened the door to place a washbasin on the stovetop, which she would always do whenever it rained like that. I knew when the rain stopped. I also knew when my brother and sister were talking. They weren't talking about what classes they were going to have that day, but about wearing shoes or not and rolling up their pants above the knees or not.

When I slipped off the bed, I came to the door only to see a pond swaying under a gloomy sky. On its surface rain was still dropping dimples.

"Send you a boat," shouted Xiaoxiao across the yard, paddling a sliver of thin wood in the water.

"Here is one for you," yelled I, taking out my paper-folded boat and placing it on the water. It couldn't move, though. Every time it was about to, raindrops stopped it right there.

Xiaoxiao's boat was beyond control. As she watched helplessly, it first circled as though in a daze and then floated into a hole in the surrounding wall. My boat never went anywhere. Once soaked, it sank.

Not until early afternoon did Mama and I head out for the Housing Management Bureau. I liked it when dirt turned into mud. Mud was in my shoes and squelched between my toes. Mud splashed onto my pantlegs, leaving stains after stains. Whenever Mama swung me across a puddle, I would giggle like being the happiest.

No one was in the office when Mama and I stepped inside a door on the left side. As we stood there, a woman cadre with short hair appeared from nowhere and said, "You again. I don't have a place for your family yet."

"I'm told to move out immediately," said Mama.

"Move out immediately? Get a divorce, maybe you won't need to move out," said the woman cadre.

"I have three children, here is my youngest," mumbled Mama, nudging me forward.

"Use children to get what you want, how old is she?" asked she, staring at me.

"Almost five," said Mama. "Too young to live on the street."

"The same age as my younger son. I have two sons, want a girl," said the woman cadre, staring at me again.

"I'm told our government cares about children," stressed Mama.

"Not your children. Even when you get a divorce, your children are still bad kind. You know that, don't you? Go, go home," urged the woman cadre.

"Divorce, what's divorce?" asked I as Mama and I walked out the Housing Management Bureau.

"You're too young, don't understand," said Mama, grabbing my right hand to go along. "You asked about baba the other day. When it's time, I'll tell you everything. But no matter what others say, remember we are *haoren*."

Haoren meant a good person. It wasn't mama. It was the word *haoren* Mama taught me to say first. For some time, I called Mama "*haoren*." I really did.

CHAPTER 5

Mama cooked sorghum flour noodle for supper, but my sister wasn't eating, sitting there with a frown decorating her forehead.

"What's the matter?" asked Mama, looking concerned.

"My stomach aches," sobbed my sister.

"Why didn't you tell me earlier?" Mama quickly rose to help her leave the table and get into bed.

Mama was before the stove again, where she made a bowl of soup with an egg. After the soup cooled a little, she started to feed my sister with a spoon.

"Dried haws ease stomachache, let me get some for her," offered my brother. After Mama nodded, he got a five-*fen* coin from our money jar and ran out of the door.

Left alone at the table, I wished it had been me that had a cramping stomach. I just didn't get sick, having never had even a sore throat. My sister, on the other hand, often had aches and pains. Every time she whined, she would get attention and eat food specially prepared for her. Afterwards, she would click her tongue, saying to me "Never get sick. I know why, you came from a rock."

I wanted to get sick too, so Mama would put her *gebei*-making aside and attend me as she had my sister. Time to time I drank rainwater on the ground and ate plaster off the wall, doing simply what Mama told me not to do, but nothing happened. Whenever I tried to knit my eyebrows as my sister always did when she was having pain, Mama would tell me to stop making faces because it was bad for a girl.

One night when it was time to go to bed, I removed my shirt but couldn't do the same with my pants fastened in the back.

"Cannot take off my pants," cried I.

"Ask your sister for help," said Mama, who was banking the stove outside the door.

"No, she is old enough to do it herself," mumbled my sister, combing her hair next to me.

"Not a good sister. Wait a minute, I'm coming," assured Mama.

By the time Mama came to me, I had been rubbing my eyes with my knuckles. She slapped down my hands and scolded, "Don't touch your eyes with dirty hands. How many times do I have to tell you?"

"They itch," murmured I, trying to put my hands back up there.

"Come here, let me have a look." Mama pulled me to the light and tilted my head to have a closer look. "This is what you get when you don't drink enough water. Too much internal heat," diagnosed Mama with confidence.

Since "heat" sounded the same with "fire," I started to image my body being a furnace with red flames raging inside. Nothing could be more horrifying, and I burst into tears.

"Don't cry like that. I can make it disappear," said Mama, holding me in her arms. After I calmed down, she took off my pants and put me in bed.

Then she looked on a shelf that had all our old bottles and broken jars. When she placed what she had found in a bowl, she filled the bowl with hot water and placed it gingerly on the stool next to the bed. As the steam curled upward, the dried chrysanthemum in the bowl slowly opened its petals to a full bloom with several thin slices of licorice root swelling little by little. Light fragrance permeated the air, and Mama looked like the fairy overseeing herbs. When the bowl became cool to the touch, Mama held it to my mouth. "Drink all of it, redness will go away," chanted she, her eyes filled with concern. I was satisfied; Mama was mine. With a warm stomach, I lied down and quickly fell asleep.

The next morning when I woke up, I couldn't open my eyes. My upper and lower eyelids were glued together by something scabby and sticky. I rubbed and poked with my fingers in vain. For a moment, I was seized with the fear that someone had sewed my eyelids together while I was sleeping. I started to kick my legs and howl at the top of my lungs.

Mama hurried over to the bed. Amused by my sealed eyes, she chuckled first but quickly placed a warm cloth on my eyes. A while later I gradually opened my eyes only to see Mama's alarmed face. My eyes were bloody red.

Mama panicked. She went to ask Xiaoxiao's maternal grandma to come over. Far-sighted, she leaned backward to have a closer look.

"Germs in there," croaked she without any hesitation.

"What should I do?" Mama asked anxiously.

"Salty water, wash her eyes with salty water," Xiaoxiao's grandma prescribed.

Mama sensed something more serious than what could be cured by salty water. As soon as Xiaoxiao's grandma left, she wrapped me up in an old bedsheet, squeezed me into the bamboo stroller that had long been too small for me, and took me to see a doctor.

It was a trip taking forever. When Mama pulled the sheet off me, we were inside a building. Before us a hallway had a ceiling so low that it seemed to lie on the floor toward the other end. Huddled up on either side were those waiting to be treated. Some groaned, and others coughed as Mama creaked the stroller through the narrow space in the middle.

Once we reached a corner, Mama went to a window to register. The young woman sitting behind the window looked up before looking down again as if Mama wasn't there.

"My daughter needs to see an eye doctor. Her eyes are red, please help," pleaded Mama.

"Help? I know who you are, why should I help *huairen* like you! Leave," insisted the young woman, who called Mama a bad person instead of giving help.

As I was telling myself we were not *huairen*, Mama was standing there stupefied. Then she yanked the stroller back into the hallway, where she asked a man where the department of ophthalmology was. He pointed at a door near the entrance through which we had come inside the building.

Crowded was the room with patients that had eye problems. Some crouched on the floor, while others leaned against the walls. Sitting at a desk in the furthest corner was a doctor in a white coat, and next to his stool was another stool for the patient he was seeing.

The doctor called a name, and a patient with gray hair slowly got up from the floor and fumbled his way to the desk. The moment he bumped into someone, a voice shouted, "You grow no eyes?" Lost in what to do, the old man kept nodding his head.

"Everybody, stay where you are, I go to you," yelled the doctor from his desk.

A small notepad in hand, the doctor went to the patient with gray hair first. He took a quick look at his eyes, said it was nothing, and let him go. Then he moved to the next patient. In a matter of minutes, the room was almost empty, and Mama and I even got to sit on a long stool near the door.

The doctor came before us. He flicked a strand of hair off my forehead with a finger and then started to play with my eyelids. His hand, so close to my eyes, was huge. I saw lines on his palm and dirt under his fingernails.

"Pink eyes," he said flatly.

"Serious?" Mama asked.

"Contagious, but some eye ointment will do," said he, scribbling in the notepad, tearing the page off, and handing it to Mama.

"Contagious?" disbelieved Mama.

"Your registration slip?" he asked.

"Don't have one. Went to register but… my daughter's eyes look really terrible," explained Mama.

"Must register first. How dare you," interrupted the doctor, trying to get the prescription back. Mama was quicker and tucked the prescription in her left sleeve.

"Someone calls the comrade in charge! Here is a woman who didn't register," hollered the doctor.

Thinking he was going to hurt Mama, I shut my eyes and started to scream. It was loud. Steps were heard running, and soon a small crowd gathered at the door.

"What's the matter?" inquired someone.

"She didn't register, call the comrade in charge," muttered the doctor.

"My daughter's eyes, I didn't mean…" stammered Mama, who just wanted to have my eyes treated and didn't expect something like that.

"Look at that little girl's eyes! Let her mother go, she did it for her daughter," shouted a woman.

"Let her mother go," echoed others.

The doctor seemed surprised, finding himself so alone on the issue. With a shrug of his shoulders, he walked back to his desk, where he began to search in a drawer as though looking for senses and then waved for us to leave. We didn't until Mama paid him the registration fee, three *fen* for a child.

Time no longer mattered. Dozing in and out, I had lost any track of it. Day and night no longer mattered. I could not tell the difference anyway with my eyes always closed. But I always knew when Mama came over. After the cloth covering my eyes was removed, her gentle fingers pushed apart my eyelids, and some ointment was squeezed in, cool and soothing. Mama murmured, "Don't touch your eyes. Try to sleep."

The window where I sang to the sweeping uncle was no longer reachable. Outside noises still could be heard but sounded so distant like in a dream. Sometime in the afternoon, there was sunlight coming in through the front window, which I could no longer catch with the tin cover of a *rendan* box and throw onto the opposite wall.

"Contagious," Mama warned my sister and brother, who started to move around like thieves and talk in whisper as if telling a secret.

I heard Xiaoxiao asking about me at the door, but Mama hushed her away. "Where are you? Are you dead? She is dead," shouted Xiaoxia before dashing back home.

It was then that I lost any desire ever to become sick again. "A dark place to be," I contemplated.

CHAPTER 6

"Cannot now, how about tomorrow?" said my sister when I asked about baba. As a matter of fact, it was Mama who I first asked, but she told me to wait until I got older. I had no idea why that was.

The next day was a Sunday. Sometime in the afternoon, my sister let an eager me sit with her, ready to tell what she knew but I didn't.

"Want to know baba? I can tell you, but try not to cry," said my sister with a straight face. "You don't have baba. Mama actually isn't your real mama. Listen, about five years ago, Mama went up a mountain to collect firewood and suddenly heard the cry of a baby. She looked around and saw a big rock that was opening up like a lotus flower. When the rock split into two, there in the center lay a baby girl. That was you! Mama tried to pick you up but couldn't, because your right buttock was stuck in a crevice. You have a birthmark there, do you know? It's from that."

Right there my sister paused, asking me to check it out, or I would never hear the rest of her story. Since I was reluctant, she pulled down my pants and pushed my right buttock further right, so I could see the mark. The size of a small egg, it was there indeed.

"The moment Mama lifted you, the rock started to close. When the two parts became one, it looked as though it had always been that way," continued my sister. "As Mama held you in the front of her shirt and walked down the mountain path, strange things happened. The reedpipe could be heard playing from the above with birds flying around, each with a jasmine flower in the beak. At the first turn, thunders rolled even though the sky was sunny, and near the second turn, a mute man started to burst out one word after another. Seeing a vendor at the end of the path, Mama weighed you in the pan of his steelyard, which read nine *jin*."

At the urge of my sister, I thanked Mama with a deep bow for having brought me home.

"What did you tell her? Not a good sister," scolded Mama.

"Had to tell her something," retorted my sister.

I kind of knew my sister had made the whole thing up, but because I liked it, for somewhile I was more than glad to tell whoever I had come from a rock.

CHAPTER 7

Summer went, and autumn came. Not until leaves were changing colors did Mama hear from the Housing Management Bureau. When Mama said we were moving, I cried. I cried easily without much of a reason those days, but this time my tears were for the swallow family that had lived in a nest under our eaves.

Early that year, on a sunny day in March, Mama asked me to keep an eye on the newly-made *gebei* drying outside on a mat. Sitting on my small stool, I was about to doze off when there came the sound of twittering. I got up quickly, wielding a stick. It was not sparrows but two swallows each with a deeply forked tail, gliding up and down around me. They were so swift that my eyes could hardly follow them. "Swallows, swallows..." screamed I. I loved swallows. The first song I ever learned to sing was about them. Once I even dreamed about becoming a swallow, so when it got cold in winter, I could fly to where it was warm.

For a while the two swallows were busy building a nest. They went and came back with their bills loaded many times a day. Watching them work so hard, I wished I could have been of help. For sure my hands would hold much more than a swallow's bill. They seemed to like each other a lot since they were always together.

They often chatted in a high-pitched tone, making me wonder why. They could be annoying too, especially when they spattered their waste on our exterior walls. Then Mama would tell me to clean it all up as though I had done it.

After the nest was finished, one swallow started to spent more time in the nest, and the other one would come and go doing something I didn't know. I became worried, thinking the one left home was ill. When I told Mama about it, she smiled. "She is fine, don't worry," she said.

Days had passed without any sign of that swallow getting better. One late afternoon, when chirps could be heard from the nest, Mama was the first to rush outside, followed by my brother, my sister, and me. Along the edge of the nest were four little bald heads, all with a big bill. My brother got on a small stool to have a closer look. He even grabbed a baby swallow and showed it to my sister and me.

Suddenly the two parent swallows returned. When they saw my brother, they flapped their wings and pecked at his hair. My brother dodged, swinging his arms in the air to keep his footing on the small stool. After managing to place the baby swallow back in the nest, he stumbled down.

For the days that followed, the two parent swallows were busy again, this time feeding their babies whose bills were always wide open for food. I tried to help. One morning when my brother wasn't home, I took out several dried worms from his bottle of fishing bait and put them outside for the two parent swallows to bring them to their babies. But they weren't interested. It wasn't long before the wind swept the worms away.

After my brother found out what I had done, he told me that swallows ate only live worms. Did they? They were so picky since I would eat anything Mama put in my bowl. Still the next day I took a small spatula, went to the surrounding wall where my brother usually got his worms, and dug.

I got several that were still wriggling when I freed them to the ground below the nest. Then I went inside to wash my hands. When I returned, they were all gone. What happened? The parent swallows took them or they crawled back to where I had found them?

The baby swallows were growing fast. About a week later, feathers started to bring grace to their bodies. Their bills had also settled into their heads, or their heads had eventually matched up with their bills. Either way, they looked lovely. They even practiced flying while their parents watched close by.

I stopped crying only when Xiaoxiao came over, swearing, not once but three times, to bring the entire swallow family to see me the next spring.

CHAPTER 8

The day we moved, I was sent to stay with Mama's friend, Auntie Chen, who lived in an attic behind what she said was a school. With a scar above her left eyebrow, she scared me at first. But I came to like her. Unlike Mama, she was patient with me. Every time I asked a question, she gave me an answer.

"Who are they?" asked I upon seeing a pencil drawing on the wall, in which a baby boy was sitting on the lap of a man.

"My son and his baba," said Auntie Chen,

"Where are they?" asked I again, having the feeling that they didn't live there because the place was tiny.

"My son in Sichuan, lives with his uncle," said Auntie Chen. "His baba in a labor camp, used to teach."

"Used to teach? Not wear eyeglasses," murmured I, taking another look at the man in the pencil drawing.

"Some teachers wear eyeglasses, some don't. You know what's a labor camp, don't you? Many teachers have been sent there," said Auntie Chen, handing me a bowl that had some water at the bottom.

When Auntie Chen said it was time to go to my new home, it was already afternoon. I had never walked so much, losing the direction at every turn. For a while we were in an alley that had wider gates and taller surrounding walls. Here a closed gate very much resembled a face with two eyes, actually two door rings that stayed forever round and upset, and there an open gate revealed nothing but a brick wall blocking any view of what was behind.

Parked along one side of the dirt road were some handcarts loaded with coal, and nearby a group of haggard men were taking a break. Covered from head to toe in coaldust, they looked just like coal. Then Auntie Chen let go my hand and stepped closer to them. She was looking for someone.

"Don't see him, not with them," mumbled she as she came back to me.

"See who?" asked I, not sure how she could tell one from another with all of them appearing the same.

"My son's baba. I guess he isn't with this labor camp," said Auntie Chen, wiping her eyes.

From one corner to another, Auntie Chen and I disappeared and reappeared. A path suddenly showed itself next to a dead end, and we stepped right in as though having that rare feat of penetrating walls.

We halted in front of a gate that had a round stone on either side when a cat charged out, arching and baring teeth. While I hid behind Auntie Chen, she stomped to scare it away. Through a dark gateway, we came to a yard, where an old woman was spinning threads in the shade of a big tree. She never looked up as we were passing.

"Aiya!" I backed out the moment I stepped inside the door.

"Don't get in yet," Mama warned, wringing a bundle of rags over a bucket. "Wait outside until I'm done."

Mama didn't choose to move there. She had to. Located in the lowest corner of the yard, the place stank with sewage oozing out the floor and mold growing on the walls.

Worried about her children getting any rheumatic diseases,

Mama came up with the idea to cover the floor with sand. On the route of the Yellow River, sand was everywhere outside the city walls. Whenever the wind blew, sand rose and sang the past woes brought by floods.

The next day four of us set out to get sand. Mama was the one who pulled the handcart with three of us children sitting in the back. Near the northern gate of the city, my brother and sister got off the handcart to lighten the burden on Mama. I didn't until they started to call me "a fool." As I trudged along with sand puffing under my feet, I got so excited that I giggled like out of my mind.

Our two chipped enamel washbasins were used to carry sand to the handcart. My brother and sister shared one, and Mama and I the other. I worked hard to show I was capable. Once Mama put down the washbasin, I would scoop as quickly as I could to fill it up.

"Ten! We are doing the tenth basin, you two only the sixth," shouted my brother and sister. Without letting Mama and me know, they had started a competition.

"One is too old, and the other too young. We aren't your match," readily conceded Mama.

As the digging went deeper and sand turned moister, a tangle of grassroots appeared at the bottom. Forgetting the reason why I was there, I jumped in and pulled a long grassroot out. After wiping it clean on my sleeve, I stuffed it into my mouth and chewed, ignoring the scowl on Mama's face. No matter what, I was going to bring some home. Sold as candy on the street, one grassroot cost one *fen*, which was a lot of money to someone like me.

It was time to go home. Mama, one hand on one handle of the handcart, pulled by exerting all her strength through the belt across her left shoulder with my brother pulling through a rope attached to the right side. My sister didn't pull. She pushed from the left side.

The handcart started to roll only when all three of them bent almost to the ground.

We made three more trips before there was enough sand to cover the entire floor. We would go back there whenever sand turned soggy again.

I had heard about a time when an entire family would sleep in one bed and under one cotton-padded quilt, which was said to be very practical especially during a cold winter night.

But no longer was this old tradition followed. Wherever we lived, my brother always insisted on having his own sleeping quarters. Before we moved, every night he would crawl into a double wall below the front window to sleep. Now, after spending several nights behind a stack of cardboard boxes, he disappeared the first Sunay morning and didn't come back until afternoon, dragging along a bundle of old mats.

"I'm going to put up a wall here," he declared, stroking the air with his hands as though a wall was already there.

After hours of mobbing the pieces clean and nailing them together, he tried to make the final patchwork stand. But it wouldn't, staggering and lurching in his hands like a drunkard. After all, he was just a middle schooler, not a wall builder.

"Her cunt," cursed he, his nose spewing heat.

"Watch your mouth!" Mama scolded from the outside through the open window.

"Someone helps me," yelled he.

"Let me," said I, standing nearby

My brother made just a face without saying a word, but I could tell he was thinking I only knew how to eat, which was what he often said to me.

"I can help," hollered my sister, hopping into the inner room.

With just two-year age difference, they two fought sometimes, but more often they were nice to each other.

Nothing else to do, I picked up some crooked nails my brother had dropped on the floor and walked outside. Right there on the doorstep, I knocked straight one nail after another with a broken brick and then went back to my brother. As he was about to make another face at me, I made a grand display of my hard work to impress him. He was indeed, which was a moment I would never forget.

"I want something around my bed too," said my sister to Mama.

"Another wall?" asked Mama.

"Maybe a curtain," suggested my sister.

Mama began to look into several carboard boxes and from one, pulled out an old mosquito net with many holes. For the next several days, whenever Mama had time, she mended the holes stitch by stitch and then, together with my sister, hoisted the mosquito net up over her bed. It was a happy day for my sister. She danced, twisting her hips.

I needed privacy too. The bed I shared with Mama was right there to be seen. I kept looking sad until one day when Mama flew up a tattered sheet along the bedside facing the door to the inner room.

"Are you satisfied?" she asked in a tone that sounded like I had done something wrong.

I nodded, knowing Mama didn't have another mosquito net even though I did wish she had had something to cover up those big cracks in the ceiling above our bed, through which webs, like festoons in the hall of devils, were always seen swinging on the rafters.

CHAPTER 9

"Go outside for some sun," said Mama when I started to pester her.

With no one else to play with, I played the house of squares by myself. After drawing a dozen of large squares on the ground, I hopped from one square to another, kicking a broken tile at the same time. I won the first round since I crossed all the squares without leaving the tile on any lines.

Hearing sniffles, I turned around only to see a girl who grinned as our eyes met. The dribbling from her nose almost reached her upper lip when she intercepted it by pulling across her right sleeve. "Just moved here?" she asked.

We ended up spending the rest of that afternoon together. First, we played the house of squares, and then we exchanged presents. I gave her a rubber band, and in return she gave me a candy wrapper. "Hui" was her name, meaning "understanding."

I liked Hui because she believed whatever I told her. Sometimes I did misuse her trust, though. It was not that I was a swindler who did it on purpose, but that I was too caught up in the moment.

"See the flower at the bottom, a rose," said I, showing off to Hui the best soup bowl Mama had.

"My mama has one too. Bigger," said she, not impressed.

"This one is a treasure bowl. It can turn one thing into two or three," explained I, unknowingly revealing my secret wish.

"Really?" asked Hui.

"I never lie. Aiya, your hands are dirty," yelled I when she tried to touch the bowl.

Hui wiped her right hand on her overshirt until it turned almost red before placing a finger on the outer surface of the bowl.

Then she ran home. When she returned, she had a one-*fen* coin and a fancy hairpin.

"Want more of them," said she, dropping the coin as well as the hairpin in the bowl, which I then covered with my handkerchief like a street magician would.

We waited. Of course nothing happened. To hide my first lie, I made another. I told Hui that the treasure bowl was taking a year-long nap, which she didn't question either.

She lived next door by herself. Whenever she saw me, her eyes narrowed, and her round Buddha face was wreathed in smiles. Her surname was "wang" and was called "nainai" or fraternal grandma.

Wang Nainai took care of things in the yard. Always the last one to go to bed, she would push on a door to see if it is bolted on the other side and check a kitchen shed to make sure the stove in there was properly banked. Then she would excise a little by kicking her small bound feet. "Make you strong," said she to Mama and me one night when we stepped outside to go to the outhouse.

Seldom did Wang Nainai allow anyone else into her home, but she let me in every time I showed up at her door. On the table against the wall stood a porcelain Guanyin in a flowing robe, holding in one hand a bottle of healing dew and in the other a twig. Wang Nainai said she talked to her Goddess of Mercy every morning to assure a nice day, but only once did I get to see her doing it. She lit an incense stick first. While a thin smoke circled in the air, Wang Nainai kneeled down in front of the table and mumbled before she rose up and mumbled again. She was down and up two more times by the time it was over. I asked Wang Nainai why I didn't understand a word she said, and she told me it wasn't meant for human ears.

Wang Nainai had two secrets. One wasn't really a secret. Just that she had a black coffin in the back of her room. I jumped in fear the first time I saw it. "Don't be afraid. Just a coffin," said she. "I had it made ten years ago. The only thing I need when it's time."

The other was about her hair.

"What does she do to her hair? So smooth," wondered aloud my sister, who was always the first one to notice anything related to looks.

"Maybe just water," said Mama.

"Water? Then why we need hair oil?" questioned my sister.

My sister had to find out what it was. One early morning, she woke me up and asked me to go with her. We tiptoed over and peeked through the bamboo curtain that was down but saw nothing. For sure Wang Nainai had heard us and moved away from the window.

Wang Nainai was right behind us when my sister and I ran back home, holding a small jar that had some water and wood dust.

"Use jujube wood," said Wang Nainai, giving out the last detail of her secrete.

"So sticky, no wonder your hair doesn't move," uttered my sister, having stuck a finger to the bottom of the jar.

His door faced ours. Although Uncle Xu wore glasses, he said he had never taught schools. As to why he was sent to prison while still in college, he said he would rather not talk about it. "Someone like me isn't allowed to teach. What can I do? I have to be fine with being a salesclerk," chuckled he when his wife said he could be making a little more money as a teacher.

"You two don't have a baby after years of trying to? I think it's his problem, not yours. Look at him, so thin. He needs to eat more, let him eat more," Wang Nainai would say whenever she ran into Uncle Xu's wife on her way to the outhouse.

Uncle Xu's wife would smile every time she saw me. Once she even invited me to have a bowl of soup with her. I didn't get to thank her because her longing eyes made me so nervous that I left before I could even finish.

When for the first time the pungent scent of herbs drifting out a small earthen pot on the stove outside Uncle Xu's door, Aunt Shan sniffed her way across the yard to find out more about it.

"For your husband? Is he ill?" she asked Uncle Xu's wife, who was attending the pot

"He isn't. Just tonics," answered the wife.

"Really? Just tonics?" asked again Aunt Shan.

"Just tonics," assured the wife.

"Just tonics," mimicked Aunt Shan with an accent.

Behind her back Aunt Shan was called "*muyecha,*" a woman to be feared. Once she was seen slapping her husband across the face, and another time she was heard exchanging insults with a vendor selling cabbages. She admitted her temper having a lot to do with her being a pedicurist at a local bathhouse because in her eyes, everyone was naked and indecent. Even Wang Nainai tried not to trifle with her. She gave away the cat she had had for years after Aunt Shan complained that it had napped on the cutting board in her kitchen shed.

Aunt Shan could be nice if she needed to. She let her husband help fix Uncle Xu's stove that had been having problems.

"My sons grow nails on their buttocks, so their pants don't last long. The fabric coupons we get are never enough. Tell your husband to get us some fabrics that don't need fabric coupons," said Aunt Shan to Uncle Xu's wife several days later.

"I will," promised the wife.

CHAPTER 10

It was that time of the month again. Before going to the shoe factory, Mama counted all the sheets of *gebei* one more time. Sixty was the number of sheets she was supposed to hand over. The last thing she wanted was to be found one sheet short by the inspector, who spared no one that miscounted. "The more people around, the louder he yells at you," complained Mama time to time.

Wang Nainai walked in with a gourdful of sorghum flour. Like at her own home, she went straight to where our flour jar was.

"I'm old and don't eat that much. Your kids are growing and need more," said Wang Nainai, dumping the flour into the jar.

"Come to thank Wang Nainai, she brings us flour," called out Mama to me.

Before I could get up from the stool, Wang Nainai came over and put a hand on me to keep me seated.

"Don't need to thank. When you have wheat flour, return me some wheat flour, not sorghum flour. I'm too old to digest that kind of stuff," said she, heading out of the door.

Once Mama finished counting, she loaded all the sixty sheets of *gebei* into the bamboo stroller at the bottom of the doorstep and covered them up with an old oilcloth. "Don't go anywhere, I'll be back soon," said she to me before squeaking the stroller away.

About two hours later, Mama returned still with all the *gebei*. After getting inside the last several sheets from the stroller, she flopped down on the floor. "There is mold, have to redo them," murmured Mama to herself. With a deep sigh, Mama started to rip apart one sheet at a time and all sixty of them. She would have to wash and dry all the rags before remaking them into *gebei*.

That night Mama didn't sleep. She tossed and turned until the break of dawn. After my brother and sister left for school, she fumbled in her camphorwood chest before bringing out a pair of silver bracelets. Slipping them into a used envelope, she said to me, "Let's go."

The small store up the alley just opened, and the storeowner was dusting the counter. I knew the place. Whenever Mama needed kerosene, I was sent here to get a *liang* or two.

Mama asked the storeowner if she could have a word with him. He nodded, lifting the door curtain in the wall made of sorghum stalks. Mama told me to wait there before going in, followed by the storeowner, who asked me to holler if someone came by.

When Mama reemerged, she was squeezing money into the same envelope that had held the bracelets. As she thanked the storeowner, he wrung out a smile, saying not to mention it. His wife also came out, adjusting the two silver bracelets on her left wrist.

CHAPTER 11

"Don't want this," said I to Mama, patting on my stomach that had been making noises.

"Don't say that again, here," said Mama, giving me half a sorghum flour *wowotou*, an unleavened bun with a hollow bottom.

I wasn't the only one that felt hungry all the time. So did my brother and sister. Upon getting home from school, if not my brother, it would be my sister who yelled something like "starved to death" even though they both always got to eat more. My brother and sister had the same-sized bowls, which were not only bigger but always fuller whenever bowls were used to eat from. On the other hand, I always ate from a smaller bowl that was never full.

Also, they each brought to school as lunch a *wowotou* or a bun weighing about two *liang*, while I always got only half a *wowotou* or half a bun at home. It wasn't that I never ate anything in its entirety. For that to happen, it had to be a potato or sweet potato or tera root.

Once at supper, when I asked Mama for a bigger bowl, it wasn't Mama but my sister who told me that the size of my bowl was decided by the government.

"At your age, you get about ten *jin* grains a month from the government. That means you get about three *liang* grains a day and one *liang* grains a meal. Your bowl is small but holds more than one *liang*. I say you have been eating my grains," said my sister, pointing her chopsticks straight at my forehead.

"Tighten your belt whenever you feel hungry. I tighten mine many times a day," added my brother, who was, with his tongue out, licking the inside of his bowl.

After my brother and sister calmed down, Mama started to tell me about Kong Rong, a grandson of Confucius, who had offered to have the smallest pear simply because he was the youngest among his siblings.

"Your brother and sister have bigger bowls because they are older and have bigger stomachs," concluded Mama.

One thing Mama never explained to me was why she always ate the least while being the oldest. I thought about it sometimes while trying to fall asleep at night. Mama had just turned off the light and lit up the kerosene lamp, a wick in a little jar placed in the corner next to the inner room door. She was making the last sheet of *gebei* for the day. From the bed, I could see her shadow on the opposite wall. Her chest heaved as she was breathing heavily. To suppress a cough, she put her left hand or the hand without too much paste, to her mouth. However little nutrition my brother, my sister, and I had, our mother always had less. She didn't mind, but her body did. Mama suffered from dropsy with her feet and legs swollen like leavened dough. Overwhelmed with sadness, I wept.

CHAPTER 12

Outside the window a cloudy sky hung heavier and heavier as the north wind kept shaking our front door as if trying to get in.

"It's cold, but who cares," murmured Mama to herself, getting ready to go to a harvested carrot field on the outskirt of the city. In those days, even someone like me knew how beneficial to eat carrots. Nicknamed as red *ginseng*, they contained whatever nutrients a human body needed.

"Want to go with you," I demanded, pulling the basket Mama was holding.

"It's outside the city, you cannot walk that far," hesitated Mama at first but gave in when she saw tears in my eyes.

Crawling along here and there in a wide field were more than a dozen of women with their heads wrapped up. Mama hurried over, kneeled down, and plowed with her bare hands, becoming one of them. It wasn't long before her fingers turned red and stiff. Now and then she blew on them. The carrots Mama had picked up were tiny and had no color at all.

To Mama's left was an older woman, who was digging fast. With her black scarf having slipped down, her gray hair one minute flew up in the wind and another minute fell on her face as she turned to drop a carrot or two into the basket at her side.

"Big sister, you're so fast! I'm ashamed," Mama said to her.

"I do it every other day, I live there," she said, looking to the right, where at the end of a trodden path were some mud houses nestling together as if keeping warm on a cold day.

Not in a mood to chat more, she went even faster. In a minute or two, she reached the other end before making a turn to start another round.

"Don't you have eyes? I'm on this furrow, this is mine," yelled a younger woman behind Mama and me.

"What you say? Who doesn't have eyes?" yelled back the older woman.

"You! You don't have eyes," yelled even louder the younger woman.

"Whether I have eyes or not isn't your business. Let me see what I can do," muttered the older woman, lifting up her basket heavy with carrots and dashing toward the younger woman.

In the blink of an eye, the basket in the older woman's hands was on the younger woman's head, bottom up with carrots falling down. Then the two women got tangled up, their hands on each other's face.

Mama and other women looked on and didn't know what to do. Only one woman puzzled loud where they got strength as the two continued to roll and tear, stirring up quit a whirl of soil.

A man was seen running toward the field from where houses were. The front of his cotton-patted jacket flapped while he bounced up and down dirt ridges. He was shouting words, but the wind thrust them back down his throat before they could come out. Words ended up like burps.

"You're here to dig carrots, not to fight," screamed he at the wrestling heap. Only when he began to kick hard at the older woman, it became clear which of the two women he meant to stop.

The older woman howled in pain and then slowly sat up. When she shook her hair off her face, there was a long scratch across her left cheek.

"Go back home! You're shameless! My brother cannot rest in peace with you behaving like this," scolded the man, pointing a long-stemmed tobacco pipe at her.

Suddenly like a little girl caught doing something wrong, the older woman sat there with her head down.

"All of you are troublemakers! I'm the brigade head, I tell you to leave, or I'll call the brigade militia," shouted the man, sweeping his hand without the tobacco pipe in the direction of the younger woman and all the rest of us.

"Just got here! How can I go home with almost nothing?" murmured Mama, continuing to pick up a carrot here and there. Only when the brigade head threatened to call the militia again, did Mama and I plod our way out of the field.

"Wait," a voice rang behind us. It was the older woman.

"What's the matter?" Mama asked.

"Nothing, just want you to have these carrots," said the older woman, holding out the basket.

She certainly didn't seem to be the same woman who earlier had fought so fiercely over some bad words and then had been so timid in front of her brother-in-law.

"No, you… keep them for yourself," stammered Mama as the older woman started to slide carrots from her basket into ours.

"I don't, don't have kids," said she, taking a quick glance at me.

The older woman walked away, swinging her empty basket. To her back Mama bowed, so did I. It was a little while before we hit the road home.

CHAPTER 13

For the meal on the Lunar New Year's Eve, there had to be some kind of meat, a good omen that things would go smoothly in the coming year.

Exactly ten days before, not Aunt Shan but her husband came home with a young rooster. Near noon the next day, it was Aunt Shan who brought out first the rooster and then a cleaver from their kitchen shed.

Mama told me not to, but I still went, hoping to get a feather or two for the *jianzi*, a kicking shuttlecock I had been putting together with Mama's help. It was just as simple as wrapping two Qing Dynasty coins in a disc of cloth cut out by Mama, who then stitched the whole thing up with a feather holder attached to the middle of one side. Four or five feathers were needed for a *jianzi* to work, but I had only two.

The rooster fought hard for its own life. The moment Aunt Shan's husband lifted the basket under which it was kept, it dodged his hands and dashed out. The chasing went from the back to the front of the yard with the rooster being just one step ahead of the long broom coming right after. Several times it was hit but still managed to escape, leaving behind a scatter of feathers. When the poor bird was finally caught in a corner, it showed a lot of skin.

With the sleeves rolled up, Aunt Shan's husband bowed to the east three times in spite of the struggle by the rooster in his grasp. Then he clapped its neck backward, quickly slid the cleaver across the throat, and held the open wound over a bowl. As soon as blood stopped dripping, the rooster was thrown to the ground to breathe its last. After it was gutted, Aunt Shan folded it up tight and bound it with a hemp string before hanging it on the wall to airdry.

"This time I'm going to cook it whole," said Aunt Shan to those of us watching with a glow on her face.

A day later, a piece of fat pork was seen dangling on Uncle Xu's door. Soon after that, Wang Nainai was excited to tell everyone she had bought a hairtail. Whatever it was would be for the meal of the year.

When I got home, Mama was reknitting a sweater before the window. Hui just told me what her family was planning to eat on the Lunar New Year's Eve. "Meat *jiaozi*," said she even though she wasn't sure what meat it would be. "*Jiaozi* wrappers made with white flour," added she, blinking her eyes. When she asked what my family would eat and I said I didn't know, she looked as though I was lying. I wasn't. It was true that Mama hadn't said a word about the meal.

"What we eat on the Lunar New Year's Eve?" asked I the moment I stepped into the inner room.

"Haven't decided yet," said Mama without looking up, her hands shuffling the knitting needles.

Hearing that, I was so disappointed that I kicked the floor. Mama looked up this time and told me to go over to her. As I stood before her, she put down her knitting and pulled me closer.

"Hard to get work lately. You know that, don't you?" she asked, looking into my eyes with her hands stroking my face. "Are you upset if Mama cannot afford a good meal this year?"

Of course I wasn't, so I shook my head. Ever since the shoe factory started to use plastic soles, Mama had been making less *gebei*. To make up for the loss, Mama put up a sign for knitting at the gate. But only a few came for the service. Often it was for a worn sweater to be reknitted, in which case Mama would unwind it, wash the yarn, and repair frayed strands before starting to knit again.

It was getting darker, and I went to switch on the light above the table. Before I could climb onto a stool, Mama rushed over to do it herself. She was knitting again. But only several stitches later, she stopped and said, "I don't have to finish this today. Let me show you how to write a character."

As I looked on, Mama brought from a cardboard box to the table a brush, half an inkstick, a piece of red paper, and an inkstone. After adding a bit of water onto the inkstone, she started to gently rub, in a circular motion, the inkstick against the inkstone. Tilting her head somewhat, she listened. What could be heard wasn't just a rustling sound. It was also a familiar sound. A sound Mama would make on a daily basis when she was young as she told me.

Mama was ready. She picked up the brush and drew the first stroke, which began with a forceful crouch that slanted a little around the shoulder, progressed with a raised even drawl, and ended with an easy, round turn. What followed was a combination of a downward dot and a phoenix beak to finish up the upper part of the character. Then the brush moved down to the left and started a short leftward sweep that was quickly braced by a vertical pillar. After another leftward sweep led to a vertical stoke, a turn at the bottom to the right ran straight up into a hook, shaping up a graceful dragon tail. The character Mama was writing was *hua*, flower.

Mama told me she liked the running style, which was not as wild and illegible as the grass style but kept the natural grace of chasing clouds and flowing water. In this style, a stroke didn't separate from a dot. Instead, it smoothened into a dot with a slightly elevated move.

After taking a deep breath, Mama picked up the brush again, calligraphing a couplet for our front door. She was telling me something I had never heard before. Calligraphy was like *qi*, which wouldn't move unless the mind and the body became one, said she. Only as one, equilibrium could rule, and *qi* could roll and leap, creating strokes that were light, heavy, slow, and swift, continued she. Even though I didn't quite understand what Mama meant, I had the feeling that *qi* was everything in doing calligraphy.

It was the morning of the Lunar New Year's Eve. When I woke up, Mama was no longer in bed. The temperature had plumped overnight. Without Mama next to me, it felt so much colder. Hearing me groaning, Mama came from the outer room and said, "Water is being heated on the stove, get you a warm bottle in a minute."

Finally, a filled aluminum bottle came. As I held it with both hands under the quilt, I felt not only its warmth but also its many dents. My sister got one too. Mama had only two such water bottles. When she told my brother she would make a warm bottle out of an old soy sauce bottle for him, he yelled, "No, a man doesn't need a warm bottle!"

"You all stay in bed, I'll be back soon," said Mama, putting on her overcoat.

"Where are you going?" asked my brother.

"There's porridge on the stove," said Mama, evading an answer.

Near noon, three of us just got up and were having porridge at the table when Mama was heard putting things away in the outer room.

"So pale, what's wrong?" asked all three of us in one voice the moment she came to the inner room.

"Nothing, just need some rest," mumbled Mama.

"Don't get sick, it's Lunar New Year!" My brother rose to help her get to the bed.

"Don't worry, I'm fine," reassured Mama, forcing out a smile.

Less than an hour later she got up. Weak as she seemed, she was in a good spirit.

"You all behave, I'm going to make you a nice meal," said she before shutting the door between the outer room and the inner room.

"A nice meal? Salty turnip and sorghum flour *wowotou*," declared my sister with her arms folded on her chest like someone who knew everything.

Three of us didn't just sit and wait. While my brother wiped clean the lightbulb, my sister found half a red candle left from the year before and lit it up. I also did what I could, which was to make sure that there was a seat at each side of the table.

"Here!" Mama walked in from the kitchen with a bowl of brown sauce.

"I smell mutton," sniffed my brother.

"Mutton? Expensive! Do we have money for something like that?" asked my sister with her tone full of suspicion. Mama kept a record of every *fen* earned or spent in a used exercise book, which my sister checked every day like doing her homework.

"Your Auntie Chen lent me," answered Mama, handing my brother and sister each a white flour bun.

With one bun left, Mama broke it into two, giving me the bigger half and keeping the smaller half for herself.

After the meal, my brother brought out a string of firecrackers wound on a stick, which he had saved for a whole year to purchase, and jumped outside.

Sparks dashed in the dark, and cracking sounds echoed. Mama, my sister, and I jammed the door and watched with fingers in our ears. We screamed together whenever my brother yanked the firing stick at us.

Then it started to snow with white flakes quietly twirling down from the sky. My brother turned his face upward and gulped as snow fell straight into his mouth. When he finally came inside, he and my sister talked.

"If only snow were flour. Think about it, we would never feel hungry again," said my brother.

"Who needs that much flour? I wish it were sugar. When was the last time we had sugar?" retorted my sister.

"Sugar is bad to your teeth. How about coins? Ah, so many coins! Then I can buy anything I want," my brother exclaimed. "I have heard a place called Old Gold Mountain, where streets are paved with gold."

"Where is that place?" asked my sister.

"Where is Old Gold Mountain?" My brother turned the question over to Mama.

"Far away," said Mama from the outer room.

"I know far away, but which country?" pressed my brother.

"You'll find out when you study world geography," said Mama.

That night I dreamed. When it wasn't about flour or sugar or coins, it was about streets paved with gold. I had a hard time waking up the next morning.

CHAPTER 14

After breakfast I put on my green corduroy overshirt. It was the third time I wore it. Long before it was mine, it had been my sister's. If not for the lowered hemlines, no one could have even guessed it wasn't new since it was worn only a day or two a year.

"Remember Grandpa Yuan? We go to see him," said Mama, combing my hair into two side ponytails with each tied up with a red yarn.

On our way out, a grinning Wang Nainai asked me for a kowtow. I ran up to her door and flopped down with my forehead touching the threshold. Wang Nainai gurgled and slid a candy into my pocket. I was disappointed. I wouldn't have been so ready to kowtow had I known there wasn't any money.

Through a narrow passage Mama and I walked into a yard, where an old man with a long goatee was shoveling snow away from the doorstep. He waved when he saw us.

"A big girl now. I won't know who she is if I see her by herself," said he, patting me on the right shoulder.

"Kowtow to Grandpa Yuan," urged Mama.

"No, it's old practice," said Grandpa Yuan, trying to stop me, but I was already on all fours at his feet.

When I got up, Grandpa Yuan fumbled out a two-*mao* bill from his pocket, which he straightened and then placed in my hand.

"Too much for a child," said Mama, signaling me to return the money. I looked away, pretending not to see. For someone like me who had never had more than two *fen* in my possession, two *mao* or twenty *fen* was a lot. No way was I going to give it up.

Grandpa Yuan's home was certainly bigger than ours. While Mama chatted with several other guests, I followed my curiosity. Behind a yellow curtain, on a lotus-shaped pedestal sat a cross-legged Buddha, who looked almost dozing off with his eyes half-closed. They were relatives, said I to myself, noticing some resemblance of Buddha to Wang Nainai's Guanyin. In a small sandbox before the statue, lit candles and burning incenses swayed like a dream. I gazed, forgetting where I was for a moment.

Wandering to the other side of the room, I came upon a wall of wooden screens hinged together. One screen depicting one scene, usually they told a story. Moving from one screen to another, I tried to figure out what the story was only to realize it was a landscape of high mountains with flowing water. Behind the screens was a bed. The moment I ran my fingers on the sheet, several of myself appeared. A closer look gave away the mirrors embedded in the enclosing boards. Next to the bed were two chairs. I sat in one for a second, slipped off, and climbed onto the other.

Before I knew it, I was browsing a shelf stacked with books. I even picked up one and thumbed through as though I could read. Then from nowhere a girl in red appeared.

"Your overshirt isn't new," said she. "Mine is."

"Yours isn't corduroy. Red is scary like devil's eyes," I fired off, upset that she was being so negative on the first day of the Lunar New Year.

Taken aback, the girl started to look sad. Feeling somewhat guilty, I gave her the candy I got from Wang Nainai. As soon as it was in her mouth, she smiled like a friend.

I couldn't help showing her my two-*mao* bill. Without any hesitation, she said her brother was interested in me.

The room suddenly turned quiet. After the yellow curtain was pulled aside, Grandpa Yuan and his guests including Mama got down on their knees in front of the Buddha statue and chanted like Wang Nainai would once a day. I didn't get to laugh, though. The girl took me behind the screens and scolded, "Don't. If you do, you'll be killed by thunders."

Half way home, it snowed again. To show off the red yarn on my ponytails, I had refused to wear my headscarf that day. Mama pulled off her own and wrapped it around my neck.

Alongside Mama I walked, holding the two-*mao* bill I felt no need to hide in my pocket. I wanted whoever saw me to see it too. An amused Mama didn't say anything, letting me indulge myself a little longer.

The road was muddy. It wasn't long before my cotton-padded shoes, passed to me from my sister, became wet and heavy. I started to walk behind Mama, stepping into her footprints to avoid my shoes getting stuck. Still, it happened. When I lifted my left foot and didn't see the shoe, I cried until Mama came to my rescue by picking up the shoe and putting it back on my foot.

On the doorstep of a closed store lied a man covered in a tattered blanket.

Only one leg did he have. Seeing us, he slowly sat up and began to play a bamboo flute. A rusty can at his side showed nothing in it. He was cold. Not only he was shivering but also his bamboo flute and his music. Mama stopped. She first looked into her bag and then looked at me.

"Don't have any money with me. How about giving it to him? said Mama, now looking at the two-*mao* bill in my right hand.

"What?" I looked back at Mama in shock.

"Help, he needs help," said Mama, tapping me on the hand with the bill.

"My money, Grandpa Yuan gave me," mumbled I, feeling Mama was asking too much of me.

"It's a good thing to help," persuaded Mama. "When we get home, Mama give you two two-*fen* coins."

That was only one fifth of what Grandpa Yuan gave me. I couldn't do it. I just couldn't. At the end, it was Mama who took my two-*mao* bill and dropped it in the can.

I sobbed the rest of my way home. To make me feel better, Mama told me a story: A man on the frontier let his neighbor use his horse to make a trip to a faraway place. Although it was his only horse, he said to his wife that helping others was always a blessing in disguise, which turned out to be true. A year later, even though his neighbor didn't return, his horse did, together with two younger ones.

For my loss I gained a lesson.

CHAPTER 15

So old was the tree outside Hui's window that she said she had no idea what tree it was. It was big. Several times Hui and I stretched out our arms to embrace it but were unable to. During summer, leaves grew so thick that the tree turned into a canopy that allowed no sunlight sifting through. One day after Hui told me she had heard a rooster up there early that morning, I slammed myself onto the tree trunk and looked up with one eye. Yes, I did see something on one of the top branches.

Hui's maternal great grandma, who was nearly ninety years old, didn't know what tree it was either, but she did know where it had come from. Even though she could no longer speak, her granddaughter, Hui's mother remembered what her grandma had told her many years ago. One afternoon, while Hui and I helped her to unwind a skein of thread, she told us what she had heard as a child:

No one knew how long ago it was when a man lived in a shed where now the tree was. One evening while knocking his shoes against each other after taking them off, he noticed something like a seed fall to the dirt floor. Without thinking much of it, he kicked it away.

That night he slept well at first but later woke up feeling his bed being pushed up in the middle. Upon seeing a tree growing under his bed, he got off, picked up his axe, and hacked.

To his surprise, no sooner was the tree cut down than it grew back again, bigger. He kept on hacking for a while until he got so exhausted that he gave up.

As the tree became bigger and bigger, suddenly the ground around it started to rumble as though crying pain from a difficult birth. Before long the tree reached the ceiling, punctured the roof, and continued to grow. The man, through the rupture, was amazed to see a night sky as he had never seen before. Clouds puffed themselves up, chasing one another like boats racing. As stars twinkled out a lullaby, the moon swayed her plump behind as gracefully as Consort Yang was dancing for the Tang emperor, Xuanzong.

Dawn broke. While trying to catch some sleep, the man was woken by the sound of wings flapping. Not only had the tree stopped growing, but right there perching on a top branch was a rooster. The moment it crowed, a gold coin rolled out of its beak to the ground. The man picked it up in ecstasy, wiping it clean before hiding it in his belt.

As days went by, the man became discontent with just one coin a day. He reasoned to himself that only a gold rooster could spit out gold coins. He had to have the rooster, so he placed a trap on the tree. But the rooster never came near it.

One night when the man climbed up the tree, trying to catch the rooster while it was asleep, it woke up and flew away. At that very moment, the tree started to grow again, so fast that the man soon found his head inside some clouds and so big that he could no longer hold on to it. Before he could utter a cry for help, he somersaulted downward all the way to his death. As soon as the man died, his shed collapsed, and the tree shrank back to the size before the man turned greedy

Much smaller were the two pomegranate trees, one outside Wang Nainai's window and the other next to Aunt Shan's door. When Hui and I wanted to play under a pomegranate tree, we would go to the one outside Wang Nainai's window. Never again did we return to the pomegranate tree near Aunt Shan's door after she yelled at us.

The two trees did seem to like each other, though. With no wind, they would try as hard as they could to reach each other. The moment the wind blew, they went all over each other like wild.

Once my brother and sister talked about them. While my brother insisted that they resemble those deities dancing on the walls of Dunhuang Grottoes, my sister claimed they were more like a couple in love after a long-time-no-see. Looking at them out of our window one time, I said to myself they were like two hungry beggars, which Mama overheard, feeling so guilty that I was allowed a bigger potato for lunch.

In spring when neither tree had any budburst on time, Wang Nainai said it had something to do with Huo, Aunt Shan's older son, who had practiced bars on both trees during the entire winter. We all were relieved that they didn't die. Before long, both were covered with a layer of tender green.

More than a month later, as if by some kind of magic, the trees blossomed overnight. After a shower brought down some petals, Hui and I got busy making ourselves pretty. Red petals were made into red pulp, which we daubed so generously on our lips and cheeks. To guarantee the best results as a nail polish, after it was applied, we wrapped the nail part of each finger in a tear of old paper and tied it up.

For the rest of that day, I refused to do any chores and later went to bed smiling. When I woke up the next morning, not only all the wrappings were gone but the color of all my fingernails also stayed the same. On her way to the outhouse, Hui stopped by to tell me a similar story. Little did we know pomegranate petals didn't stain fingernails.

Not until August did pomegranates begin to peep out behind leaves. It took a few more weeks before some of them grew a rosy tinge with a few even cracking a grin as though to show off their not-so-white teeth. One day Hui and I counted how many pomegranates on the two trees. Hui counted thirty, and I more than twenty. With some still tiny, it was hard to account accurately.

It had been a while since Wang Nainai started to collect money to help get a coffin for Hui's maternal great grandma. "Have some pity. She is hanging on because she doesn't have a coffin," said Wang Nainai to whoever she ran into in the neighborhood. Not that Hui's great grandma had never had a coffin. As a matter of fact, the one she once had was said to be quite good. The saddest thing was that she had to use the coffin for herself to bury her daughter, Hui's grandma, who died while giving birth to Hui's mother.

"Still several *kuai* short for an unfinished coffin. Let's sell this year's pomegranates," said Wang Nainai, going door to door. When my brother got home from school that evening, he and Hui's brother were given the task to pick pomegranates from the trees.

The next morning two baskets of pomegranates were brought outside our gate. While Wang Nainai made sure that smaller ones were not mixed up with bigger ones, Hui and I held a cardboard with two different prices on it. The Mid-Autumn Festival was near, and pomegranates were the fruit for it.

"Put down that sign, cadres from the residential committee," said Wang Nainai when a middle-aged woman and a young man were seen striding their way toward us.

"Do you have a sale license? I'm sure you don't, you are breaking the law," said the woman in a stern voice.

"A sale license? It's a one-time sale, sell them to get a coffin for a dying great grandma. She won't breathe her last until she has a coffin," explained Wang Nainai.

"Coffin? Tell her to get cremated. Confiscate them," yelled the woman first at Wang Nainai and then at the young man, who was already putting our pomegranates into a sack he had brought along. After the young man swung the half-full sack on his right shoulder, he and the middle-aged woman left like they had just bought them.

"*Qiangdao*," mumbled Wang Nainai, staring in their direction.

"*Qiangdao*, what's *qiangdao*?" asked I.

"Who knows?" said Hui as she and I followed Wang Nainai into our yard.

Upon getting home I asked Mama about *qiangdao*. She didn't explain the word. She just told me never to take anything that wasn't mine.

The day some circular bits or *yuqian* appeared on the young elm near the male outhouse, Aunt Shan hurried over to pick.

"*Yuqian,* extra money," hollered she since *yuqian* meant extra money. She even called the tree "my elm" because she said she herself had planted it after moving there.

But Aunt Shan couldn't tell whether *yuqian* was her elm's fruit or seeds. "Don't care as long as it isn't poison," declared she.

Although I never had any *yuqian*, I got to eat locust flowers for the first time. The two locust trees outside our gate didn't seem to belong to anyone, so anyone able to climb a tree could get up there to pluck some when it was time.

It was a Sunday, and my brother was home. Right after finishing his bowl of porridge, he raced out, followed by me carrying a basket.

The first locust tree was already taken, so my brother went to the second one. The hero I always admired kicked off his shoes, spat in his palms, and climbed up as fast as he could. From the crotch he moved closer to a branch where white locust flowers glistened in the midst of green leaves. As my brother got busy up there, I got also busy down below, catching clusters he dropped.

For a moment my brother was a little beside himself up there. He sang the song *Nanniwan* and even adorned a garland he made with twigs.

When another boy got on the same locust tree, my brother started to move to another branch, which shook hard as he was trying to sit on it.

"Come down," shouted a voice. It was Mama, who had come out to check on us. It was too late. My brother was in a situation where maneuvering down was as risky as maneuvering up. While he was swinging off, the branch broke with a loud crack.

Mama uttered a cry of relief when my brother rolled up from the ground. A sprained ankle was the only injury. He was fine after a few days of walking like a cripple.

I wanted to do it too as Mama was removing locust flowers from their stems. While I could pluck several flowers at a time,

Mama could get as many flowers off as a long cluster with just one pull. After flowers were rinsed clean, some sorghum flour got mixed in.

Streamed locust flowers smelled nice but tasted bland. No matter what, I got to eat a full bowl for supper, which had never happened before.

CHAPTER 16

Besides my brother, Auntie Chen's son Xuan was the only other boy I got to spend time with. Not a lot of time, though. I met him for the first time just several weeks ago when he was brought back from Sichuan.

On this day when he lifted our door curtain and hopped in, followed by her mother, he was holding a paper cylinder. He shook it, put it to his right ear, and grinned before telling me to come closer. As I did, he yanked the cylinder away.

Xuan didn't give me the cylinder until Auntie Chen asked him to. I opened the lid only to find a pack of grasshoppers wrestling with each other like armored warriors.

"Taste good," said Xuan with a Sichuan accent before handing the cylinder over to Auntie Chen, who said those were Sichuan grasshoppers, the most nutritious among all insects.

While our mothers cooked in the outer room, Xuan and I played at the table in the inner room.

"Read," ordered he after scribbling something on a piece of paper.

"Can't," said I.

"Of course you can't. It's foreign language. I can," retorted he, starting to twist his tongue and utter sounds that were completely incomprehensible to me.

By the time he finished, I was so amazed that I couldn't help staring at him with admiration. He tilted his head and laughed, his eyes turning into two fleshy puffs, each with a short seam. Furious about being fooled, I threatened to tell his mama.

A little while later, in the middle of teaching me numbers, Xuan opened his legs and pulled out his *ji* or penis, which looked like a dried date.

"Do you know why I have this?" asked he.

"Who doesn't know? Pee," said I.

"Pee? Sow seeds," swaggered he.

Before I could figure out how that ugly lump could possibly sow seeds, Xuan went on to say he would like to marry me someday.

"No, you're too young," rejected I.

"I'm not, I'm two years older than you," insisted he.

"At least four years older than me!" I gave a specific number just to show Xuan how clear I was about what I wanted.

After supper, we all went outside to get some cool air. Sitting on my short stool with another short stool next to me, I asked Xuan to come over and tell me a story. He ignored me by running to Auntie Chen, who was chatting with Mama on the doorstep. He even cuddled up at her side like a baby.

I had no idea what Xuan thought of me. One minute he made me feel I was the only one he cared about, and the next minute he behaved as though I didn't exist.

With nothing to do, I tried to get some rest on a mat Mama had rolled out at the base of the doorstep. As voices around me were fading, I felt a finger touching my face. It was Xuan, who grinned once I opened my eyes. I didn't say a word and closed my eyes again.

"I have a story, want to hear?" asked he, lying down next to me.

"No," said I, mindful of his arrogance a moment ago.

"It's about two monks in a monastery, once upon a time, an old monk was telling a young monk a…" started Xuan like reading a book.

"… story that once upon a time, an old monk was telling a young monk a story," interrupted I with what I knew would come the next.

It was one of those stories that could go on and on. In this case the old monk just kept repeating the same line.

Xuan became quiet. He wasn't falling asleep since his eyeballs were rolling beneath his shut eyelids. Then he nudged me and whispered, "Want to touch my little *ji*? Touch it, here."

Before I had time to say anything, he grabbed my right hand and pressed it on the front opening of his pants. For sure something wasn't right here. If it wasn't Mama, it was Wang Nainai who had told me not to touch that thing of a boy.

I tried to snap my hand away, but Xuan wouldn't let me. I sat up and strained hard to free my hand. For a minute, we two were like in a tug war testing each other's strength. He gave up only when I scratched him with my other hand.

"I'm not going to marry you," cried he.

That was pathetic I thought. Who wanted to marry him in the first place? Not even six years old, how could I know a boy like Xuan probably would be my only choice as a husband when it was time? But I did know that girls got to act like swans in front of boys or so-called warty toads. Instead of saying I liked a boy, I had to make sure he knew I didn't. The young nun who sometimes came to visit Wang Nainai told Hui and me that she preferred having a shaved head than getting married.

She swore she didn't mind sitting cross-legged all day long, knocking on a wooden fish and chanting scriptures.

As I got up to sit with Mama, Auntie Chen came over to find out what was the matter with her son. "She's mean," whined Xuan to Auntie Chen, who shook her head, knowing her son too well to believe his nonsense.

Believe or not, that was how Xuan had literally reduced himself to a little *ji*, which never failed to zoom in in the back of my mind whenever I saw him or his name was brought up.

CHAPTER 17

Without any reason, my brother came home from school haughty one afternoon.

I was folding paper at the table when he stood next to me with his two legs squarely apart like a giant. He squinted his eyes before shaking his head as though something was pitiful about me or about what I was doing.

"Don't need them anymore. From now on, I read only books with no pictures," said he, going behind the mat wall and coming out with a cardboard box that hardly held together.

The second he dropped it, a dozen of old picture books fell to the floor.

I had seen my brother and sister fighting over those books. Neither of them seemed sure who owned this one or that one. But half a year ago, my sister voluntarily gave all hers to my brother, who later showed his gratitude by helping with her homework.

More than ten picture books! The number was enormous by any stretch of my limited imagination. "Aiya," cried I, throwing myself onto the floor to scoop them up.

Later in the day, I mended what suddenly belonged to me with Mama aside to show me how. I smoothened out pages, fixed loose spines, and made new book covers. I couldn't write words well yet, so Mama wrote the title with me adding what resembled a flower to each cover.

When I bragged to Hui about my picture books, she insisted on having a look. She was so amazed that she clicked her tongue every time I picked one book up and showed it to her. I was so pleased with her reaction that I didn't hesitate when she asked to borrow a couple. But I made it clear that she had to return them the next day.

She didn't. One day later when Hui came with two of my picture books and a timid smile, I gave her a harsh look and then my back. In the days that followed, I refused to talk to her. Whenever I saw her on her way to the outhouse, I would slam our door with such force that she shuddered from head to toe.

Hui couldn't bear it any longer. One morning she stopped Mama, who was going somewhere, to pour out her grievances. I didn't know what she said to my mother, but I knew that Mama later returned home very upset.

She pulled me up from where I was sitting and spanked. It was the first time that Mama used corporal punishment on me. I cried as loud as my lungs allowed. Even Wang Nainai came, asking what was going on.

The truth was that I made it sound far more painful than it was. Mama stopped slapping long before I stopped crying. To make up for the hurt my buttocks endured, Mama later gave me a whole *wowotou*. Even though filled with undeserving guilt, I didn't say anything. I was always hungry those days. Everyone was.

Hui and I were friends again, which wouldn't have happened without Mama pushing it. She brought me to Hui's door, telling me to apologize. Stubborn as I was, I murmured something of that nature to Hui, which was enough to make her happy again.

CHAPTER 18

Two days after her coffin was bought and brought home, Hui's maternal great grandma died. The day before, lying on a wooden board next to the coffin, she had a smile on her face, as Hui told me. I wouldn't dare to go near her.

The last time I saw Hui's great grandma was months ago. She was making strings. With one of her bound feet as a stake to hold a thread in the middle, she bit on one end and twisted the other end between her hands. Then she stopped, picked up the bamboo scratcher at her side, and waved it at Hui, who took it, stuck the scratcher down her collar, and plowed.

Through the open door the coffin was seen with the lid on. Next to it, on her knees was Hui's mother wearing a hempen vest on top of a not-so-white bedsheet. She howled. She literally did, her hands up in the air and then down on the floor. As neighbors gathered, she turned louder and even began to strike her chest.

Hui, still in her usual clothes, stood outside, looking around as though it wasn't her great grandma that had died.

"You aren't crying?" asked I, going over to her.

"My mama is doing it for all of us. My baba works today, I don't know where my older brother is," said Hui. "You know, she died after my mama told her to."

"Who told your great grandma to die?" asked Aunt Shan, who was standing nearby.

"No one," said Hui. "My great grandma was dead in her coffin when I woke up this morning."

A day later Aunt Shan was heard telling Wang Nainai that the dead great grandma was made to die. "She'll come back to haunt us," warned she.

When something in the ceiling dropped to the floor and rolled, Mama got up and lit a match to see what it was. Nothing was there. Soon after she returned to bed, the roof began to rattle with a screeching noise. This time my brother rose and switched on the light, which miraculously stopped whatever was going on up there. If it was a ghost, the ghost ran just one round, and the rest of the night was quiet.

"Did you all hear? She is back, her ghost," yelled Aunt Shan the next morning. Not until Uncle Xu got home from work in the evening did he start to talk about his close encounter with a ghost the night before.

Uncle Xu was on his way to the male outhouse sometime after midnight when he ran into a white figure that had a huge head without a face. As if surprised by his sudden presence, the figure fell to the ground, but as Uncle Xu slowly approached, the figure rose again with two white wings as expansive as those of a flying vulture. Uncle Xu said he got so scared that he dashed back home without going to the outhouse.

"Have another funeral, a bigger one," said Wang Nainai to Hui's mother, who once again set up a mourning shrine, without a coffin this time and outside to have more space. The wooden board that had been Hui's great grandma's bed were propped up as a table, on which were a tablet with her name written in black, a plate of corn flour *wowotou*, some paper money, and four incense sticks inserted in a bowl of dirt.

Both Hui's parents, her stepbrother, and herself were there, kneeling in a row with their heads down. Wang Nainai was the first to come and bow, followed by Aunt Shan and her husband. Although Mama didn't believe ghosts so much, she brought me over anyway to bow. Uncle Xu and his wife arrived the last and bowed.

The second funeral didn't seem to appease Hui's great grandma at all, whose ghost returned several days later and every other week afterwards. Since it didn't hurt anyone in anyway, everyone kind of got used to it.

Between the backwall of Hui's family and the surrounding wall lived Hui's stepbrother Baobao, who was the same age as my brother. Ever since he dropped out of school, he had wandered the neighborhood, collecting anything he could sell.

Now and then Hui and I played outside Baobao's shanty. In the junk scattered there, we could always find something either Hui or I would like to keep. Several old buttons, two tiny cases for mint ointment, and half a pencil eraser had ended up in my possession this way. Of course, Hui had more stuff. It was her stepbrother, and she could go there any time.

Baobao just left. When Hui waved from her side of the yard, I jumped off the doorstep and ran over. Stenchy as the place was, we rummaged through when a cane handle poking out a pile of waste-paper caught my eyes. As I tried to pull out the basket underneath, something like a bedsheet fell onto my feet. Crumpled and dirty, it was white.

"What's this?" asked I, showing it to Hui.

"My brother's," said Hui as if it was nothing. But it was something to me.

The night when the ghost was supposed to run its round, my brother and I, barefooted, sneaked over to hide in a corner near Baobao's shanty and waited.

The tarp on the shanty moved, and Baobao stepped out. As he got closer, he was seen carrying that basket with that bedsheet in it. When he reached the elm, he placed the basket bottom up on his head with his chin resting on the handle and then threw the bedsheet on. Draped in white from head to toe, Baobao looked exactly the ghost Uncle Xu had talked about. Once he tied the loose part of the bedsheet around his waist, he was ready to leap onto the elm tree, only to be grabbed by my brother.

Next to her coffin, Wang Nainai had made a bed out of some straw for Baobao. Even though it wasn't really a bed, it was much better than sleeping on dirt. Baobao even started to eat with Wang Nainai. Not to rouse any suspicion that Baobao had badmouthed his stepmother, Wang Nainai declared how badly she, a single old woman, needed a grandson like Baobao to keep her company.

Baobao's misery began after his own mother died and his father remarried. Hui's mother was nice to everyone else but her stepson, who was never allowed to get inside the home. He slept in that shanty and ate whatever he could afford with the little money he made. To give his stepmother a bad name, he played the ghost.

"The second funeral worked!" cheered Aunt Shan, clapping her hands after the ghost seemed to have vanished.

CHAPTER 19

The day I turned six, Mama talked about me going to school. Believe it or not, I already had a school in mind. Not the elementary both my brother and sister had gone to and graduated from, but the one inside what had been a *yamen* or a county office at the time when men were still wearing pigtails. According to Wang Nainai, who had lived nearby during the short reign of the last Qing emperor, even though the *yamen* had a dungeon, the punishments for criminals were always staged under two pine trees outside the entrance. Without much entertainment at the time, Wang Nainai said those punishments were like shows to local residents. For a lesser crime, a criminal was tied to a bench with the pants down and the buttocks up. While the skin was being lashed open, blood spattered like petals of plum blossom. The one sentenced to die was always hanged on one of the pine trees with the dead body not being taken down for days. Wang Nainai even told me the county magistrate liked the sight of a dangling corpse, which reminded him of the roasted whole lamb he and his extended family enjoyed on the Lunar New Year's Eve. Not until sometime in 1917 was the *yamen* shut down and turned into an elementary school.

However, my wanting to go to that school had nothing to do

with its *yamen* history but everything to do with being a six-year-old. My best friend Hui was going there, so I wanted to go there too. Mama also wanted me to go there because it was a key elementary school with its most graduates going to better middle schools.

On a hot day in July, Mama brought me to the very school to apply for admission. Following an arrow sign, we came to a classroom where a woman sat behind a desk blocking the door. She handed Mama an application form. While Mama was filling it out, I was taking an oral admission test. The application took longer to be filled out. After I answered the last question who was the greatest leader of the country, Mama was still writing in that form.

For about a month, nothing was heard from the school. Two weeks before the new semester was to start, Mama and I went to the school again. The woman who had handled my application took us to see the principal. I didn't really get to see him. Only Mama did. He had me shut out of his office, saying it was a matter to be discussed among adults. A few minutes later, Mama came out and grabbed my right hand to leave. On our entire way home, Mama never said a word.

"How about going to the elementary school your brother and sister went to? A better school, has a bigger schoolyard," said Mama, pulling me to her side as I was getting ready for bed.

"Hui's going there, I want to go there too," groaned I.

"Hui? Her father a worker, our father isn't," squealed my sister, who just got back from the outhouse.

"Tell her, tell her not to want this or that. People like us just don't get what we want," grunted my brother behind the mat wall.

At that time, I already knew my father was in prison but still had no idea he would be the reason for me not to get into the school I wanted.

CHAPTER 20

The first day of school I made a friend, Dahua.

When our names were called one after the other, we went to the same desk and sat down on the same long stool. Like me, Dahua had applied to but didn't get accepted by the same elementary. Also like me, Dahua had never seen her father. But unlike me, she knew more about her father than I did about mine. Her father was arrested four months before he was executed, and she was born the day after his execution. One day Dahua even showed me a page of calligraphy by her father, which I could only stare at, unable to recognize one word I knew.

"So good, isn't it? My mama says only *haoren* can handwrite like this," gushed Dahua with a grin.

"I know, my mama says in ancient times a government official had to pass a calligraphy test first," enthused I.

Soon Dahua and I stopped going home at noon. Sitting at our desk, we ate what each other had brought as lunch, which almost always was half a *wowotou*. Whenever Dahua said my *wowotou* tasted better, I would say the same about hers.

One afternoon after lunch, we gave up a nap on our desk, running four blocks under the glaring sun to see a boy said to have a memory that was hard to believe.

With a crowd before us, Dahua and I held hands and squeezed our way to where the boy was sitting just steps away, in an old chair. Although surrounded, he didn't seem nervous at all, darting glances, wiping his nose, and scratching his neck as if he had been there all by himself.

"Name five heroes from *Water Margin*," asked a middle-aged man while handing over a five-*fen* coin.

"Song Jiang, Wu Yong, Gongsun Sheng, Guan Sheng, Lin Chong," spat out the boy in one breath.

"Tell the story about Liu Bei's three visits to Zhuge Liang," asked an older man, walking up to the boy with two five-*fen* coins.

The boy proceeded with ease and didn't stammer a bit through the entire story.

"How about Bai Juyi's *Song of the Piba*? It's my favorite," hollered a woman in the back.

The boy nodded but didn't begin until three five-*fen* coins jingled into the jar he was holding on his lap.

It was a long poem. The moment the boy recited all the eighty-eight lines of it, a round of applause rose with some yelling praises. Pleased with the reaction he got, the boy started to sway his body and clap his hands, chanting out the dynasties from Zhou to Qing. His mother, who was sitting on a stool nearby, wasn't happy about what her son was doing. She got up and started to stomp her feet.

"Why isn't he in school?" asked the same woman.

"I'm a neighbor, they don't have any money. Eat first before going to school," said the woman standing next to the mother.

"His father, where is his father?" asked the young man behind Hui and me.

"Where? In a labor camp. He was a high school teacher who taught classics.

He taught our son," sobbed the boy's mother with her eyes red.

I dug my right hand deep into my shirt pocket and fumbled for that one-*fen* coin Mama had given me as my weekly allowance. After I dropped my one *fen* in the jar, Dahua also dropped hers, which she said was her biweekly allowance.

"His baba taught his son well," said Mama when I told her about the boy after I got home that day.

"Where is my baba?" asked I.

"I told you, in prison," said Mama, straightening my shirt.

"In prison, which prison?" pressed I.

"Which prison? I don't know," said Mama.

"He was a teacher who taught classics?" asked I, trying to find out more about my father.

"A teacher but taught something else," said Mama.

"When he comes home?"

"Don't know. Wait, just wait. I'll tell you more about him when it's time," promised Mama drearily.

CHAPTER 21

The first day of my second grade wasn't that different from that of the first grade. Await were the same classroom, the same teacher, and the same classmates but without Dahua. I did run into her in front of an herbal store the other day. She told me she had to skip school to take care of her mother dying from ovarian cancer.

The bell rang. It was not the same teacher but another teacher in a blue outfit with bluntly-cut short hair who strode into the classroom. I knew her, and so did every student of the school. She was Teacher Li, the counselor for the Young Pioneers organization. At a special ceremony before the summer break, she was awarded a model teacher for grooming new members

"Your class teacher cannot be here today," mumbled Teacher Li as if to herself. Then in a louder voice she called the roll, fifty-six names. By the time she took out a red scarf from her pocket, she was almost shouting. Every student in the class kind of sat up to hear what she had to say.

"Mine when I was your age," said she, tying the red scarf around her neck. "Its red color never fades because it's blood from revolutionary martyrs."

For the rest of that first class, the Young Pioneers was the only subject Teacher Li discussed, from when the organization was founded to the importance of becoming a member.

I listened with my eyes wide open. I could even feel my heartbeat. For a moment Teacher Li looked as radiant as the Chairman Mao in the portrait high on the wall behind her. I was in awe.

About a month later, after the first class in the afternoon, the entire school gathered in the schoolyard to witness some new Young Pioneers pledging their allegiance.

Two of my classmates were among those marching onto the platform.

Standing at attention before the flag of the star and torch, with the right hand high above the head, they repeated, in unison, after Teacher Li. Then each had a red scarf tied around the neck by Teacher Li. It was glorious to be on that platform. It was glorious to wear a red scarf around the neck. I also wanted to be a Young Pioneer.

That evening, I wrote my first ever application. In just two sentences I made clear my desire to become a Young Pioneer. The next day I went to Teacher Li's office and handed it to her. Then I waited for Teacher Li to talk to me, which was what she would do if she approved a member. This inside information I had learned from a classmate who, as a member, knew every detail of the process.

When weeks passed without hearing from Teacher Li, I went to her office again.

"Teacher, have you looked at my application?" asked I.

"Yes," responded she without turning her head.

"A Young Pioneer, can I become a Young Pioneer?" blurted out I with eagerness.

For sure she didn't like my question. As her face changed from inattentive to frosty, she glanced at me up and down as if she saw an enemy.

"You don't know? You must know your father is a counterrevolutionary, you are from a very bad family," said she with knitted eyebrows.

"I've never met him," said I.

"Well, you are his child, you two are the same," growled she, getting up from her chair.

"I get good grades, the best in my class," said I.

"Grades? Grades aren't important, your family background is. Revolutionary thoughts are everything. Tell me what that red color means," asked she, pointing to the red Young Pioneers flag on the wall.

"Blood," quickly replied I, remembering what she had said of the red Young Pioneers scarf.

"Revolution. Revolution means blood. Anyone against revolution is an enemy and deserves to die" said Teacher Li, her face turning red.

When I left Teacher Li that day, I was as unclear about what revolution was and why it always led to bloodshed as I had been. What did become clear to me was that my father was a counterrevolutionary. Even though I didn't know what made him a counterrevolutionary, I knew a counterrevolutionary always ended up being either prisoned or executed. What also became clear to me was that not my grades but my father would determine my fate.

CHAPTER 22

Only once did Mama bring me along to her study session on Wednesday night at the residential committee, which was just a short walk away, but Mama insisted on leaving home more than an hour earlier.

On the doorstep of a two-story building sat a man who was coughing into one of his hands. He knew who Mama was and waved the other hand for us to enter.

When Mama and I fumbled our way up the stairs to the second floor, outside the only door open two women were chatting. The moment they saw us, they followed each other inside to sit at a table.

"Director," greeted the two together as another woman strode past us into the room.

"You two are early," chuckled the director, who then noticed me.

"Are you taking the study seriously?" asked she, looking at Mama.

"My two older children aren't home yet. She's afraid to be alone late in the day," explained Mama.

"Your self-criticism for this week," demanded the director.

"Here," said Mama, handing over two pages neatly folded together.

Sitting down in a corner at the near end of the hallway, I started to eat the boiled peanuts I had saved from supper. One by one I shelled them, turning three unshelled peanuts into five shelled ones and then ten halves. Placing one half into my mouth, I rolled it all over my tongue before crushing it between my teeth. The chewing was slow, and the swallowing even slower. Still, they didn't last as long as I had wanted. After staring like a fool for a while, I got up to check how many doors there were. Three of the six doors had a sign, and I was pleased I could read them all.

Back in the corner I slipped down again when someone patted me on the shoulder. It was Mama with several women dressed in black. I wondered to myself why I didn't notice them coming.

"What time is it?" asked I, rubbing my eyes.

"My youngest daughter," said Mama without answering my question. Her eyes were tearful, and she was in pain.

"Haya," uttered the women in one voice, quietly looking at me. While their eyes, big and sunken, didn't have any luster, their long and pointed faces showed gnarls of veins beneath the translucent skin. As I was trying to remember where I had seen them since they all looked familiar, slobber slowly dripped from the corners of their mouths. I was scared.

"Mama, go home," I cried.

"Maya, go home," dry coughed the women once again in one voice. They were mimicking me.

"Let's go home," said Mama, pulling me up.

"Who are they?" asked I.

"Who are you talking about?" puzzled Mama.

"The women in black," said I after we went outside the building.

"You're dreaming," said Mam.

CHAPTER 23

The new textbook I just got had a story about Pangu, the giant said to have created space and mankind. "If he has fathered mankind, he is my father too," reasoned I. "Since he isn't a counterrevolutionary in prison, I, as his child, would have no problem joining the Young Pioneers!" For a moment, all I could think about was my father Pangu.

Pangu went hunting on the longest day of the first lunar year. When he spotted a cave at the bottom of a mountain, he stumbled right in without any hesitation. After a thousand *li* of darkness, he came to an open space, where rows of peach trees in full bloom grew horizontally like logs lying in a lumberyard and birds flew vertically, looking alarmingly suicidal. While spring water gushed out from nowhere, comets of time shot through the air right in front of his eyes.

Curious, he set out to learn more about the place. Taking one hundred strides to the east, he slammed his forehead onto the sky that had two layers: a light blue and a dark blue. Even though nothing was on the light blue, shiny objects dangled from the dark blue. When he ran his huge hands over them, they knocked on each other, making jingles. A hundred strides to the west, he bumped his nose into the earth, where peach trees anchored their roots, water springs hid their eyes, and soil enriched itself with protein, vitamins, minerals, and more. He grasped a handful and tasted, yelling "*Xiang ji le*" or extremely delicious, one syllable at a time.

"How can this be?" Pangu recognized the chao and decided to do something about it. Arms and legs open, he stood in a big way like the Chinese character "*da*," one hand holding the sky and the other the earth. Moving his arms clockwise, he lifted the sky up and pushed the earth down, one *cun* or bit at a time. It was a slow and heavy process. Months passed before the sky and the earth were locked, with a huge click, into their right places. Pangu laughed his satisfaction when he saw the sky over his head and the earth under his feet.

The first year in the cave was lonely, which Pangu found hard to bear. What he wanted was kids running around his legs and playing with his toes. "I need a woman," he said to himself. At the foot of the Kunlun Mountain, he found Nuwua, who was busy firing five-colored rocks at the time. Bringing her back to the cave, he lay with her, and soon she got pregnant.

An impatient man, Pangu thought one child a year would take too long to fill the place up. When his crotch itched again, he thrashed himself among peach trees, squirting his white juice while shouting, "More kids!"

By the time Nuwua was about to give birth, the peach trees were also heavy with babies. According to historical records, the date of birth was marked exactly the same for all Pangu's children.

With the place suddenly crowded, lack of space became a serious problem. Glancing around, Pangu had an idea. One morning, after having a good breakfast, he tightened the belt around his waist and started to push in every direction. Miraculously all the sides retreated, yielding more room. While working on his project of expansion, Pangu never took a break. When his arms turned sore, he used in turn his feet, his head, and his back. The moment he finished, he died of exhaustion, leaving Nuwua a single mother to take care of all their children.

However, Pangu made every part of his body beneficial for his children. His left eye turned into the sun, and his right eye the moon. Perfect as wind was his breath with his hair scattered all over the sky as clouds. His sneeze made lighting, and his voice thunders. His limbs grew into all kinds of trees since he knew his children would need them. His sweat fell as morning dews and evening showers. Where his penis lumped to the side at the moment of his death, the most powerful remedy for men, *renshen* or *ginseng*, was discovered centuries later.

CHAPTER 24

In the back right corner of the inner room sat Mama's camphorwood chest. The metal strappings around it had gone rusty. The metal lock in the front, rusty too, featured a ferocious dragon face with a ring hanging through its nostrils. As Mama told me, all I needed to do to lock the chest was to click the dragon's nose back into its place.

It was Mama's because it was passed down from her grandma to her mama and then to her, which for sure made my older sister think about owning it one day. She had said to me many times it would be her camphorwood chest, not mine.

Even though Mama seldom allowed me around when she was looking inside her camphorwood chest, she let me know its story. The camphorwood had been donkey-transported from the deepest mountains of Jiangxi to Ningbo, where the best chest makers resided. Also, there was so much hassle to bring it all the way from Shanghai to the northern city where my father was teaching at the time.

One day after I returned home from school, Mama said she had something to show me. Along with a whiff of camphoric aroma, she brought to the table a tin box, in which were old photos that appeared to have been removed from a family album.

I recognized Mama. Her short hair, in one photo, was parted by a straight line in the middle, and a thick bang almost reached her eyebrows in another photo. Underneath some small photos was a larger one that showed Mama wearing a black robe and a flat hat with a long tassel. She seemed trying hard to keep a straight face.

"Like a Daoist priest," chuckled I.

"My graduation photo," said Mama, taking another glance at the photo.

"Fudan University," read I, looking at the embossed impression in the lower right corner of the photo.

"My university," murmured Mama.

"Who is this?" asked I as she picked up a photo in which she sat with a baby on her lap and a man standing behind.

"Your father," said Mama. "We took this photo when your sister was one hundred days old… you take after your father."

"I don't," mumbled I, resenting the comparison.

"Kind of small, let me find another one. Here this one, his forehead and your forehead, his eyes and your eyes, you resemble your father," concluded Mama after turning her head back and forth between the photo and me.

"I don't," insisted I, wanting to cry.

Without saying anything, Mama continued to rake through the photos with a dreamy expression on her face. Clearly her mind was drifting far back into a time I knew little about.

Several photos also showed the man being with my brother. The little boy was on his father's lap or in his father's arms. As he was making his first steps, his father was right there cheering him on.

When I saw a photo in which the man was dressed in a long robe that almost reached his feet, I asked why he wore something like that. Mama said it was a common attire among men at that time. To make her point, she went to pick up a *qipao* from the chest. “Years ago, I wore this all the time. Isn’t that pretty? Now pants,” said she, dropping the *qipao* before pulling up the legs of her pants.

CHAPTER 25

Before I had a bed to myself, I always slept in the same bed with Mama. Even though Mama detested me lying too close to her, the old coir bed had its own way of rebellion. We often fell asleep apart but woke up nestling together in the low-lying middle.

Even after my brother and sister started to eat and spend the night at school during the week, I felt no need not to continue to sleep right next to Mama. I liked it when she asked me to scratch her back while trying to fall asleep because that hand of mind used to scratch could easily make a quick detour to her breasts. Not often but it did happen that I got into bed before Mama just to steal glances as she was undressing herself. Once she lay down, I would cling to her like a vine to a tree until she nudged me away.

The bed creaked, and Mama was shifting the side. Not knowing if she was asleep or awake, I fanned a hand over her face. Immediately she grabbed it.

"What you're doing?" asked she in a weary voice.

"Cannot sleep," mumbled I.

"Count numbers," Mama readily coached.

"Cannot sleep," mumbled I again.

"Told you to count numbers," said Mama impatiently. I became impatient too by banging the bed with my legs.

"Stop doing that." Mama sat up and held my legs down with her hands.

"Tell me a story!"

"It's time to sleep."

"Tell me a story!"

"What story you want to hear?"

"How you and he met?"

"Who is he?" asked Mama, pretending not to understand my question.

"The man in the photo," said I.

"… your father and I met at Fudan. His father, your paternal grandpa once paid a visit to Shanghai from his village in Anhui to see neon lights, tall buildings, and foreigners he had heard so much about. But while there, he was made fun of by some locals, who didn't like the way he looked and talked. Upset as he was, nothing he could do. After returning home, when he saw his only son, he had an idea. His son would get his higher education right there in Shanghai. Several years later at the age of eighteen, your father passed the entrance exams and was admitted to Fudan University.

"I was a sophomore when a friend of mine introduced to me your father, a senior who was looking for help with his English pronunciation. I tried, but he just couldn't get rid of his heavy accent. I almost gave up on him when a cousin of his suffering from leukemia came to Shanghai to seek treatment. Since he couldn't afford a hospital stay, your father let him move in with him. While his cousin slept in his bed, he got some sleep on the floor. Whenever his cousin needed to see a doctor or go to a place, your father would go with him. I was so moved that I changed my mind. Instead of stopping tutoring him,

I tutored him more often. By the end of that semester, your father's English pronunciation didn't improve much, but we had become inseparable. Your father graduated first. Soon after my graduation, we decided to get married.

"At first my parents didn't like it. They felt your father's family was too old-fashioned. 'His father is filled with old stuff. He's going to ask you to follow the three obediences and the four virtues,' protested my mother. Your father's parents were horrified when they learned my father had studied abroad. 'Son, you cannot do this to our family. She has foreign ink in her blood, which is bad for our future generations. Does she look foreign? Even if she doesn't, our grandchildren will,' pleaded they.

"Realizing our mind was made up, my parents were the first to give in. As long as she was happy, they reasoned. Your father's parents felt relieved after I paid them a visit since I looked just like everyone else and even spoke some local dialect.

"Your father and I couldn't care less about a formal wedding. We even thought about having a bicycle trip instead. That was an idea inspired by the love story of Marie and Pierre. Have you heard about them? They were foreign scientists.

"If only we could have had our way. Both families insisted on us having a formal wedding. What they couldn't agree on was the color of the wedding. My parents desired a white one, the color of purity to symbolize the beginning of a long marriage. We had had a white wedding when we got married, exclaimed they. Your father's parents couldn't believe their ears when they heard about it. That color is for funerals. A wedding should always be red, and only the red color could lead to a happy life together. To accommodate both families, we let go our bicycle plan and had two separate weddings.

"The white wedding was held in a restaurant on Sichuan Road

in Shanghai. I was in a flowing white gown and surrounded by white flowers. Champion instead of Maotai was served. As a band played foreign music in the background, we waltzed and then cha-ch0aed. Of course, no one from your father's family attended that wedding.

"A month later, we went to Anhui for our red wedding. Your father's parents had heard about the white wedding and were determined to minimize the negativity brought by the white color.

"I, in red from head to toe, was led into a hall that was completely decorated in red. Just like me, your father the groom was in red from head to toe too. Red was not just the wedding ceremony but also the bedroom. After the wedding, for quite some time, my eyes couldn't stand anything red."

Mama paused, and her eyes gazed into darkness, perhaps seeing herself first in a white gown and then in a red dress, frolicking and whirling with her new husband from a ballroom dazzling white to a bridal chamber draped in lavish red. It was a world once real but forever shattered. That night Mama let me have a glimpse of it.

Mama also told me more about my grandparents that night. During the land reform, my paternal grandparents were beaten to death in the very hall where their only son had held his wedding ceremony. Their bodies, dragged through their own rice fields, were thrown into the very pond that had been the family's source of water for more than one hundred years. Getting wind of what was happening while visiting Malaysia, my maternal grandpa decided not to return. His wife, my maternal grandma tried to join him, but the boat she took was intercepted off the coast.

At the same time, my father was being reeducated at a camp. Months later he was sent to teach at a university in the north, where two years later, Mama, together with my brother and sister, joined him.

During another sleepless night, Mama told me more, about my father.

It was late and raining hard, and Mama, seven months pregnant with me, was already in bed, while my father was working on a lesson plan at the desk. Suddenly thumps were heard from the gate with my father wondering who would be out there at that hour in that kind of weather. When Mama said that someone might need help, my father took an umbrella and hastened out. Minutes later, it was not my father but a militiaman carrying a rifle who pushed the door half open. Without getting inside, he delivered the news that my father was wanted for questioning. By the time Mama got off the bed and struggled to the door, he was gone.

The next morning Mama went to one militia station after another, looking for my father. But the militiamen she ran into had no idea who my father was as he was just one of so many that had been arrested. A warm-hearted militiawoman at one militia station took pity on Mama. "You'll know, go home to get some rest," consoled she with one hand on Mama's belly.

CHAPTER 26

When I walked in, a cheerful Mama was scaling a fish she bought in the morning market. My father would be home that evening, which was all Mama had been talking about for some time. But instead of being excited, I felt numb and even strange about meeting for the first time the man called my baba. Not saying a word, I sat down at the table and did my homework before stepping outside.

On trees cicadas were still singing even though already after five o'clock in the afternoon. The sun wasn't as bright as an hour earlier but still blinded eyes. I sought the shades along the walls as I hurried along.

Even though I wasn't sure where I was going, I avoided the direction that would take me to the residential committee. The residential committee wasn't a problem, and the problem was the neighborhood police station, which was officed on the first floor of the same building. My father would be brought to the neighborhood police station first before he was allowed to come home. The last thing I wanted was to run into him.

Out of another alley after our alley, I found myself not far from our waterman's door. I had been sent here several times to pay the water money we owed him. Even though it wasn't much, almost always even not much we didn't have. Whenever my brother said he could bring water home on Sundays to save money, Mama told him to study harder. The waterman needed to make money to support his family, explained she.

Every time our waterman came to deliver water, he would pull his watercart, a handcart strapped with two water barrels, as close as possible to the gate. Once two buckets got filled up, he would carry them by using a shoulder pole all the way to our door. He came and went twice, emptying altogether four buckets of water into our vat behind the door. That was only one barrel of water. The other barrel of water went to two of our neighbors, two buckets for Wang Nainai and two for Uncle Xu.

At first the vat was just a water container to me. But once I noticed the reflection of my face in there, it became something else, a mirror. Mama never understood why I started to dawdle around the vat. Whenever she saw me there, she would push me away, telling me to be extra careful.

Outside our waterman's door parked his watercart that was still wet and dripping. He just got home, said I to myself. Over there next to a crooked tree was the well. A hand pump well that was. The young woman trying to get her basin filled was working hard at it. Only after she cranked the handle three times was there water spouting out. Every time our waterman came late, he would complain about how old that hand pump was. "More than a hundred years old, it takes forever to fill up my water barrels," hollered he before maneuvering his buckets one after the other out of the door.

To the side several barefooted women were doing laundries. Their washboards were weathered bricks from the city wall some distance away. Not much had been left of some sections of the ancient wall, but their bricks carried on.

Two women were passing by, and one asked the other what kind of girl would be away from home by herself, which bothered me. I got up from the brick I had been sitting on and headed in the direction I had come.

Under a tree two little girls were playing with dirt. When I walked over, they were so focused that they didn't even give me the side eye. I didn't care as long as I wasn't alone. "Time for supper!" called their mother. They didn't just leave. Together they stomped on what they had been working on, which quickly fell back to the ground as though it had never been there. Since they couldn't have it, no one would.

It was getting really late, and the first star had jumped to the sky. For the reason I had left home, I wasn't ready to go back yet. I started to dig dirt too. Wriggling beneath my fingers was an earthworm eating and emptying at the same time. Once exposed, it was in a hurry to thrash back into its native surroundings. I didn't put a foot on it even though I was in a mood to. As its pinkish body was disappearing, I looked on with envy. It had at least somewhere to go.

Then I heard Mama calling me. I sat up and quietly waited for her to approach. Then she saw me.

"Your father is home, let's go," said Mama, grabbing my right arm. No matter how hard I tried to free myself, she wouldn't loosen her grip.

There he stood, his back toward the door. The moment he turned around, his tanned face was all I could see in that split of a second. I looked away as his eyes searched for mine. I didn't want to be here, cried I to myself. With Mama's hands tight around my shoulders, I couldn't move.

Suddenly wrinkles crowded the corners of his eyes and a slight smile broke out on his face as he stepped forward. Before I knew it, he held my right hand in his and shook it up and down as if guessing its weight.

"Call baba," urged Mama. My heart stopped. How impossible that sounded! My mouth dry and my tongue numb, I couldn't utter anything.

"Ba," murmured I as Mama leaned over my head with her eyes on my lips. Even though it was only half of what Mama had wanted, it was good enough. She gave me a pat on the back and let me go.

CHAPTER 27

I was told to go to a movie with my father the next evening.

No sooner did I follow him outside the door than I slowed down. When he noticed me trailing behind, he stopped for me to catch up with him. Since I would stop too, he resumed his way, turning his head to check on me now and then.

I entered the cinema together with my father because he had my ticket. But rather than sitting in my seat next to him, I sat several rows behind him. Only when an usher held a flashlight to my face and asked for my ticket, did I go to sit with him. Throughout the movie, I stared ahead at the screen. I wasn't watching the movie; I was waiting for it to end.

Once the lights were back on, I left my seat and went outside, where I crossed the street to stand under the eaves of an already closed store. In front of the cinema gathered those eager to get in for the next movie. But they wouldn't be allowed in until the place was cleared. Through a side door, those having seen the movie were slowly coming out. Now it was their turn not to worry about being late.

I saw my father, a lonely figure standing conspicuously at a lit spot near the side door. He looked at everyone passing him. He was looking for me.

I went home by myself. Along the way were blocks that were dark and had few people. So scared was I that I ran as fast as I could. What if my father didn't know to come home? I thought at one point only to dismiss it by concentrating on my footsteps.

"Where is your father?" asked Mama, who was surprised to see only me.

"Don't know, maybe at the cinema," said I.

At that Mama threw on a shirt and hurried out. Now I became really worried, starting to regret what I had done. All I hoped was that my father was still at that lit spot, so my mother could easily find him.

At the table I sat listlessly with our old alarm clock right in front of me. Its every tick took so long and so much effort, and one minute was like an hour.

When the door opened and both my parents walked in, I let out a sudden cry of relief. Then tears streamed down my face, an outpouring of grief that had been held for some time. I lived just fine without this man. I didn't need him. He had brought me nothing but troubles.

CHAPTER 28

Across the yard Uncle Xu stood up, took another glance at the sky, and went inside. And seconds later, his wife went inside too before shutting their door.

"Where are your brother and sister? They should be home," murmured Mama, sitting next to me on the doorstep. Through the open window, seen at the table was my father, a dark figure against a darker room.

When my brother and sister were home last Sunday, Mama reminded them of the Mid-Autumn Festival this Sunday.

"Your baba is home next Sunday, let all of us watch the moon together," said Mama to my brother before he went out of the door on his way back to school that Sunday evening.

"Do come home to watch the moon next Sunday," said Mama to my sister as she was leaving for school next Monday morning.

As the moon gradually climbed higher, it slowly floated toward me, getting closer and therefore bigger. For a moment I felt I could almost touch it or walk into it if I wanted. No longer did it look as solid bright as it was afar. Those intertwined shadows were said to be the grand palace where Changer had been dancing alone for years and years.

"The moon palace for Changer!" said I, pointing to a dark spot on the moon, which to my eyes, looked like a big house of exquisite construction. In addition to a laurel tree, there was a rabbit. Not any rabbit, though. It was a jade rabbit as the story went.

"Really?" Mama wasn't so sure about what I saw.

"Changer is coming out, she is going to look down at the place where she once lived. She misses her husband and regrets having taken elixir," continued I, assuming Mama knew little about Changer.

Rustled the pomegranate tree outside Wang Nainai's window. As Mama and I looked on, someone slowly stood up from a squatting position. It was my brother.

"Come, come to watch the moon," said Mama, edging closer to me for my brother to sit next to her on the other side.

For a while, none of us said anything. His head on his lap, my brother kept stroking his hair. Then he removed his glasses and wiped them on his shirt before putting them back on.

"I have to show I have nothing to do with him," mumbled my brother. "It's not good to be found out watching the moon with him."

"Do what's the best for yourself, I understand," said Mama, her eyes on the moon.

After my brother put his left arm around Mama's shoulders for a long squeeze, he got up to leave. Not once did he look sideways towards the window, where my father had become part of the room.

By the time Mama and I went indoor, my father had gone to bed behind the mat wall. His time home would come to an end at five o'clock tomorrow morning when he was expected at the neighborhood police station. It was already close to midnight.

CHAPTER 29

"A *jin* of hairtail," said Mama to the saleswoman behind the counter after she and I stepped inside the store for rationed groceries.

At that the saleswoman turned around and gave a kick to a gunny sack on the wet floor. As several hairtails slipped out, she used her right foot to sweep a hairtail into the pan of the steelyard.

"Don't do that," gasped Mama, who seldom picked on anyone but couldn't help this time.

Immediately the pan of the steelyard was flung down on the counter with a loud bang, sending the hairtail flying toward me. I dodged, and it landed on the floor behind me.

"You, the stinky wife of a counterrevolutionary is finding fault with me," exploded the saleswoman.

Mama didn't say another word. She paid, I picked up the fish, and we left.

It was something Mama had become long used to. She just couldn't allow herself to be bothered by it anymore. But for me it was still so hard.

"What do your parents do?" asked Teacher Huang, the new class teacher.

"Workers," said the girl classmate sitting in the first row.

"Your parents?" Teacher Huang had come up the aisle to where I sat.

"My mother…" said I.

"Your father first," interrupted he.

"… works from home," said I, ignoring what he said.

"Don't you have a father? Your father first," insisted he.

Talking about my father was impossible for me, not to mention in front of all my classmates. I didn't say another word, which Teacher Huang apparently didn't expect from a student. For a minute he tried to stare me down, but I stared back. My eyes! I wouldn't have blinked had it lasted for the entire class time, forty-five minutes. Then he looked away and stepped to the next student.

Teacher Huang no longer needed to ask the question about parents. He just went up to a student, who would tell him what he was there for.

"My father is dead, my mother a salesclerk," said the boy classmate to my right across the aisle. Teacher Huang gave a nod and continued his way.

Dead, his father was dead! That was all he had to say! I thought to myself. That moment I envied the classmate whose father was dead.

Teacher Huang returned to the front. He pinched his nose and scratched his head before opening a folder.

"You get out, your father is a counterrevolutionary, a class enemy, you get out," shouted Teacher Huang, throwing his right arm toward the door behind me.

When I didn't move, he marched over. Lili, who sat with me at the same desk, sprang up to the side.

"Get out," shouted he again, grabbing me by my left arm,

I was determined not to leave. I couldn't use my left hand and arm, so I used my right hand and arm as well as my feet and legs to hold onto to my desk.

Many of my classmates left their seats. They looked on as Teacher Huang was trying to drag outside a girl classmate whose father was a counterrevolutionary.

"What's going on?" asked a voice outside the classroom.

"Our new teacher is fighting with ..." yelled a boy classmate standing on his desk. He didn't finish the last word, but I knew what it was, an enemy.

Then Teacher Huang loosened his grip. While he was walking back to the front of the classroom, he was rubbing his right hand with his left one.

Lili came over to help me get up as I was on the floor with my right hand clawing the inside of my desk drawer and my body coiling around my side of the desk. It was then when I felt something on my low lip. I licked and tasted blood.

CHAPTER 30

When I leaned over Mama's shoulder to see what she was reading, she pushed me away without looking up. Laid before her on the table was a piece of paper written on both sides. More than a year had passed since my father left, and a letter from him to Mama had finally arrived.

"It was beneath the door, someone left it there," said Mama, still not looking up.

"Can I? said I, trying to read too.

"No, it's for me, you shouldn't," said Mama, still reading.

Later that day I found the letter inside the table drawer. Still, I didn't get to read it. Mama took it from me and shoved it under the wok sitting on the stove. The smoke rose and dissipated, leaving behind no trace of the letter my father had written to Mama.

I understood why Mama burned that letter. She didn't want to turn it over to the residential committee, which would prompt a word-by-word analysis of the letter, bringing more troubles to my father. However, Mama did tell me a few things from the letter, which I couldn't stop thinking about until I started to write them down. It was the first letter I ever wrote, and it was a letter to Mama on behalf of my father:

My dearest, I was mostly indoor while in prison. But here in a labor camp, we are always outside. Unmarked on the map, it's located in the middle of a desert with sand stretching as far as the eye could see.

The temperature between day and night is so different, quickly turning icy cold after sundown and a hot pan at noon. We shiver at night and swelter during the day.

Before dawn, at the scratching sound of a whistle, we crawl out of our shed half buried in the sand. After the roll is called, each of us receives a sorghum wowotou, one half for breakfast and the other half for lunch. We toil in the fields until dark.

Mentally-active men who desire free thinking are being numbed through heavy physical labor. Their hands accustomed to holding pens and flipping books are reclaiming the wasteland that has slept for who knows how many years. We burn grass, cut down bushes, and dig wells. We plow and sow. We do everything without any help from either animals or machines. We have only the simplest tools such as hoes, plows, and spades. We use our hands, our backs, and our shoulders. Our hands blister time after time until calluses turn so thick that they no longer feel. Our backs bend for so long under so much weight that no one can stand straight anymore.

The dry wind has left our faces with cuts and bruises. We look darker than dried cow dung. When it gets warmer, insects are everywhere, making their ways into our clothes. I stumbled into a pit one day, and a swarm of wasps left my head swollen with bites.

Since I got here, I have written ten autobiographies, and every week I also hand over a self-criticism. We are asked to watch each other. Every other week we are called one by one into a room to report on each other. If you have nothing to report, you'll get nothing to eat that day. I have had twenty such days.

I miss you always. The other day, during the short lunch break, after half a sorghum wowotou was thrust down in a matter of minutes, I got some time for relaxation. Lying face-up in a cornfield with the sky above so high and so blue, I felt being lifted and became part of that vastness like a cloud. Through a green sieve of corn leaves, golden eyes of sunshine danced on and around me. They were flirting with me, like you. And the soil beneath suddenly smelled womanly sweet, and something warm started to brew inside me. While my heart was pounding, my blood was racing down until a panicked me rolled over to lie on my belly. After a minute or two, I got up to go back to work.

CHAPTER 31

"Let's go to have some stir-fried bean jelly," said my sister standing at the door.

To me, it was like the sun suddenly rising from the west since she never spent one *fen* on me. To prove she was not kidding, she showed me her money, two five-*fen* coins.

Outside the gate I was surprised to see Huo, Aunt Shan's older son who worked at a sewing factory. Only then did my sister tell me that he was going too.

Three of us strolled down the alley. With me in the middle, they two talked to each other over my head. Something was wrong with my sister, who giggled at everything Huo was saying.

Passing a stall selling fresh dates, we went straight to where bean jelly was sizzling in a pan on an earthen stove. As I was eating, Huo asked my sister what she wanted while he played with a five-*mao* bill in his hands. My sister appeared not right again, turning her head first to the right and then to the left, which probably was her way of saying not wanting anything. When Huo started to look sad, my sister tried to make a full turn on one foot, which wasn't very successful, though. Half way, she was throwing her arms around to maintain her balance. When she finally came to a halt, she was pointing at a man wearing a dirty apron.

"Fish stew, fish stew," chanted the man, starting to stir in the wok with a ladle. Fish stew actually had only eggplant without any fish in it. But any dish that included ginger and green onion was a fish dish because ginger and green onion were considered fish flavor.

"I like it too," approved Huo, asking for two bowls.

"Yes, two bowls," shouted the man again before picking up two small bowls. Huo finished his in no time, while my sister sucked a bit at a time from the bowl, showing no teeth.

Later in the evening, as Mama was telling three of us to get ready for supper at the table, there came loud curses outside our front door.

"Your mother's cunt! Want to seduce my son, a revolutionary worker? Who are you? Black trash from a counterrevolutionary family. Use your urine as a mirror to have a look at yourself..."

"Who is that?" asked my brother.

"Sounds like Aunt Shan. What's matter?" said Mama, looking out of the window and then at my sister.

"I didn't do anything," grumbled my sister.

"What is she talking about?" demanded Mama.

"Ask her," said my sister, pointing at me.

"I ate... stir-fried bean jelly," stammered I. But that wasn't what my sister wanted me to say.

"I took her to have stir-fried bean jelly earlier. Huo saw us and asked to go with us," lied my sister.

"Let me talk to your Aunt Shan," said Mama.

"Don't, don't try to add oil to the fire. I'm hungry, let's eat supper," chipped in my brother, who always knew what to say in a situation like this.

Aunt Shan's anger was subsiding. After taking a look around, she lackadaisically walked back to her side of the yard.

My sister sobbed at the table with her shoulders up and down in a rhythm. Seldom did I see her crying so hard.

Later she confessed to Mama what had been going on. For some time, Huo whistled at her whenever he saw her. Tantalized by the attention from a young man, my sister returned his flirting glances. The past Monday morning, he stopped her while she was on her way back to school and offered her a ride on the rear rack of his bicycle. She didn't refuse. Six days later, that very Saturday afternoon, Huo waited outside her school to take her home. She accepted. Then he asked her to eat something together. My sister hesitated at first. After some sweet talk by Huo, she agreed to go but under the condition that I would go with them.

CHAPTER 32

The waterman came and left.

"Let me boil some water," said Mam to herself, starting to ladle water from the vat to the wok on the stove.

In the wooden washtub at the base of the doorstep was my brother's bedsheet. Mama told him to put it there when he brought it home from school the day before.

"Why so filthy?" asked Mama.

"Well, after sleeping in my school's pigsty for two nights," said my brother.

"You slept in a pigsty? Don't tell me you slept there by yourself!"

"Yes, I did sleep in a pigsty, not by myself, a classmate was with me. His father is an old rightist."

"Were you told to sleep there?"

"No, I just wanted to show I'm not bad. My father is bad, but I'm not, I can endure all kinds of hardship," said my brother.

The air smelled heavily alkaline after some brown soda paste and hot water were added to the washtub. Sitting on a short stool with the washtub between her feet, Mama rubbed the sheet against the hardly visible ridges of the wooden washboard.

Ever since my sister stopped coming home on Sundays, Aunt

Shan had started to talk to us again. When she saw Mama outside, she came outside too.

"Find a man who can carry water for you," yelled she, snapping her fingers. Mama grinned and didn't say anything. It was Aunt Shan's husband who, once a week, would use a carrying pole to bring home water from the same hand pump well as our waterman. So would Hui's father.

Aunt Shan was teasing of course. She would be the first to call out anything inappropriate by a married woman and report it to the residential committee. One time she almost reported Hui's mother when she saw her chatting with a man outside the gate. Only after she learned that was Hui's uncle, did she not bring it up while in a monthly meeting with the cadre in charge of women affairs at the residential committee.

The moment my brother said he was going back to school to study for an exam, he disappeared. After hanging the washed sheet outside the window, Mama said she wanted to go to the temple fair.

She didn't just go. She tidied herself up first. After damping her hair, Mama rolled up one strand at a time with a hairpin. When she finished, she seemed to have a Buddha head.

Pulling out a light blue *qipao* from her camphorwood chest, Mama slipped it on and went to the mirror, which she jerked off the wall and held up to look at herself.

"Still fits," declared Mama, straightening here and there with the other hand.

"Cannot wear it outside," warned I.

"I know," murmured Mama, starting to remove those hairpins.

She kept combing her not-so-curly hair for a while before tucking it behind her ears.

Under the bed was a pair of black leather shoes Mama had never been seen wearing. They were from the past of course. Picking them up, she hit one with the other really hard and then put them on. They also still fit, and Mama smiled.

Just seconds later Mama quietly took off the *qipao* and the leather shoes. By the time we left home, she was wearing her usual faded clothes. They would fit so well on the streets.

The temple fair had for sale everything from rat poison to threads and thimbles. A stall could be as simple as a dusty figure squatting next to a page of old newspaper on the ground. There was even entertainment. With a sudden burst of the gong beating, a young man started to sing Beijing opera in falsetto, followed by a little girl who contorted her body into one ring after another.

Mama and I came to a handcart, where a man was printing a door picture of two dragons playing with a fire ball. He brushed red ink on the carved woodblock and then placed a piece of straw paper on it. After repeatedly pressing the paper, he carefully lifted it up before clipping it to the side of the handcart to dry.

Mama asked for a door god. In just a matter of minutes, the door god came off the woodblock in wet red. Mama was pleased, saying just a look at it could make us safe.

With the man Mama chatted. Even though Mama didn't say, I felt that they had known each other. On the way home, I kept wondering if he was the reason Mama went to the temple fair. I just wondered. I didn't actually ask.

CHAPTER 33

The small room in the gateway had always been vacant since we moved there. The half-hinged door squeaked whenever a gust of wind was passing. Now and then I dumped garbage there, too lazy to walk to the pit half a block away. I wasn't the first to do that, though. Hui started it.

Coming home from school on afternoon, I couldn't believe my eyes to see a lock on the newly fixed door and a full-page old newspaper covering all the cracks and dents. When I told Mama about it, she hummed something like not good to sniff around like a little dog.

For the next several days, the sole purpose of my life had become to find out who had moved into that room. Hui and I hanged around there whenever possible, but that door was always locked shut.

One evening Hui ran across the yard like smoke and without saying a word, dragged me to the gateway. The lock on the small room's door was gone, and the *erhu* was heard playing inside. I tried to look inside. Before I knew it, the music stopped, and I was staring at a man wearing glasses. He said something, but I didn't hear. Hui and I were racing as fast as we could to our safe haven, the female outhouse.

When Mama suddenly scolded me for peeking into a neighbor's room, I thought Hui had betrayed me. But soon I realized Mama not only knew the man who just moved into that small room but well.

One day on our way out, Mama talked with him. Without his glasses, I recognized him as the man making door pictures at the temple fair. I didn't like the way he looked at my mother. When Mama introduced him as "Uncle Xia," I turned my head away.

Midnight wasn't that quiet for sure. The moon could be heard shining, and stars tinkling. Outside our window some crickets were singing something really annoying. Then a mosquito dashed head-on against my bed curtain with a high-pitched buzz. While two dogs barked at each other in a duel from the other side of the surrounding wall, a cat, perhaps lost, kept mewing somewhere on our roof or Wang Nainai's.

I shifted the side only to find Mama no longer next to me. She had gone to the outhouse and would come back, I thought. When she didn't, I became worried. I got up and came to the window. As the moon up in the sky was drifting away with its palaces, I was gripped with the fear that Mama had flown away like Changer.

From the direction of the gate two people approached. As they got closer, I saw Mama and Uncle Xia, who came to a stop in front of our door. While they stood as one casting only one shadow, they looked up at the moon.

It was then that I left the window, relieved that Mama didn't go to the moon and was still with us. All her three children needed her, and I needed her the most.

The next day I didn't say anything about the last night, nor did I tell anyone about it. It was Mama's little secret, I sensed. When it happened again, I wasn't even bothered, knowing where Mama was.

CHAPTER 34

Aunt Shan waved for me to go over to her as I was getting out of Wang Nainai's door.

"You like stories, don't you? I have one about a hen spirit," said she, pushing me down on a small stool next to her.

Late at night, the student was preparing for his exams under a dim light when there came a knock on the door.

"My good brother, open the door," said a woman's voice.

"I have to study for my exams," resisted the student at first.

"My good brother, I won't stay for long. I have brought you a *shaobing* stuffed with chicken meat. So late, you must be hungry," pleaded she.

When the door opened, a stunning woman in a white silk dress floated in, with a *shaobing* in one hand.

Right there the student lost all his mind. He first ate her *shaobing* and then went to bed with her as he was told to.

Early next morning, the woman got up and hurried away, saying she would return that night.

The student wasn't interested in his study anymore. Day after day, he waited for the woman to show up so that he could eat the *shaobing* as well as share the bed with her. Day after day, in a strange way, the student became paler and weaker, struggling to even stand up.

One day a Daoist priest came to the village. The moment he saw student, he shouted, "Possessed, possessed!"

The student was so scared that he kneeled down and begged for help. After some hesitation, he told the Daoist priest about the woman in a white silk dress.

"Don't worry, I'll help you," said the Daoist priest, who gave the student a ball of red yarn and instructed him what to do with it.

That night the woman in a white silk dress showed up as usual. When she handed the student the *shaobing*, he placed it in a tray on the table, saying, "I'm so tired, let's go to bed."

After the woman fell asleep, the student sat up and gingerly tied the loose end of the red yarn to her right ankle and dropped the remainder in an urn under the bed.

The student didn't sleep at all. No sooner did the woman get up and leave at dawn than he went to the table. What he saw in the tray were some chicken droppings.

When the Daoist priest arrived later, he and the student followed the red yarn to a chicken coop on a nearby farm, where a white hen stood out with a red yarn tied to her right shank. Before the white hen had time to run away, the Daoist priest waved his whisk at her, casting a spell that paralyzed her ability to turn into a human ever again.

Never had I heard a story like that. But I didn't tell Mama as Aunt Shan had wanted me to. I wouldn't.

Days later I returned home from school only to find the door to the inner room shut. When it opened, Aunt Shan and the cadre in charge of women affairs from the residential committee marched out. At the table Mama was wiping her eyes.

That night and the following two nights, Mama didn't go anywhere. Then the fourth night, a Saturday night, when my brother returned home from school, he said the man living in the gateway was outside. Mama didn't say anything. Once she finished doing some chores, she was knitting again. After three of us children went to bed, she turned off the light and came to bed too. However, she didn't lie down. With her eyes closed, she sat with her head against the wall.

On my way out to school next morning, a weary Mama asked me to hand a sealed self-made envelope to Uncle Xia. I didn't actually hand it to him. I slid it under his door.

That evening and every evening after for two weeks, the sad *erhu* music could be heard from that small room, one moment a man's sighs and another moment a woman's cries.

For two weeks, Mama didn't go so far as near the gate until Uncle Xia moved away. The small room turned vacant again.

CHAPTER 35

My brother lay motionless on the floor with his head on the quilt he had just brought home from school. He was awake even though his eyes were closed, and his glasses sat legs up on his chest.

"Are you ok?" asked Mama, stirring in the boiling wok on the stove in the outer room.

"Are you ok?" repeated I, sitting at the table.

"I'm fine, just tired," groaned my brother as if from another world. "I haven't had much sleep."

"Go to lie in bed. The floor is wet, don't get sick," said my sister, walking in from the outside. Unlike my brother, she moved back home from school two days earlier right after the college entrance exams.

"Tell me how your *gaokao* went," said my brother with his eyes still closed.

"I think I did well, better than last year. How about you?" asked my sister, sitting on the edge of her bed, her feet next to my brother's.

"I think I did well too," said my brother, opening his eyes. "My *gaokao* scores are good, I'm going to college!"

"You know someone like us with a father like ours can't get into college, don't you?" said my sister, who took *gaokao* the year before but wasn't accepted even though her *gaokao* scores were above the admission requirements. She took *gaokao* for the second time after two semesters of auditing in the same high school.

"Who doesn't know? It's policy," said my brother, making a yawn.

"Don't see myself get accepted this time either. What I'm going to do? Maybe kill myself," said my sister, staring ahead.

"Don't, don't say that. Why kill yourself? Cannot go to college, cannot find a job, let's go to Heilongjiang. Have you heard about the Heilongjiang Production and Construction Corps?" asked my brother, sitting up before patting off the sand on his back.

"Of course I have. But it's so cold there, I don't want to be frozen to death," said my sister.

"Don't think too much about death. Try to live as long as you can," said my brother, stretching his legs after getting up.

"Can't find a job, can't even find a husband. Who wants to marry someone like me?" said my sister, her voice starting to crack.

"Someone will marry you, just wait," said my brother behind the mat wall.

On a cloudy day in September, my brother left for the Heilongjiang Production and Construction Corps. He didn't have to leave so soon, just two months after graduating high school. But he kept saying he couldn't wait to earn his own *wowotou*.

It was like every time he went to school either early Monday morning or late Sunday afternoon during his high school years. But every time he always came back. This time no one knew when he would come back or if he would ever come back.

With tears in our eyes, Mama, my sister, and I quietly followed my brother to the gate, where waiting was the same classmate who went to sleep in the pigsty with him. He also had a bad family background but was blessed by Old Heaven with a distant uncle who worked as a tractor mechanic in one of the farms affiliated with the Heilongjiang Production and Construction Corps. The uncle, no matter how distant a relative he was, could make life easier for two new high school graduates.

"Write to me as soon as you get there," cried Mama, wiping her eyes.

"I will, I will," assured my brother, his free hand on Mama's left shoulder.

Mama, my sister, and I didn't go back home until my brother and his classmate made a left turn at the end of the alley.

My sister didn't know where to go yet, but as long as she was home without a job, she was a street youth under the supervision of the residential committee.

She was always mean to me, and now she was meaner. When no one was around, she pinched me or yanked my hair or kicked my behind. I tried to avoid being alone with her, but it was hard to do.

One day when I came home from school and didn't see Mama around, I hesitated to get inside the door. It was then when my sister asked me to get her some water. She was thirsty, she said. As I brought a bowl of water to her at the table, she didn't take it. Instead, she shoved the bowl, which landed on my chest with water all over me.

Fearful of what my sister would do next, I went outside to sit on the doorstep. Little did I knew she was right behind me. She pulled me up by my right ear and pushed. I tumbled but didn't fall. When she tried to push me again, I ran to the gate.

I was waiting for Mama to come home when my sister came. As

she grabbed me by my left arm to go home with her, she smiled at any neighbor who happened to be outside as if nothing was going on.

Once we got inside, my sister bolted the door before kicking me to the floor. I cried while her feet rained on my back and sides

"Stop crying," muttered she. Angier, she pinched me up by my mouth and wrung. At that point I could only whimper.

Not wanting to endure another minute of it, I struggled free and dashed to unbolt the door, but my sister was one step ahead of me. She stood against the door and began to slap me on my head.

"This is good, leaves no marks," she laughed as my head turned left and right between her hands.

When she stopped, she gave me another push. I stumbled, my face crashing onto a short stool nearby.

The next thing I knew I was on the floor with my sister wiping blood off my nose. Then she applied purple alcohol to the bruises on my forehead. Her touch was gentle, and her face softened.

It was quiet for a while. My sister went to the outer room and then came back to the inner room to stand before the window.

Tears blurred words in the textbook, and hardly could I keep doing my homework. I didn't know why my sister would try to hurt me like that. She was older, many years older.

"You fell yourself, didn't you? I had nothing to do with it," said my sister, looking at me.

I quickly nodded. I didn't want to be hit again.

"I fell," said I to Mama when she asked me about the bruises after she got home from having paid a visit to Aunt Chen in hospital. Like a doctor, Mama held my forehead to the light and examined. She even blew air on it to soothe my pain. To some extent her presence did.

CHAPTER 36

As rainwater was climbing up the doorsteps, Mama and I busied ourselves with moving the things under the beds onto them.

The camphorwood chest was on the floor. Mama emptied most of it before two of us lifted it and put it on the table.

"Do we need to get to the roof?" asked I, mindful of a scene from a movie, in which terrified people were stranded on rooftops.

"Hope we don't," said Mama, placing a washing basin on top of the camphorwood chest for a leak in the ceiling.

So worried Mama was about my sister that she kept looking out in the direction of the gate. Since my sister joined the propaganda team organized by the residential committee, seldom had she been home during the day. Sometimes she didn't come back until midnight.

Hui's father was taking Wang Nainai to the gateway, the only place the flood hadn't reached. No one knew what would happen if it kept raining like that, and the fear was that the Yellow River would crest, inundating the city like a rathole.

Under one oilcloth, Mama and I were splashing our way toward the gate. In the bundle Mama slung over her left shoulder were a thin quilt, an old sweater she was going to reknit, and a *wowotou.*

Not every neighbor wanted to leave home. Uncle Xu and his

wife were trying hard to scoop out the rainwater that was turning their small dwelling into a small pool. Kept wide open was Aunt Shan's door, through which she and her husband were seen squatting on the bed against the sidewall.

The small room in the gateway had turned into a shelter of a sort by Hui's mother, who was attending an earthen pot of ginger soup on a makeshift stove. Sitting down next to Wang Nainai on a pile of straw, Mama took out the sweater in the bundle, shook it open, nipped off a knot at the bottom, and started to unravel it onto her left elbow.

"Where is your older daughter?" asked Wang Nainai, sewing a sole.

"Don't know. She tells me nothing," complained Mama.

"All daughters are like that. Without telling me, Hui went to spend summer with her paternal grandparents," said Hui's mother.

As it was getting darker, Hui's mother lit up the kerosene lamp she had brought and placed it on the windowsill. Immediately mosquitoes could be heard buzzing. Almost at the same time, a lizard appeared on the wall and crept toward the window with its eyes rolling outward. Once it got near the lamp, it darted its tongue several times before it turned quiet again.

"All is well! All is well," called Hui's father like a night watcher after finishing a cigarette outside the door. That was the last thing I heard before dozing off with my head against Mama's side.

I even dreamed. Once a fallen tree was removed from me, I started to run for no reason. Several steps later my body lightened, my feet went off the ground, and I was flying higher and higher, two wings flapping where my arms were. Below were winding rivers, green trees, rugged mountains, terraced fields, people so tiny like ants, and my sister, who happened to look up with one hand on her forehead. I shouted, "No more your bloody menstrual cloths! You wash them yourself!" Her face turned dark as I cast a long shadow over her.

"Rain has stopped, let's go home," rang a voice. It was Mama, who was putting her bundle back together.

Lingering in the air was a fog so light that it seemed almost not there. Early as it was, it was another day. Wading before Mama and me was Hui's father, once again carrying Wang Nainai on his back.

When I woke up the next morning, it was almost noon, and Mama could be heard doing something in the outer room. Was I late for school? No, no school on a Sunday. Then the sheet was yanked off me, not by Mama but my sister who just got home.

"Don't tell anyone," said my sister, lying down next to me. "He didn't go to high school. Well, his parents are municipal cadres, they'll find a job for him. He and I played *pingpong* last night. He kept winning but conceded the last round to make my happy... he wants something from me."

"Something, what?" asked I.

"Not, not sure," stammered my sister, gesturing for me to lie on top of her.

Why did she want me to do that? I really didn't understand. But my sister insisted even after I told her I was too heavy and would crush her to pieces.

"Let me have a look," said my sister the moment I came off her.

"At what?" asked I.

"That," said she, pointing between my legs.

"Why?" asked I.

"Just a look," croaked she, grabbing my legs and trying to remove the underwear.

"No," said I, kicking to free my legs.

"Just a look," demanded my sister, not letting me go.

"No," screamed I at the top of my lungs.

"Go to your own bed. Don't bother your younger sister," said Mama outside the window.

After giving me a hard squeeze on the thigh, my sister rolled off the bed and went to her own bed.

CHAPTER 37

I really didn't want to, but Mama insisted that I go with her to the train station to see my sister off, who was joining the Xinjiang Production and Construction Corps. I would be turning deserts into cotton fields as she had been saying for days.

The train was starting, but Mama was still holding onto the open window, through which my sister just climbed inside the train. I would send you some Xinjiang raisins once I got paid, yelled my sister in a high-pitched voice. Xinjiang raisins were raisins that didn't have seeds.

"Sign," hollered the mailman.

"What happened?" asked Mama, looking at the package.

"It was like that when I got it," said the mailman, leaping on his army green bicycle and pedaling away.

"From Hong Kong," uttered Mama, seeing the sender's address on the package.

The package was damaged and appeared as if it had been dropped in mud and stomped on. All the stamps featuring the crowned head of a woman had been scrawled on with her eyes gouged. Tears here and there revealed aluminum cans inside.

Mama opened the package, and the four dented small cans slid onto the table. She read the two largest English words on each can: Condensed Milk and stared at the two Chinese characters scribbled on the top of the last can.

"She still remembers me," murmured Mama.

"Who?" I couldn't wait to know.

"My sister, bolt the door," said Mama.

"Another sister?" asked I, dashing back from the door. I was surprised. I had always thought Mama had only one younger sister, who was a school teacher in Shanghai.

"Another sister," confirmed Mama.

"Where is she?" asked I.

"United States," said Mama.

"Does she know me?" asked I.

"No, she left long before you were born," explained Mama, scooping the cans into the table drawer.

I never saw them again. Two days later, as I was looking into that drawer, Mama said she had handed them over to the residential committee.

By that time, I had learned a lot about the United States of America at school. It was an imperialist country that had invaded many other countries. It had two very bad presidents, Kennedy and Johnson, who had sent American troops to Vietnam, a neighboring country.

Waiting for the first class to start in the morning, we often sang a song that began with "American imperialists are guilty of monstrous crimes and do bad things everyday..." It was understood that if we sang that song loud enough, it could be heard across the ocean, scaring the hell out of American devils.

CHAPTER 38

In the waiting room of the local railway station, fifty of us, each with a roll of bedding, sat on the concrete floor between a sidewall and Teacher Wang, our class teacher. Steps away was a rusty iron gate padlocked, behind which sections of rails formed a narrow passage to an empty platform. We were taking an evening train to Lankao, where Jiao Yulu had worked as the County Party Committee Secretary. A commune outside the city was where we always went to help with the autumn harvest. For six days straight, we would walk there at dawn and walk back late afternoon. The death of Jiao Yulu from liver cancer had changed all that. He became a national hero for everyone to learn from, so the school was sending us to Lankao.

Suddenly the loudspeaker announced the arrival of a train. When a woman emerged with a cardboard showing the number of the train we were supposed to take, Teacher Wang told us to line up.

It was already dark by the time we got on the train. A slow train, it stopped at every station. Sometimes just as it started to speed up, it slowed down again to a halt, clunking and shaking.

Outside the window, whatever out there was hardly seen. Only a light here and there twinkled like creepy eyes. Now and then a tree stood so close to the track that its branches scratched against the train. I wondered if they were paulownias, trees hollow inside and easy to grow. Jiaoyu Lu was said to have made it a mission to change the alkaline soil of Lankao County by planting such trees.

"Where will we end up if the train keeps going?" asked Xiaoya, my deskmate that semester. She, Lili, my deskmate during the previous semester, and I often hanged out together.

"Fall into the sea," blurted out Lili as if she had long had the answer ready.

"What sea?" I didn't quite understand what she had just said.

"Don't you know? The earth is a square board on four sea turtles," Lili couldn't hold back a sneer at my ignorance.

"The earth is round. If the train keeps going, it will get to where it started," argued I.

"My grandpa is always right. If he says the earth is a board, the earth is a board," insisted Lili.

"Both of you are right. The earth changes its shape. Sometimes a board, sometimes a ball," mediated Xiaoya, striking a middle ground.

As I stared into the darkness through the window, my aunt came to my mind. Not the aunt in Shanghai, but the aunt who had sent my mother condensed milk. I wondered if the train could crank all its way to where she was.

"Can this train get to the United States?" I murmured.

"To the United States! Are you crazy?" Xiaoya leaned over, slapping her a hand over my mouth.

None of us spoke again. The train was slowing down, and ahead was the Lankao railway station.

When I went to have breakfast with Uncle Zhang's family for the first time, he was smoking a dry pipe at the door. Seeing me, he got up and took a step forward, showing a sturdy figure and a limp in his left leg. "The student is here," hollered he in a gruff voice before letting me into the shed, where on the mud stove three bowls of porridge were being cooled. Flies were shooed away when his wife hurried out of the side room.

"Here," said she, handing me and Uncle Zhang each a bowl before taking the last one for herself. My tongue went in and licked up a little without my lips touching the bowl.

Flies returned. They circled, tried to land, and cried foul when I flapped a hand at them. While I was fighting flies, Uncle Zhang and his wife seemed to be having their best breakfast ever. It was then when I realized I had a problem. Without looking, I opened my mouth and slurped. At the same time, a bowl of milk appeared in my head with my American aunt drinking from it and flies circling around. Flies were always part of a meal, which was true in both Lankao and the United States.

All the girls of our class left the field early and followed Teacher Wang to the brigade office located on the side of a dirt road. For a demonstration scheduled later that day, we were there to make hand flags. While we were busy cutting red paper into triangles and gluing each to a sorghum stalk, Teacher Wang was writing slogans on them. It wasn't long before small red flags were everywhere in the room to be dried.

On a cardboard the brigade accountant had just finished drawing a head that featured a fat nose, two wicked eyes, and three horns.

"Who is this," asked I, standing next to him.

"The president of the United States, a big bad egg," explained he, retracing the lines around the eyes.

"People there all look like this?"

"Who knows?"

As the sun was setting, about twenty brigade members including the brigade head and the brigade accountant plus fifty of us elementary students and Teacher Wang gathered in front of the brigade office. Everyone had a small red flag in hand except for the brigade accountant, who was holding the cardboard he had worked on. With the brigade head leading the way and the brigade accountant next to him, the demonstration went down a winding dirt road.

One slogan after another we shouted after the brigade head, at the same time raising the small red flags. Our voice rang through the usually quiet fields, startling crows and sparrows. I couldn't help thinking about my aunt in the United States again. She had to be an imperialist too since she had been in the United States for so many years. I also wondered if she had any idea that she wasn't liked in her home country.

Uncle Zhang didn't come for the demonstration. When I joined him and his wife for supper that evening, he had a small red flag stuck out from his collar with Teacher Wang's handwriting on it.

"I got it from my nephew. He didn't want to give me, I just took it," said he with pride. "What does it say?"

"Down with Johnson!"

"Johnson? Is that a name?" asked Uncle Zhang with knitted eyebrows.

"Yes, the name of the president of the United States."

"The United States… a country?"

"A country on the other side of the earth under your feet," added I, remembering my argument with Lili.

"Under my feet? Where?" He lifted his feet one at a time and checked.

To explain myself, on the dirt floor I drew, with a chopstick made from a sorghum stalk, a circle as the earth and two figures one on each side. Of course, I didn't say one figure was my mother and the other my aunt in the United States.

After the meal, Uncle Zhang paced from the mud stove to the side room and back. At first his steps were light as though he was afraid of hurting someone beneath. But soon he started to stomp, his feet coming down so hard that soot fell from the walls.

"What's wrong with you?" scolded his wife.

"I didn't go to demonstrate, but at least I can say I have done my part against imperialists," said he in a serious voice.

The small red flag flew from Uncle Zhang's collar for several more days until the wind tore it to pieces. Then that stick was paired up with another to be used as chopsticks.

CHAPTER 39

When I met my maternal grandma for the first time, she was seventy-five, and I just turned nine.

She had been ill and was in bed. Seeing me peek in through the door, she waved for me to come over. I did. I crawled in and cuddled against her. For a while neither of us said a word, and together we listened to the passing of time. She coughed. With her eyes closed, she told me something I had never heard before.

"You're a boy in your mother's belly. Just before you came out, Old Heaven changed his mind and made you a girl," said she.

"Really?" I winked and wasn't convinced that a boy could change into a girl just like that.

"When your mother was having you, she often dreamed about a dragon. That's the sign of having a boy. Your mother dreamed of a phoenix while having your older sister and a dragon while having your older brother. Ask your mother, go to ask," continued she. "You see, you were born in the year of dragon. That's the year for bearing boys. Boys are strong and can protect themselves and their families. You are a boy, that's why you are taller than other girls."

"Why, why me?" puzzled I.

"I know why, have you heard the story of the white snake?

Because Old Heaven wanted to have a girl who would grow up like that white snake. Wait a minute, not the white one, the blue one," mumbled my grandma, somewhat confused about which snake Old Heaven meant me to be. "The blue snake was a girl but had the strength of a boy. You know, she rescued the white snake. Only a boy could do something like that."

At the time I wasn't sure what my maternal grandma was saying. Maybe I was really a boy in spite of the fact that I wasn't born in the year of dragon and looked every bit a girl. And no longer did I need to feel embarrassed when the physical education teacher asked me to stand at the tall end of a line with boys.

Not until a year later did I realize it was impossible for an unborn baby to alter sex the last minute, which I could no longer tell my grandma, for she had already passed away.

Not until another year went by did my maternal grandma's story finally sink in. She meant to tell me that things would be tough and require the strength of a boy to go through. She wasn't a sexist. She just didn't know a better way to convey what was on her mind.

Here the story about the blue snake: It had to be many thousand years ago because only then there were all sorts of spirits around. In the deep mountains near West Lake lived two snake spirits, a white one and a blue one. Day after day they roved beside streams and played beneath trees, carefree but unsatisfied because they secretly admired the earthly world and dreamed some day they could live as *fanren* or humans.

They did turn themselves into human forms by mastering some difficult incarnations. On their way to a downtown district, they were warned by the master monk who had authority over snake spirits not to get attached to humans or face severe punishments.

For some time, they enjoyed their life among humans. They

visited all the opera theatres in town, was in and out every teahouse that allowed women, and never missed a seasonal party organized by the county magistrate.

The evening of the Lantern Festival that year saw the two snakes going out early to seek a good time. As they strolled down the main street lit up by lanterns of various colors and shapes, they came upon a group of scholars who were there to show off their poetic talent. Among them was a young man who caught the white snake's eye. His manners were as elegant as pines on Mount Yellow, and his words as refined as pearls in the East Sea. He composed the best poem within the least time. Transported, the white snake chanted out an incarnation to match his poem. Seeing a pretty lady so gifted, the young man fell in love also. After just two more dates, they tied the red knot, and a year later, they had a son.

As the couple was celebrating the first one hundred days of their son's life, the master monk learned about the white snake's marriage. He looked down from his temple in midair, swearing he would tear the family apart. A fierce fight between him and the white snake ended up with the latter being captured and locked up under a pagoda.

When the blue snake learned what had happened, she told her friend in her dream that she would come to her rescue one day. It took years for her to strengthen all her muscles, be able to use all the weapons, and memorize all the important incarnations. At the same time, she ate nothing but mushrooms to keep her body light, so she could tumble up and down in the sky as she pleased. No matter how tired she was, her promise to the white snake kept her going.

The day she felt she was ready, she came out of the mountains to fight the master monk. After six rounds of knife flashing and spear glinting, she defeated him. She didn't stop there and chased him all the way to his temple, where she placed a foot on him and recited an incarnation that completely resolved his magic power. Then the blue snake went to the pagoda. With just one kick, she overturned the pagoda and freed the white snake, who was once again united with her husband and son. Protected by their friend, the blue snake, the family lived happily ever after.

It was the blue snake that my maternal grandma had wanted me to be.

CHAPTER 40

One afternoon in June 1966, dust flew up, and an army green propaganda truck tooted to a halt not far from our gate. So loud was the loudspeaker that the Red Guards singling along in the back of the truck could hardly be heard.

Around the truck some little boys capered. It didn't take long before several climbed up, hanging their bellies on the side railings and even baring a few chapped buttocks.

The army green truck started moving again from our alley all the way to an alley on the lower side, leaving behind a trail of big character posters. The last time I saw a poster like that was at the two funerals for Hui's great grandma. Written in black ink on a large sheet of white paper was one big character. Mama wrote that big character, which I was told meant paying respect to the dead. This time was different. Instead of just one poster, there were so many, and they were everywhere. Written on them were slogans and condemnations.

"Destroy the four olds!" read Hui, pointing to the poster plastered on the opposite wall.

"Down with the feudal…" continued I but couldn't finish because I didn't know the last character in that poster.

"*Nei, yunei* means old evils," explained Hui, eager to tell me what she knew.

"What are old evils," asked I.

"Things from the old society," said Hui.

It was then when I came to understand why Mama never wore the clothes in her camphorwood chest. Because they came from the old society and because they were evils.

"Who did this? Where is the bastard," screamed Aunt Shan, who just got back from work. At her feet was the oleander that had been crashed out of its pot. Spitting curses, she squatted down trying to put the plant back in the pot.

"Ask someone in your family," said Wang Nainai from her doorstep. She had been standing there for a while but didn't utter a word until then.

Xiaoer, Aunt Shan's younger son hopped outside holding a fishbowl, which he raised and smashed with full force to the ground. Following a shattering sound, some goldfish could be seen bouncing in a pool of water and glass shards.

"Four olds must be killed," yelled Xiaoer, stepping on a goldfish. As its bloody inside oozed out, a cold smile appeared on Xiaoer's face. He was in his second year of middle school and became a Red Guard just that morning.

By the time I got up, Mama was already gone. Ever since she started to work at the city museum, we had stopped having breakfast together. She said she wanted to be the first to arrive at work and the last to leave. She had been doing just that.

Minutes later I was on my way to school. Striding along, I brought out the half *wowotou* I had left in my pocket the day before and devoured it all in just two or three bites. I didn't even flick off crumbs on the front of my shirt not to slow myself down.

Ahead of me was Dafeng, the boy who sat three desks before me in class. Just the other day, passing by my seat, he mumbled "*hei-wulei*" before pretending to cough. I had been called many things but hadn't heard this one. A black category was always a bad kind, but what *heiwulei* or the five black categories actually meant, which I wondered as I was crossing the street to the other side and ran.

I was on time for the morning self-study. Sitting down at my desk, I noticed, through the back door, the gable wall across the schoolyard had turned black and white. Even though big character posters were everywhere on the streets, this was the first time they appeared in my elementary school.

The bell for the first class rang, but the arithmetic teacher wasn't walking into the classroom. Not knowing what it was, the class just sat and waited, which didn't last long.

"No teacher, let's go," shouted Dafeng, pushing open the window near his desk and jumping outside. The rest of the boys followed suit. In the matter of minutes, only girls were left in the classroom. Looking at each other, we got up from our seats and filed out. Xiaoya didn't forget to close all the windows and shut the two doors. A class cadre, she was on duty that week.

Those of us that didn't leave right way hung around in the schoolyard. A playful push between the two girl classmates led to a chase around the north end of the basketball court. Playing in the sandpit were some first-grade boys, who kicked one another's butts and pinched one another's ears with sharp cries going off like alarms.

The double door to the conference room opened. Teacher Li walked out first, followed by three rows of teachers, who stomped their feet and swung their arms like PLA soldiers. Our physical education teacher came out the last, holding a red flag, the fly end of which draped over his head like a bridal veil.

Onto the platform they marched. As Teacher Li called out a series of commands, they marked time, stood at attention, and then turned to face a schoolyard of their students, who had long quieted down and were stupefied by what was taking place.

There stood our arithmetic teacher, who was a head taller than the two teachers before him. He was new to the school, which might explain the sweat on his forehead. I didn't see Teacher Wang, who had been our class teacher for more than three semesters, Teacher Xie, who had been teaching us science once a week for more than one semester, and Teacher Zhang, our music teacher who could sing some really high notes like a bird. Teacher Xie taught only parttime and didn't have any class that day, but where were Teacher Wang and Teacher Zhang? Then Teacher Li stepped to the front of the platform.

"A great revolution has begun! No more classes from now on," announced she as if she had been the school principal. "As revolutionary fighters, we must carry out our task to expose class enemies among us and fight against them to the end!"

While her voice shrilled through the dusty air, another row of teachers emerged from the same double door to the conference room. Stooped and crumpled, each had a placard hanging from the neck.

One by one they bumped onto the platform to line up behind Teacher Li, who then turned around to stand near the first teacher in that row.

"A big landlord who deserves to die a thousand times," shouted Teacher Li, looking at what was daubed on that teacher's placard. Even though that teacher had never taught me, I knew he wasn't a landlord. He couldn't be. When there were landlords, he was still a child. But once his father or grandfather was a landlord, he as a son or grandson was one too.

"A bad element from the old society!" called out Teacher Li, holding up the placard on Teacher Wang's chest.

"A bad element, what's a bad element?" asked I, giving Xiaoya a nudge.

"Not sure, I've heard his grandpa was a church member," whispered Xiaoya to my right ear. "He was executed after the liberation."

"Church members are bad elements," murmured I to myself.

Teacher Xie didn't come to school that day. If he had, he would have been up on that platform with a placard hanging around his neck too. Written on it would be "counterrevolutionary" because his father had been executed as one. He passed college entrance exams but wasn't admitted into any college. He was allowed to stay home only to take care of his mother, who had been bedridden after a stroke.

After I was rejected for the third time by the Young Pioneers, Teacher Xie wrote me a little note that said "Strive for your best. Nothing else matters." I wasn't sure what the second sentence meant but completely agreed with the first one.

The last in that row of eight teachers was Teacher Zhang, who, instead of a usual grin, wore no expression on her face. She was a rightist according to her placard, but no way could she be one. Every song she had taught my class was a revolutionary song, from "Socialism Is Good" to "The East Is Red." We even learned a song called "Beautiful Havana" from her, which was a revolutionary song too. But because her father was a rightist, she was one too.

All those on the platform were going back to the conference room. But no longer were they teachers. They were either revolutionary fighters or class enemies. "Down with class enemies! Our fighting continues," shouted Teacher Li before hopping off the platform from the west side. She didn't use the four-step stair. She was in a hurry.

"What do we do tomorrow?" asked I, my eyes following Teacher Li as she entered the conference room.

"Who knows?" said Xiaoya, playing with the Soviet watch on her left wrist. The first time she wore it to school, she let every girl classmate try it on for two seconds, saying she got it from her father, who had bought a new one. No one else I knew even had a watch, not to mention a new Soviet watch.

"No school for how long?" asked I again, gripped by a sense of nothing to do from then on.

"Who knows?" said Xiaoya again, pulling me by the arm toward the gable wall.

Listed on one of the big character posters on that wall were the five black categories: landlords, rich farmers, counterrevolutionaries, bad elements, and rightists. No longer was *heiwulei* just uttered. It was written in black ink on a large piece of white paper. Even though the poster didn't say anything about a child of a *heiwulei*, it was clear that a child of a *heiwulei* was a *heiwulei* too.

"Let's go," said Xiaoya. She pulled me by the arm again, this time leaving the gable wall for the school gate.

CHAPTER 41

On the kneading board were the noodles I made earlier. My first time of course, and of course under the watchful eye of Wang Nainai, who had been telling me being able or unable to cook meant life or death since the day I no longer needed to go to school.

"Too much water. Sprinkle, don't pour. Don't poke, use the heel of your hand," said Wang Nainai while I was mixing flour and water into dough.

It was Wang Nainai who wrapped the dough up in a wet cloth to get some needed rest as she said. When she went home and came back, she was holding the round stick she sometimes used as a cane.

After rubbing some flour on both the dough and the round stick, Wang Nainai stepped aside to let me try my hand at rolling the dough into a sheet and cutting the sheet into noodles.

I went to get salt. The sundry store around the corner wasn't open, so I turned around and headed for the one four blocks away. The empty jar on the counter and a five-*fen* coin next to it, I was waiting for the saleswoman to come over when a commotion erupted behind me. Rushing out of the alley across the street were a throng of Red Guards with a man wearing a white dunce hat in the front. I didn't realize it was Grandpa Yuan until I saw his name in black on a white banner. Stepping outside the store, I pushed through the crowd that was gathering on the sidewalk to get closer.

Gone was Grandpa Yuan's long beard with blood dripping out of his nose. Dragged to go along through a rope tied around his neck, he convulsed every time a Red Guard poked him in the waist with an iron rod. Behind were more Red Guards, carrying displays of old photos and loads of old clothes, both from the old society. The last two Red Guards pushed a handcart, in which an upside-down Buddha continued to emit grace even though all his hands and feet were missing.

I was moving along. I wasn't sure what I was trying to do. Maybe I just wanted to give Grandpa Yuan a smile if he happened to look up. Not for a second did I sense it would be my last time to see him.

I tripped on a sewer cover and fell. When I got up, the Red Guards were no longer in sight. Only their shouting of slogans could be heard.

I didn't know how I went back to the store, and I didn't know how I returned home. All the way all I could think of was what I just saw happening to Grandpa Yuan, who was a kind old man, knowing nothing but kindness and even being kind to something so miniscule like ants. "He just doesn't step on them," Mama once told me.

As it was getting late, I filled the wok with some water and sat it on the stove. Minutes after Mama got home, a bowl of just cooked noodles topped with chopped green onion would be brought to her at the table. I would tell her I had made them from the scratch. Of course I would also tell her how Wang Nainai had helped me. Would I tell Mama about Grandpa Yuan? Of course not, I said to myself.

I tried not to but still felt asleep while waiting for Mama to come home. When I woke up, it was already so dark, and there was no Mama. I became really worried.

"Mama," called I. I called again in case she didn't hear me the first time. Still it was so dark, and still there was no Mama. Getting up from the table, I looked around, not wanting to believe Mama wasn't home. It couldn't be true, I murmured. But it was.

Those photos came to my mind. How could they not? Photos, taken before 1949, had been declared evidence of nostalgia for the old society. Not just evidence. They were ironclad evidence. Of course, Mama understood the risks of keeping her old photos. She had been thinking about burning them for some time. That tin box containing them was no longer inside the camphorwood chest. It was next to her pillow. Every night for about two weeks, she went to bed saying she was going to burn them the next day. But she never did. She simply couldn't.

I found myself also saying I was going to burn them, not the next day but right that moment. My heart pounding, I brought the tin box to the outer room, where at the scratch of a match, the first photo I picked up caught fire and curled up like a dry leave before it was dropped into the washbasin before my knees. Without light, I couldn't really tell who was or were in that photo, but I knew it had, if not one member, two or three or four members of my family. Even though I wasn't in any of them, those in them were my flesh and blood.

I didn't hesitate, though. For me at that moment in time, no longer were they photos. They were troubles, and I was burning troubles.

It didn't take long, and it wasn't that hard. One photo after another was burned to ashes. In ashes was my family.

The rest of that night was long, and the next morning seemed never to come. All the time I was gripped by the fear that what had happened to Grandpa Yuan had also happened to Mama. That day was the third Monday in August 1966.

"Come over," yelled Wang Nainai from her door. She had gone to run an errand but turned around the moment she got to the gate. After she pulled me into her room, she shut the door and lowered the bamboo curtain on the window, which was further shielded by the pomegranate tree outside.

I didn't get to ask what it was. I saw. Being shoved forward by two Red Guards was Mama, whose head rested listlessly on the wooden board hanging down her neck with the word counterrevolutionary scribbled across it. She had no shoes on, perhaps having lost them somewhere along the way.

Mama was pushed to stand against the outhouse wall. When she saw our opened door, she couldn't help taking a step forward. Realizing I wasn't inside, she gave a small sigh of relief. The Red Guard who appeared to be in charge asked, "What are you looking at? Isn't this your black nest?" With one hand, he thrust Mama back to the wall again.

Two Red Guards rushed inside the door. The first thing they hauled out was the camphorwood chest. One of them removed a brick from the doorstep and hammered on the lock, the dragon head. The lock didn't break, but the dragon head was knocked off in its entirety together with the wood it was attached to.

While one Red Guard rummaged through the camphorwood chest, another with closely-cropped hair brought outside two cardboard boxes. After he dropped both to the ground, he lifted one with the bottom up. Falling out were my picture books. Not interested, he shuffled them aside and squatted down to check the other box, which stored Mama's scrolls of calligraphy. One after another he browsed, and now and then he read with a finger moving down the lines. He was looking for something, confident he would find it.

"Ah," grunted he, standing up. With one hand holding the top and the other pulling down the bottom, he opened the scroll like showing off a trophy.

What he found was a couplet by a Song Dynasty poet, which read "As I doubt any road lies amid those mountains and rivers, there comes a village with bright blossoms and shady willows." For centuries this couplet had been quoted as words of hope and optimism. Mama copied it the day she got a job at the city museum.

"She is a counterrevolutionary, here the evidence," yelled that Red Guard before marching over to Mama, who slowly writhed to the ground as he kicked her in the shanks.

Behind the bamboo curtain I watched between my fingers while my heart flinched at every hit Mama endured. Tears trickled down my cheeks into my mouth, and I swallowed them all. Wang Nainai asked me to leave the window. I didn't because it was my way of being with Mama.

"Nothing else," hollered one Red Guard through the window to the one in charge, who signaled for all the Red Guards to gather around Mama in a semicircle. Right there a struggle session started. One Red Guard cursed, "She has a granite skull! Deserves to die!" Another denounced, "Married to a counterrevolutionary, she a counterrevolutionary too. She must be executed!"

As it went on, they seemed angrier with the only female Red Guard getting out a pair of scissors from her army green bag. When Mama used her two hands to shield her head, two other Red Guards each grabbed one and squeezed. With Mama's hair gone, the same female Red Guard picked up the bottle in which Mama had kept ink, held it over Mama's head, and poured. The ink paused for a second and then slowly dribbled down Mama's forehead. Unable to wipe it off, Mama simply closed her eyes and let it run its course. Into an inkstone Mama froze.

Before taking off with Mama and her scrolls of calligraphy, the Red Guards set on fire the camphorwood chest and everything in it. Mama was again pushed to go with them. Passing by Wang Nainai's window, Mama turned her head a little and flashed a grin out of her ink-covered face, knowing I was behind it. I wanted to run out to her but couldn't with Wang Nainai's arms tightly around my shoulders.

The fire burned through the late afternoon and was still burning after the sundown. A quick wind passed, sweeping more smoke toward the sky. Hanging around were some neighborhood kids, whose faces glowed like lit lanterns in front of the fire. Now and then they got so excited that they babbled.

When I tried to join them, Wang Nainai came to stand between me and the door. Holding my face in her hands, she said I had already seen too much and didn't need to see more.

CHAPTER 42

Wang Nainai took me in. I ate with her and slept in her bed. Every time I cried in a dream, she would shake me awake, telling me about a better place on the other side of a suffering sea, and I would go back to sleep with one arm around her.

I kept asking where my mama was, and Wang Nainai became so worried that she even slapped me in the face once to see if I was delirious. Of course I wasn't. One afternoon while Wang Nainai was taking a nap, I sneaked out with several coins in my pocket and the red band Wang Nainai had sewn for me around my waist.

Into this alley and out of that alley, I ended up on a quiet sidewalk, where a woman was selling roasted sunflower seeds in the shade of a tree. I asked her how to get to the city museum, and she spat out a seed shell, telling me to walk four blocks down before turning left.

In front of me was the closed gate of the city museum. The signboard that should have been on the lintel was lying on the ground. I gathered myself, stepped to the gate, and knocked. When no one answered, I looked through a crack but saw nothing.

"Uncle, when does the place open?" I asked when a man came out of the side door next to the gate.

"When it opens? No one knows," said he in a low voice. "A mess inside. Red Guards were here, burned a lot of things."

"Where are those who work here?" interrupted I.

"Some are dead, some have been taken to a cowshed. Who are you looking for?" asked the man.

"My mama," said I, giving him Mama's name.

"I know her, a *haoren*. Sometimes Old Heaven lets good people suffer..." murmured he, his voice trailing to a sigh.

When he said he was the gatekeeper there, I knew he was the one for whom Mama had been saving grain coupons month after month. A peasant from a nearby county, he came to the city to escape poor harvests. Even though he had a job, he didn't get monthly grain coupons like a city resident would. Without coupons, grains were expensive, and few could afford them.

"You're still here," yelled his wife from the door. She looked somewhat embarrassed once she learned who I was. Inside his tiny room, the gatekeeper told me more about Mama.

"Once they brough her back here, they started another struggle session that didn't end until after midnight. They said they had new evidence to show she was a real counterrevolutionary. The following day, they forced her to walk back and forth in the yard, beating a urine pot. After pouring urine all over her, they made her stand on a stool in the hot sun for hours. All the time she was given little water and almost nothing to eat.

"The director hanged himself. So afraid she would do the same, I went to talk with her the night I found out which storage room she was locked in.

"I grabbed the iron bars in the window and got myself onto the sill. It was all dark in there with only a square of moonlight, striped and with my head in it, on the lower part of the opposite wall. I narrowed my eyes and scanned like a cat. When I saw something in a corner, I whispered your mother's name. With no response, I tried again, a little louder. This time I heard the sound of crawling toward the window. As your mother got closer, I dropped what I had brought, a corn flour *wowotou* and a boiled egg wrapped in a cloth.

"She thanked me. Her voice was so weak that I could hardly hear her. I told her to have hope. I didn't feel good about saying that when I wasn't the one that was going through hell. Even in that kind of situation, your mother was concerned about my safety. She urged me to leave."

"Let me show you," said the gatekeeper, getting up and taking me outside to a wall covered with big character posters. On one of them, I found Mama's name and the following:

A counterrevolutionary, whose major crimes include holding meetings with other counterrevolutionaries, supporting her counterrevolutionary husband, copying counterrevolutionary poems, and refusing to accept revolutionary thoughts. Her true colors as a counterrevolutionary are absolutely undeniable. She deserves to die a thousand times, and even death will not expiate her crimes.

CHAPTER 43

New on the wall next to the gate were two big character posters. Wang Yinhua, as one of them claimed, had been the secret concubine of a wealthy merchant. Drawn on the other was a cartoon showing an old woman with a pair of tattered shoes dangling on her chest.

Not for long did the big character posters stay on that wall. Later that day Wang Nanai pulled them down and brought them home. After tearing them up, she mixed the bits with wet coal. Then she sat me down and told me her story:

"Remember what I'm telling you. A maid, I was a maid, not a secret concubine. I came from loess hills of Shanxi. When I was six, the village was hit by the severest draught it had ever had. Since no crops were harvested, villagers started to die from starvation. The alive didn't even have the strength to bury the dead, and bodies were everywhere.

"Along the side of a dirt road lived my family of four. We hadn't had anything to eat for a while, and my father was dying. Too weak to speak, he waved his bony hands, urging my mother to leave. After he died, with my younger brother on one side and me on the other side, my mother staggered out of the door and joined a sparse line of those trudging east.

"The second day on the road, my mother could no longer move. She pushed my brother closer to me before slipping down to the ground. She was resting, I thought.

"A man pushing a small handcart stopped by. He checked my mother's pulse before uttering 'dead.' Then he put my brother and me inside the handcart before saying he was also heading east. He didn't look a bad person, so I felt safe.

"Three days later we came to a small town, where the man got me out of the handcart to sit at a streetcorner and left. When he returned, my brother was no longer in the handcart. He handed me a *wowotou*, telling me my brother was staying with a family that had food.

"He and I continued the trip as green fields started to appear along the road. One afternoon we stopped in front of a big house, from which a woman with a powdered face stepped out. She looked at me up and down before pulling the man aside to have words. Later he told me we would stay there for the night.

"The next day I woke up to find my feet being bound up by the woman with the help of a man said to be her husband. When I screamed in pain, the woman thrust some bandages into my mouth. By that time, long gone was the man who had brought me there.

"For more than ten years I waited on her. She was evil. Whenever she felt dissatisfied with me, she would beat me up with a stick. I had scars all over my body. Then all of a sudden, she died. Two days after the funeral, her widower called me to his room, where he was in bed, smoking opium.

"'I'm in charge now, you listen to me,' ordered he, sitting up. 'Come here, come closer.'

"'My bad blood can make you sick and die' yelled I, trying to scare him. 'My parents died, the lady of the house just died, I don't know who'll die the next.'

"The widower snapped back his right hand, rubbing it on his robe as if it was covered with blood.

"I decided to leave and go where I could find work. The day before my departure, I asked the widower for the money his household had owed me for so many years. Afraid of me just as he had been of his late wife, he paid me in full.

"On my way eastward, I ran into a group of opera singers who happened to head in the same direction and offered me a ride in their wagon. Whenever the group stopped to perform, I cooked and did chores for them. When I told them I didn't have anyone and wanted to stay with them, they let me. They became my family."

"They are here," said a hushed voice through the door as Wang Nanai and I were about to have lunch. Wang Nainai immediately stopped what she was doing, threw me the basket that had *wowotou* in it, and told me to go back to my own home. Before I knew it, I was outside with my back against a closed door.

"Beggar, get out of the way," hollered one of the Red Guards, seeing me with a basket.

Then he noticed the picture of the door god, the one Wang Nainai had insisted on having after Mama brought it back from the temple fair. She said she needed the protection from the door god. Although the lines and colors all had faded after two years, the door god was still visible. With one grab, the same Red Guard tore it off the door. Clearly it was a useless god who couldn't even protect himself, not to mention someone else.

The door was kicked open. Once the Red Guards jostled in, the first thing they went for was Wang Naina's Guanyin, who, in fine porcelain, stood in the middle of a lotus flower with a flask of healing dews in one hand and a willow twig in the other.

A Red Guard turned the Guanyin statue upside down to see if it was hollow with an old title deed hidden inside. Disappointed that it was solid, he flung it against the back wall. It was then when he noticed Wang Nainai and her coffin.

"A ghost," screamed he, running out of the door.

After he and the other three Red Guards calmed down and re-entered, they turned the light on first. Feeling fooled, they swooped on Wang Nainai. They cursed her and ripped her hands off the coffin before dragging her outside, her bound feet plowing the floor.

One of the Red Guard was checking under the plank bed and behind the coffin. When he found nothing that interested him, he turned around and removed the lid on the wok. He smirked as he was pouring water from the wok into the stove, extinguishing the fire.

With nothing else to take, the Red Guards took the coffin heavy as it was. "Who needs a coffin? Free," howled they while loading it onto the handcart they had brought along. They seemed to be having a good time.

Against the sidewall Wang Nainai sat motionless with her eyes closed and her gray hair in disarray over her shoulders. Her lips were moving, but there was no sound being uttered.

That evening, I waited on Wang Nainai. She liked gluten soup, so I made a bowl on Uncle Xu's stove with the wheat flour I had found in a broken jar. But Wang Nainai didn't even look at the bowl held to her. She hadn't said a word since she told me to go back home. Her mind was no longer with her, having drifted away to a place where she was free to be herself and no one could do anything to her anymore. I kept calling her and patting on her hands, but neither worked. She didn't want to come back. She really didn't.

I sat there at her side in case she needed me. I didn't know what happened next. When I opened my eyes, Hui and her mother were looking at me, and there was no Wang Nainai.

That morning Hui and I walked from one end of the alley to the other end, asking about Wang Nainai. That afternoon we went to the temple Wang Nainai had sometimes visited. The gate was sealed with two long banners. On our way back, we stopped by the post office to find out if Wang Nainai's friend, an elderly man who wrote letters for those who couldn't, had any idea as to where she was. He had not shown up for more than a month, said the postal clerk behind the counter. Not knowing where to go next, we ventured to the public security bureau, which didn't seem to exist anymore with its signboard no longer there.

The following day Hui and I went as far as the Ku River looking for Wang Nainai. Residents cooling along the bank told us about an old woman wandering on the city wall the day before. They couldn't see her face, but they could still see her hair, long and gray. When she was facing the wind, it all flew behind her in one mass. The moment she gave the wind her back, it spread like flames around her head. She was seen gesturing, and she could be heard singing an episode from the opera *Grandma She*, the story of an old woman warrior who, after her son, a general and all his troops died in battle, commanded all the women in the family to fight against the foreign invaders.

Hui and I didn't cross the bridge to the other side, where strewn on an arid terrain along the foot of the city wall were unmarked graves and where on a moonless summer night, fireflies swirled forming a glowing parade or a funeral procession, each accompanying a spirit. Among them were the spirits of unborn or new born babies who, naked or wrapped, had been left there already dead or to die. Even though no one seemed to care who they were, their spirits were out and about. So were the spirits of those who didn't want to live or were made not to live. The former generally climbed up the city wall and jumped head first, and the latter were always brought there and executed on a bare slope near the city wall. Whenever an execution was to take place, in wait were also those who were there to get some brain tissues. According to the folk medicine for epilepsy, one slurp of that stuff taken while still warm was the most effective.

A total of six days passed before Hui's parents learned from Hui about the old woman on the city wall. They said they had to find out if that was Wang Nainai, and Hui and I tagged along.

It was the first time that I set my feet on that old bridge, which creaked with my every step. A long draught had dried up the river-bed, but Hui was still afraid to look down. With her eyes half-closed, she dashed to reach the other end.

We wound among graves. We paused at each grave we came to and bowed at each grave. Close to the foot of the city wall, Hui's father first stopped and then fell to his knees. Before him, laid side by side on top of some loose dirt were two black cloth shoes. They were not just any shoes. They were shoes for bound feet. Sewn to the back of each shoe was a red bead. They were Wang Nainai's shoes. Every year Wang Nainai would make two pairs for herself: the pair without padded cotton for summer and autumn and the cotton padded pair for winter and spring. My feet got to feel seasonably comfortable, said she.

A shadowy man appeared, wearing a long robe so dirty that it was hard to tell what color it was. Passing us, he said not to us but to himself, "She is alive, she sings every night."

Wang Nainai was alive, which was all I wanted to know.

CHAPTER 44

Auntie Chen came. With a sigh she came over to the table and started to comb my hair with her fingers, one strand at a time. It was always Mama who did my hair. Then for twenty days Wang Nainai did. Now it was Auntie Chen, who didn't ask me about Mama, nor did she ask what had happened. She knew.

She brought two eggs. With one she made me a bowl of soup on Uncle Xu's stove. The last time I had a warm meal was with Wang Nainai. Since then, I had been eating the *wowotou* she left me, several bites a day.

Auntie Chen came to tell Mama she was going to Sichuan to see her son, who had been infected with typhoid, a fever disease. Seeing me all by myself, she decided to delay her trip for a few days.

That evening Aunt Shan walked in with two steamed sweet potatoes. Placing them on the table, she began to speak words that made sense.

"Your mama is a good person, Wang Nainai harms no one," said she. "I'm a proletarian but have no idea what's going on."

Auntie Chen had to leave. She pretended not to hear me when I said I would see her to the train station. The minute she stepped outside, she turned around and locked the door. That was not all.

She gave the key to Uncle Xu's wife, telling her not to let me out until sometime later. She knew I wanted to go with her all the way to Sichuan.

Of all my fears, spending a night by myself was the worst. Lying there with my eyes wide open and my ears plucked, I tried to detect any sound that would surely send chills down my spine. Every time my head would end up under the pillow.

Mice started to visit. During the day, if it was quiet for several minutes, gnawing could be heard. One morning I woke up to see a mouse standing on its hindlegs not far from me. The moment I tried to sit up, it scampered away.

They were indeed thieves. I couldn't think of who else would make the food Uncle Xu's wife or Hui's mother gave me either disappear or uneatable by leaving droppings in it. Even when I hid the food under a bowl or in a hanging basket, they could still find it.

I told Hui about my crisis. She ran home and came back with some white powder on a broken tile

"*Liuliufen*, don't eat it," said Hui seriously.

"I know, it's poison," said I.

Hui started to scatter the white powder *liuliufen* along the back-wall, boasting, at the same time, that she knew exactly what she was doing after having seen her mother doing it so many times.

Believe it or not, that *liuliufen* worked. For quite some time, while a pungent smell gave me headaches, I neither heard a mouse nor saw one.

It was on one of those nothing-to-do days when I got on a stool and kicked my left leg up to see how high it could go. Even though I ended up crashing down, the feel of the wind stirred by myself was stronger than pain. I got back on the stool and tried again. I was doing what I thought was Shaolin kicks.

I also tried to bend forward with my fingertips struggling to touch my toes, which was only at the beginning. A couple of weeks later, it was my palms that I could place not on my toes but in front of them while in the same pose.

When a boy schoolmate living just two gates down the alley watched me walk by and then called "*heiwulei*" to my back, I had to do something. Turning around, I marched towards him and kicked him in the knee. As he plopped to the ground, he howled like a family member had died. For the rest of that day, I kept saying "self-defense" to myself. It was.

"I have something to tell you," said the girl with a ponytail, looking aside to avoid eye contact.

"What?" asked I, stepping onto the threshold with my head almost touching the lintel and either hand on either side of the doorframe. Unknowingly I was trying to appear as big as I could before a schoolmate from the same grade. We had never spoken to each other, but I knew who she was.

"A meeting, meeting in the music room, two o'clock," stammered she before taking a step backward to leave.

"What meeting," shouted I to her back. Not only did she not give me an answer but she started to run. Her ponytail swirled side to side like dismissing me as nothing.

Leaning on the door, I thought about this meeting I was just told to go to. What meeting? A meeting only for *heiwulei students*? Why did she come to tell me? Probably because she lived nearby. I decided to go.

The gatekeeper sitting in a chair didn't say anything as I passed him, which kind of assured me of the meeting. He would have stopped me if I wasn't supposed to be there.

Away from other classrooms, the music room was located in the upper right corner of the schoolyard. Besides distance, it also had such sound proof features as a solid wooden door and no windows. Whenever the music teacher couldn't find help to bring the old organ to a class, that class would come to where it was. The room was small. With the organ and a stool taking up the front area, the entire class just stood packed, singing at each other.

Shut was the door with no one around. I was the first to arrive, said I to myself as I pushed the door open and stepped in.

A hand pulled me further in before kicks began to rain on my legs and lower back. They were swift kicks and curvy kicks. They were kicks that really hurt. Falling to the dirt floor, I saw stars with long tails flying, a sign of my soul trying to escape. But it only lasted seconds.

"Help, help," screamed I upon noticing three figures panting over me. Startled, one of them silenced me with an arm around my mouth. It was an arm thinner than mine. I was sure I could break it like a sorghum stalk or bite into it as a sweet potato. I did the latter. The arm snatched away with a loud cry that sounded familiar. It was that boy I kicked after he called me "*heiwulei*." With all my strength, I jumped up and threw my fists left and right as swiftly as I could. I didn't stop until the door swung open and the daylight poured in. Turning around, I found myself the only one in the room, while footsteps were heard hastening away.

CHAPTER 45

After a light knock came Mama's voice calling me. I got up and unlatched the door. There in the moonlight stood Mama, a skeleton. What had remained of her hair was a *yin-yang* cut with one side cropped short still black and the other side shaved bald showing the scull.

"So late?" asked I.

"No one around," said she, stepping inside.

Mama told me, for the same reason, she took the route along the Ku River. She also told me that for a moment, she was so exhausted that she longed to slip under to be caressed, leaving all hysteria behind. But she dismissed the thought when her youngest child came to her mind. She plodded on, telling herself she had to live as a mother.

"They cut it again during a struggle session," said Mama as I was touching first the *yin* side and then the *yang* side of her head, feeling her at least one hundred thousand wounds.

"You'll have more hair, better hair," said I, bringing out a slight grin to Mama's face.

Mama kept asking me questions. How were you? Had you heard from your brother and sister?

A long pause followed after I told her about Wang Nainai. She quietly got off the bed and went to the window, where the moonlight quivered like silver. She then turned around to pick up her shirt. She pinched both pockets, bringing out half a cigarette from one of them. Lighting it up, Mama went back before the window and kneeled down. She murmured as the cigarette held above her head sent up a thin smoke. Outside the window, the moon took a glance and glided away. The messenger between the high above and the down below was to pass Mama's words to Wang Nainai.

It was a while before Mama got to her feet and came back to the bed. Her knees were so cold against mine.

Mama was getting ready to leave. She folded a thin quilt and her cotton-padded jacket into a bundle before asking me to come to the table.

"Let them know if something happens to me," said she while writing down, on the back of an old envelope, the addresses of my brother, my sister, and the aunt in Shanghai.

CHAPTER 46

January 1967.

Someone was outside. Through the window I saw Xiaoya in an army green overcoat that had a brown pile collar.

The moment I opened the door, an excited Xiaoya plunged in, sending me stumble backward. She looked around and then looked at me.

"When this happened?" asked she like an adult.

"Hum," I twitched my mouth unable to say anything.

"They made a mess of my home too. My baba is no longer a revolutionary carder, he is a capitalist roader now," said she, shrugging her shoulders as though not being bothered.

"Really?" said I, not sure what to say.

"Have you heard about the big connection?" asked Xiaoya.

"Yes, go to Beijing on foot," replied I. Just the other day Aunt Shan's Younger son Xiaoer was heard saying he was walking to Beijing to see the great leader Chairman Mao.

"Beijing? Let's go to a place not too far first, then Beijing," suggested Xiaoya.

"We aren't that old to be Red Guards," said I.

"We are Little Red Guards," said Xiaoya.

"Need to bring a quilt and something to eat on the road?" asked I.

"Do need to bring a quilt. My brother just got back from Beijing. He says reception stations are everywhere. With an introduction letter from his school, my brother and his teammates always had a place to eat and sleep," said Xiaoya, whose older brother was one of the first Red Guards in his school.

"Free to eat at a reception station?" asked I.

"Not free, but you know what, my brother's school reimbursed every *fen* he spent during the trip," explained Xiaoya. "I'm going to get an introduction letter from our school. I think I can get one."

"H*eiwulei,* I'm a *heiwulei*. A *heiwulei* cannot be a Little Red Guard," I felt I had to say.

"Aiya, who cares? I don't care, I don't think the girls who go with us care, just go," said Xiaoya, patting me on the back.

I had been by myself for months. More than anything, I wanted to get out and become part of something. Xiaoya asked me to go, so I would go.

A trip was planned. There were eight of us girls with in charge Xiaoya and Minmin, a girl from another class. Not sure If we could really reach Beijing or not, we would just walk as much as we could each day.

About six in the morning, I hurried all the way to the school gate only to see two of the girls already there. Then Xiaoya arrived. Even though we all were shivering, our spirits were high. Cheers erupted when Minmin and her classmate Lanlan were seen trotting toward us. The school gatekeeper opened the gate, letting us wait in his room for the arrival of the last two. But they never came.

We first headed east to get to a main road outside the city wall. At that time of the day, only a few people were out and about.

Whoever we passed turned around to give us another glance. Little did we realize, even in all our seriousness, we didn't look like Red Guards at all.

Once on that main road, we found ourselves surrounded by teams of real Red Guards who each wore not only an army green jacket but also a red armband. The red flag each team was waving showed a team name as well as a school name. Some teams came from faraway places, and all the teams had spent a night at the reception station on the outskirt of the city.

"Younger sisters, which kindergarten are you from?" jeered a male Red Guard, which led to a burst of laughter.

We blushed, lowering our heads.

"Give a round of applause to our younger sisters! They are so courageous," shouted a female Red Guard who seemed offended by what that male Red Guard just said. Few hands clapped. It was a moment I had tried very hard to forget.

Near noon, six of us were the only ones left on that dusty road. More than five hours had passed since we started. During that time, we stopped only once to release ourselves behind a mud wall. When I took out the *wowotou* I had brought with me, it was icy cold. A bite left only the prints of my front teeth on it and not much in my mouth.

"Two *fen* a bowl, boiled water," yelled an old woman on the side of the road as we were approaching.

The water was lukewarm. I drank a little and then dropped the *wowotou* in. After it soaked enough water and turned puffy, I used the spoon I brought to poke it into pieces. It didn't taste bad at all.

"Girls, you don't look old enough to be Red Guards," said the old woman from where she was sitting. "My grandson a Red Guard, he is in high school."

"Little Red Guards, we are Little Red Guards. No difference," snorted Xiaoya, raising her chin.

"Too young, something wrong with your parents," continued the old woman, sounding like a grandma.

"Nothing wrong with our parents, your thoughts are too old," retorted Xiaoya, gesturing for the rest of us to get up.

The old woman was quiet this time, but her face darkened like the sky before a storm.

"See you again on your way back," shouted she, waving her hand as we hit the road again.

"Meddlesome," mumbled Xiaoya, walking next to me.

"She means well," said I, defending the old woman, who reminded me of Wang Nainai I missed so much.

The road in front of us kept playing tricks. The more eager we were to end the day, the further down into distance it seemed to extend. As the sun was setting, a sea of shades rolled out from nowhere, and it was getting dark fast.

Several low houses appeared along the roadside with smoke floating off their thatched roofs. Without telling anyone, Lanlan started to run toward the one that had a dimly lit window. Minmin made a dash, pulling her back. For a while we trudged along in silence. Xiaoxiao cleared her throat, trying to sing something, but she never did.

A middle-aged man on an old bicycle rattled by. As he was about to disappear, Xiaoya shouted to his back, "Is there a reception station nearby?" He made a U turn and stopped before us. "There is one but not nearby," said he. When we moaned, he asked us to follow him. Changshun was his name.

"My wife," introduced Changshun, yanking his chin toward the narrow-faced woman squatting before the mud stove. She didn't say anything when the husband told her we needed a place to sleep that night. Then she got up, went to a corner, and picked up some sweet potatoes. She wiped them with her shirt before adding them to the wok on the stove.

"Don't have something better?" asked Changshun, rubbing his nose.

Once again, the wife didn't utter a word.

"A mute," whispered Minmin to Lanlan next to her.

"Who? Who is mute?" growled the wife, rolling out all the whites of her eyes.

Changshun's five-year old son shrieked in from the side room. After staring at us for a minute, he held out a hand. We looked at each other and then into our pockets or schoolbags. Xiaoya brought out a handkerchief knot, in which was a boiled egg badly crushed. As if he was collecting some kind of fees, he came to each of us, and each of us gave. At the end with his two hands full, he grinned, and the face of his mother softened.

As each of us was having the warm supper of a boiled sweet potato, Changshun could be heard begging his wife to let us stay for the night. But she insisted that we go somewhere else.

Changshun looked embarrassed when he came out of the side room. He thought for a second and then told us about a *wowotou* shop down the road.

"We're closed, come in the morning," yelled a man's voice from the attic window when Changshun banged on the door.

"Some girls, Little Red Guards need a place to sleep," yelled back Changshun, looking up.

Minutes later, a man holding an oil lamp opened the door. As Changshun turned around to leave, we stepped inside to a mud stove next to a kneading board. Like a home, it smelled leavened dough and mold.

"Don't have another room, try to get some sleep here," said the shop owner, throwing a barefoot toward the stove.

Too tired to unpack our quilts, we curled up near the stove as soon as the shop owner went up the attic. About the same time, the glow from the oil lamp breathed its last.

It was a short night. Before dawn, first the shop owner and then his wife came down the attic and moved around as though we were not there. He poked the stove, showering cinder dust, while she smashed the dough like spanking an unruly child.

We crawled up, thanked them, and left.

CHAPTER 47

The fourth day on the road seemed to be the fourth week. With blisters on our soles and between our toes, we all walked in pain. No one complained, though. It was shameful to cry hardship those days. We simply kept shouting Chairman Mao's quote: "Be determined, fear no sacrifices, and overcome ten thousand difficulties to win the final victory."

At dusk we came to a small town and asked a young woman on a donkey-pulled cart for directions to a reception station. Following what she said, we limped up and down the same dirt road twice to get to the middle school the young woman claimed she had graduated from.

The schoolyard teemed with Red Guards getting registered. Those having arrived earlier were already eating with their faces resembling frozen pumpkins in the light of a single bulb hanging from a wooden pole.

We stood the last in a long line to get food. When the Red Guards before us stomped their feet, the man looking like a cadre in charge came running and then walked away shaking his head.

The meal consisted a *wowotou* and a ladle of boiled cabbage. By the time we reached the window, no cabbage was left. We each got a *wowotou* before hastening over to the boiler, where a tussle was going on for the only faucet.

I squeezed through and got a mugful of lukewarm water but spilled almost all of it while trying to squeeze out. As the last resort, we went to a faucet on the other side of the schoolyard for some cold water.

The straw-strewn floor of an empty classroom was the bed for six of us and four groups of female Red Guards that night. Since all the better spots away from the two doors and four windows were already taken, we found ourselves resting at the base of a wall under a broken window.

I got almost no sleep, very likely so did everyone else in that classroom. Always someone was on her way in or out, and always several in a row were stepped on, causing loud screams.

Toward dawn, Xiaoya rolled inside my quilt with something to tell me.

"Let's take a shortcut, our day will end earlier," whispered she.

"You know a shortcut?" asked I.

"The railroad," mumbled Xiaoya.

"Are you sure? Not safe," said I before a voice telling us to shut up.

At that Xiaoya and I went under my quilt and didn't come out until it was time to get up.

As we walked out of the reception station that morning, two trees outside the school gate swung their leafless branches in the wind as though waving goodbyes. We all were cheerful, due to the nice weather, a new route, and most of all, the prospect of getting to a city none of us had never been to.

The railroad track lied among debris and overgrown weeds. As it went further west, it sloped up onto a ridge covered with pebbles, where harvested fields below could be seen extending into distance with peasants plowing like in a dreamland. Lanlan removed the scarf around her neck and let it flutter. We all laughed, drinking a lot of dust.

In a single file we walked with the crossties of the track lying passive for us to step on, but soon we all felt their control over our pace. The distance between two crossties was less than a stride of ours. Not to slow down, we sped up in smaller steps. We flapped, and we flew.

The track trembled. Behind us, a train was coming fast toward us. Immediately we jumped off the track to stand on the slope. We held onto each other tight as the train was passing by. Although shaken, we smiled at the passengers looking out of the windows, but not one of them smiled back.

The train was gone. We were climbing back to the track when Lanlan dropped to her knees with her head held in her arms. Asked what was wrong, she said she felt dizzy.

At noon we stopped at a railroad station that had only a ticket booth. Seeing soot-covered us, a man in a railroad uniform asked, through the window, how old we were and where we were going. When none of us gave him an answer, he suggested we take a train to wherever we wanted to go. Feeling belittled, we all crawled up, slung on our quilt packs, and stomped toward the track.

We could tell we were getting closer to a bigger railroad station. One railroad track was branching into two with some concrete buildings emerging on the right side. They were factories turned into ghost towns after factional violence shut them down.

Minmin and Lanlan needed to pee. They got off the track, hopped across a ditch, and disappeared into a thicket of dry weeds. They could be heard deciding who would do it first while the other was on the lookout. The rest of us didn't stop to wait for them. It had been too often an occurrence to cause any concern. Besides, two of them was enough a team to brave anything.

More tracks appeared. Seeing a railroad platform to our right, four of us raced as fast as we could before collapsing onto a concrete floor.

"Where are they?" asked Xiaoya after all four of us sat up, looking in the direction we had come, where loomed an ominous sky streaked with deep orange and dark grey. Where were Minmin and Lanlan? We were dying to see them. The very moment they were spotted, we would cheer just as we had at the school entrance in the early morning on the first day of our trip.

When the loudspeaker announced the delay of an express train to Beijing, we were not surprised at all. Seldom was a train on time those days.

We all got up when an ambulance drove onto the platform through a side gate. Just as it came to a screeching halt, the express train to Beijing, with its dazzling lights in the front, whistled into the station.

Once the ambulance left, the express train also cranked away, leaving the platform as deserted as before. Then the loudspeaker started to call Xiaoya's name, asking her to go to the station office.

A railroad worker took a glance at the introduction letter Xiaoya showed to him before kicking open the door behind him. There on the floor sat Minmin, who uttered a long cry when seeing us.

On their way back to the track, Minmin and Lanlan noticed a trodden trail which seemed to run in parallel with the track. They took it, thinking they could catch up with the rest of us faster. But the trail ended abruptly, leaving them without any choice but to climb up onto the track. Lanlan was ahead with Minmin pushing her up from the below. After she reached the track, she turned around to pull Minmin up. But she couldn't hold on. She took a step backward, falling faceup onto the track. As a coming train suddenly turned around a curve and approached, Lanlan tried hard to get up but was unable to. She did manage to roll off the track, but her left leg got caught under the train. So that ambulance we saw earlier was taking Lanlan to a hospital. Which hospital? Where was that hospital? We asked. Could we go to see her? She had been on this trip with us since day one. We were her friends, schoolmates, and fellow Little Red Guards. We pleaded. But the railroad worker sitting behind a desk in the office looked clueless. He didn't know what we were talking about at all.

Early next morning, a female railroad worker brought five of us onto a train that had just come to a stop. One by one, we squeezed into a compartment that had only half a window. When the train started to move, we huddled together on a wet floor, trying to get some sleep.

The moment the train came to a stop, the same female railroad worker opened the door and told us to leave the train. Quietly we followed one another through an isle packed with passengers, off the train, across the platform, and out of the train station. On the sidewalk Xiaoya looked having something to say, but she didn't say a word before crossing the street and disappearing into an alley on the other side.

I never saw Lanlan again, but she had been in my dreams. The siren from a train was always followed by a loud scream with a flashing light revealing a dangling leg from a still body. Around her neck was that scarf she always wore. How was she? And where was she?

Whenever I thought about Wang Nainai, I also thought about

that old woman selling water on the side of the road. Her wrinkled face always closed in like in a blown-up photo. Perhaps she was still waiting to see us on our way back. One hand on her forehead as a sunshade, she kept gazing down the dust-shrouded road. She was worried, and she was worried about us.

CHAPTER 48

"Go with me," cried Hui outside.

"Where?" asked I while trying to unlatch the door.

"My baba, find my baba. He didn't come home last night," said Hui, grabbing my both arms. "My mama has gone to see a relative, I'm by myself."

Like a summer storm had just swept through, the debris of a fierce fight between two factions littered the street leading to the fertilizer plant where Hui's father worked. Not one gate or door on either side was open. Only a few shadowy figures sneaked along with their heads down.

"Dead, let's go," said a man's voice as we were approaching an intersection.

To our right, crouching over what looked like a body were two men, each holding an iron stick. After they hurried away, we edged over.

In a pool of blood was a dead man. A gape in his head had emptied all his vessels, leaving him as pale as a blank big character poster. Frozen in terror were his eyes with a mouth so wide-open crying pain that even death didn't shut it up. He had only shorts on. Likely he had been called on to join the fight while taking a nap or eating supper at home.

I tried to turn around, but Hui held my right hand and stepped closer. She wanted to make sure it wasn't her father.

More bodies lay further down the side. While I stood there with my eyes looking away, Hui tiptoed among the dead, checking their faces. She was quiet as if otherwise she would wake them up.

We were almost at the gate of the fertilizer plant when several workers, each in a rattan helmet, appeared before us. They seemed surprised to see us. One of them even called us "little loyalists," at which Hui's hand tightened around mine, for her father belonged to a faction of loyalists.

"Catch him," shouted one of the workers nearby, pointing at a man coming out of a small pond off the road. Sludge dripping all over him, he looked fully camouflaged. Apparently, he had been hiding underwater and was spotted while taking a breath. The workers before us and more inside the gate ran toward the pond. They jumped in on all sides, wielding sticks and belts. The man howled.

Without a word to each other, Hui and I fled in the direction we had come. Fright lent wings to our feet, and we flew as the wind whizzed by and the trees lining the road went blurred. A man at a bus stop stomped, pretending to chase us, and we just kept running.

Once around the corner into our alley, we were so exhausted that together we plunged to a wall and collapsed. It was some time before we rolled up to go home.

On the doorstep Hui's father squatted, head in a bucket. The night before, he managed to hide in a ditch covered by weeds once he sensed his side was losing the fight. Only after the other side left did he dare to get out and head home.

"Where have you been? I'm worried," yelled he, snorting water from his nose when he saw us.

Not saying anything, Hui and I held each other's head and cried.

Hui cried perhaps feeling relieved that her father was safely home, and I cried surely to wash off those images of death.

Never had death been real to me. It was just a word uttered in a hushed voice that led to a funeral. On that day I got so close, and I saw. No longer was it a word. It was open wounds, pools of blood, seized eyes, twisted faces, and lifeless bodies. Now and then in a dream, I was even able to count those bodies. Always among them was that man in the pond, whose desperate howling echoed on.

CHAPTER 49

August 1968.

"Middle school students, we're middle school students," said Hui before hopping inside the outhouse.

Two minutes later she came out, clutching two slips of paper. She handed one to me.

"Admission notice? Mine?" asked I in disbelief as my name was smudged up by too much ink from the school stamp.

"Yes, here is mine. We go to the same middle school," answered Hui while tapping her feet in excitement.

I had to make sure. When I held the slip of paper up to the sky, the red mess faded away with all the strokes of my name showing up.

"I'm a middle school student," screamed Hui again, waving her admission notice.

"I'm a middle school student," I also screamed.

"We're going to middle school," laughed Hui and I together.

Holding each other's hands, Hui and I swirled back and forth from one side of the yard to the other.

For more than two years I had no idea if I would ever go back to school again. Now I knew I would. It was so easy in a way. Without finishing all the elementary studies and taking any exams, I became a middle school student.

"You two! Xiaoer has been a student there, no big deal," hollered Aunt Shan from her door. Behind her stood her younger son Xiaoer, who would soon start to work at the same factory as his father. While many like him had to go to the countryside, he could just stay in the city as a worker.

"Not a good school! Many stinky intellectuals," shouted Xiaoer as a Red Guard would.

The morning to register, even under an overcast sky, I felt only sunshine. Hui walked next to me, and her eyes sparkled like stars. Ahead of us, a boy was singing to himself as he jumped over a fallen wall and hurried eastward in the same direction. When two girls stepped out of the gate we were passing, I recognized the girl who had come to trick me on behalf of those mean boys. But I didn't have a thread of shade in me that moment. I smiled at her when she looked at Hui and me. Who cared if she didn't smile back?

Before an open window stood a long line that zigzagged all the way to the school gate. Cordoned off was the schoolyard still belonging to the three-old-grade students, many of whom were still wearing a Red Guard armband.

Hui reached the window first. She handed over her admission notice to the female staffer, who then looked in a registration book before telling Hui which class she was in. It was quick. Then my turn came. However, the same staffer couldn't find my name in the same registration book. She again read my name in the admission notice and again looked in the registration book by moving the tip of her right forefinger alongside a column of names from one page to another. As impatience grew louder behind me, the staffer, pointing to the wall to her left, told me to go to the next door.

The man in charge of student affairs got up from his chair as soon as Hui and I entered. When he learned that my name wasn't in the registration book, he asked with a southern accent for my admission notice. Holding it close to the buzzing fluorescent lamp on his desk, he examined.

"Real," said I, nervous that he would think it wasn't.

"Let me find your application form," said he, turning to open a cabinet against the wall. Clenching a stack of forms, he started to check the name on each. When he pulled out one that showed a dark correction, I knew it was mine. In the blank after my father's name, I first wrote a prisoner and then changed it to a counterrevolutionary. I was just trying to be as honest as possible. I would have no chance of getting into any school if I was found lying,

He turned to Hui and asked for her name after taking a glance at my application form.

"Very good, your father is a worker," said he to Hui, placing her application form next to mine on his desk. "Keep an eye on her, report her counterrevolutionary words and deeds."

"Don't, don't pay attention to what he said," said Hui to me once we got outside that office.

She was right. If I did, I wouldn't be able to live for very long. But I did hope he would add my name to the registration book as he just promised.

CHAPTER 50

Younger than my brother, I thought as a PLA soldier strode in to stand in the front of the classroom. The red star on his cap and the two red tabs on his collar shone in stark contrast with his grass green army uniform.

He lowered his head to clear his throat. When he looked up, a shy grin dawned his youthful face. But still, like the sound switch of a radio was turned off, a chattering room fell silent. For a moment I could hear my own breathing.

During the orientation the day before, both the head of the soldiers propaganda team and the head of the workers propaganda team spoke. They announced that either a soldier or a worker would come to lead each class in the morning. My class had a soldier.

The soldier cleared his throat again, this time with the class roster in his hands. Hui's full name was called. Not sure how to respond, Hui slowly got up while looking to the right at the soldier, who gestured for her to sit down while calling out the next name.

As one name after another echoed throughout the classroom, one student after another stood up as Hui did and then sat down as Hui did. My name was the last one to be called, and I was the last one who stood up and sat down. This time being the last had nothing to do with my height. My name was added at the last minute, and I had barely made it.

"Everyone, open your red treasure book," said the soldier, holding a copy of Chairman Mao's quotations. It had a plastic cover that glimmered the same red as the star and tabs on his uniform.

The whole class fidgeted. Then Hui got up, telling the soldier that she had a copy but didn't bring it to school that day.

With a sigh the soldier opened his own red treasure book and started to read, in a singing voice, the first quote in the first chapter of Chairman Mao's quotations.

"Read the next," instructed the soldier, placing the opened red treasure book before Hui, who started to read in a singing voice too. But this time the rest of the class tittered, and Hui also tittered, leaving the soldier the only one who didn't titter in that room.

After Hui finished, the soldier pushed the red treasure book over to the other girl at the same desk. Slowly she read. Upon a word she didn't know, she looked up at the soldier.

"Skip it," said he without finding out which word. The girl continued but could hardly be heard. When she looked up at the soldier again because of another unknown word, the soldier picked up the red treasure book and went to the desk across the aisle.

The red treasure book was passed, by the soldier, from one student to another, from one desk to another, from one end of the row to the other end, and from one row to another row. Each row had four desks and eight students, and there were seven rows in total.

The school gatekeeper was swinging his handbell again. This time was for a ten-minute break. The boy who was in the middle of reading a quote abruptly stopped, but the soldier clapped his hands twice, telling him to continue.

One face after another started to appear in the windows facing the schoolyard. They were students from the class next door. As if no one could hear them, they loudly chatted among themselves. One wondered why a PLA soldier was teaching this class, not theirs, and another swore that only fools didn't take a break when it was time. The soldier was annoyed. He made a run out of the door, shooing them away.

The opened red treasure book was put before me with two quotes on one page and one on the other page. Not sure which quote was for me to read, I looked at the soldier, who thought for a second and then told me just to read one.

After fifty-seven quotes were read out including the one by the soldier, the soldier said he needed to find eight class cadres, two for one group of fourteen students.

"A class cadre must have a good family background. Do you know five red categories? Let me write them here" said the soldier, turning around to use the blackboard, on which a drawing, although fading, was still visible. Under the heavy boots of a Red Guard was a frightened teacher, whose glasses were flying off his face.

The soldier took a step backward and looked at the drawing. After taking another step backward, he leaped outside the door. A minute later he was seen charging into the office building across the schoolyard, and another minute later he reemerged with a small blackboard under his right arm.

As the class watched, the soldier hung the small blackboard next to the large one and scribbled out, one after another, the five red categories: poor and lower-middle peasants, workers, revolutionary soldiers, revolutionary cadres, and revolutionary martyrs.

Again the soldier picked up the class roster, in which after a name and gender was the family background. Once again Hui's name was called first. One after another, eight members of the class each with a good family background, were chosen as class cadres.

But not everyone of the eight wanted to be in charge. When three shook their heads, three more names were called out. After some seats switching, Hui and the boy sitting two seats behind her would lead the first group, and the boy four seats before me and the girl sitting with me at the same desk would the group I was in.

"Municipal cadres," said she to me of her parents.

"Municipal cadres? Aren't they revolutionary cadres?" asked I.

"Yes, yes," chuckled she, nodding her head.

From the far end of the schoolyard a team of construction workers emerged. They were coming towards Hui and I as we two slouched behind our classroom, taking turns to bite on a raw sweet potato.

Five men followed by two women were passing before us, none wearing any shoes and none looking either up or around. The sun was almost overhead, and they cast almost no shadows. They themselves were shadows, moving but making no sound. Once reaching the wall on the right, they turned left, disappearing into a corner.

"There used to be a dorm for teachers, now a cowshed. I've heard some cow devils are allowed to teach again," said Hui into my left ear.

"Really? Teach again," uttered I.

"More teachers are needed to teach new students like us, let's go to see the cowshed," said Hui, grabbing my left hand.

A narrow pass between a backwall and a sidewall led us to a small junkyard. Piled up in the weeds were some dorm furniture like plank beds, two-drawer desks, and chairs, so weathered after being outside so long that they turned grey and grim. Even the sunny sky above couldn't lighten them a little bit up.

A door on the east side opened. One of the two women seen earlier stepped out with an old bucket. After closing the door, she slowly shuffled along a path toward the west side, where a rusty faucet looked struggling to stick its head out of a crumbling wall. Still, she didn't have shoes on. Still, she didn't look up or around. Like a shadow she made no sound. Then the downpour started, shattering the silent thrall like thunders.

She used the bucket to knock her door open. Before she could close it, a room with almost nothing showed itself, so typical of a cowshed for cow devils those days. A cow devil would never need to sleep in a bed or sit at a desk. While in the cowshed, Mama, night after night, simply sat with her back against the wall, which was, she later told me, better than lying on the dirt that was cold and damp.

There came a cough. Only then did I notice the open door next to me. On the floor sat an older man looking through some papers. He didn't put on his glasses even though they were right there at his side. While his right leg stretched out listlessly, his left leg bent at the knee. Instead of shoes, he wore sandals woven with straws. If a Red Army soldier on the Long March could wear them, a cow devil could too, no matter how much they hurt the feet that had them on. The moment he put down the papers and tried to get up, Hui and I ran away.

The afternoon sunlight followed the same older man into the classroom door, simmering on the right side of his grey hair. Down was his head as he stood there. If he had looked up, he would have seen half the seats before him were empty.

Through the door in the back a middle-aged man walked in. He wore a red armband that read "Workers Propaganda Team."

"Your math teacher," said he, strolling to the front with his hands in a clasp behind him.

"Not a teacher, not a teacher. Criticize," hastily responded the math teacher.

Putting on his glasses, the math teacher unfolded the papers in his hands and began to read. He was denouncing himself.

"Cannot hear you," complained the worker, leaning against the front wall.

The math teacher raised his voice when he continued to read. He denounced his grandparents who had owned land and hired helpers as wealthy peasants until the land reform; he denounced his parents who had operated a department store before 1949; he denounced the education he had received from a private primary school and then a Catholic university in Beiping, now Beijing; he denounced his first job as a teacher in the old society. As his voice turned hoarse, he sounded more determined. At one point he even raised his right fist, declaring he would forever hate his long-dead grandparents and parents.

"The cowshed is good, allows me to see my true self," continued the math teacher, reading out another page. This time he was expressing his gratitude. Behind him the worker sighed, pacing back and forth.

"What happened to your forehead?" asked the worker when the math teacher finally finished reading all the pages in his hands.

"Hm," hesitated he while the long scare above his right eyebrow glistened.

"What happened to your right leg?" asked again the worker, stepping closer to the math teacher

"Fell, I fell," stammered the math teacher.

"You still live in a cowshed?" pressed on the worker with some anger in his voice.

"In a cowshed, in a cowshed, I'm a cow devil," murmured the math teacher, stooping lower and lower with his arms going up backward like an airplane in a nosedive. For him, it was just another struggle session.

The worker was taken aback. He went to the front corner and grabbed a stool. After he dusted it, he let the math teacher sit down, who still wasn't looking up.

"Who knows what's going on," said the worker, glancing around before fixing his eyes on the drawing on the blackboard. "Why I'm here? A worker or a middle school graduate who has no idea how to teach."

The math teacher limped outside. For every step he took, he threw his upper body to the left and dragged his right leg forward. As soon as the worker dismissed the class, he hastened outside too. Tears welled my eyes when I saw him placing a hand on the back of the math teacher.

My father came to mind. Had there been someone like the worker with him? He, he had died. My father, my father had died, which Mama learned while she was in the cowshed. It wasn't that she got notified of his death as his wife. She heard it from the Red Guards who had gone to the labor camp to question him about Mama's past. No one knew when he had died and how he had died. That her counterrevolutionary husband had died was all Mama was told. Mama didn't say if she cried when she heard the news. If she did, it would be when no one was around. Shedding tears for a counterrevolutionary was another thing not allowed no matter who that counterrevolutionary was. Mama cried while telling me about it after she returned home from the cowshed.

"A *haoren*," sobbed Mama. "He didn't do anything, he just wanted to have a better land reform. He said it wasn't right for so many landlords to be beaten to death."

I cried too. For the first time I cried for my father.

CHAPTER 51

"Don't have classes today," said Hui as we were hopping along.

"Don't have classes? Why?" asked I, only then noticing Hui didn't bring her schoolbag.

"Attend a sentencing rally. I have my red treasure book," said Hui, patting on her pocket.

"A sentencing rally?" asked I, looking inside my schoolbag to see if my own red treasure book was there. It was.

"A sentencing rally," said Hui.

"The city stadium?" asked I just to make sure.

"The city stadium," said Hui.

Near the school entrance a small crowd gathered. A struggle session? No, it wasn't. Who was that girl? It was Yuanyuan, a student from another class. She was on her knees. She was on her knees sobbing. She was sobbing with both hands covering her face. Also a *heiwulei*, she happened to sit with me at the first meeting for *heiwulei* students. No, she didn't tell me her name. During the entire time, we didn't utter a word to each other. I learned her name when she stood up in response to her name being called out.

"The second one, her brother," said a man standing next to the sentencing poster on the wall. Underlined were the names of the four active counterrevolutionaries to be executed right after the sentencing rally on that day.

"An intelligent young man, took *gaokao* twice, each time got the scores for Qinghua and Beida but was never accepted," mumbled the same man, shaking his bald head.

I had heard about him. He had gone to the same high school as my brother. Unlike my brother and others, he couldn't, he just couldn't bear not going to college. He had to do something. He tried to overturn his father's death sentence first. On the eighth anniversary of his father's execution, he wrote a letter to the authorities, in which he argued that his father's criticism of the system was intended for a better system. When he got arrested as a counterrevolutionary, that letter was the only piece of ironclad evidence.

I had no idea that he was Yuanyuan's older brother. Squatting down next to her, I wanted to say something to her. Maybe just a word or two, but there existed no such a word or two. What could I say to her, who had lost her father and was about to lose her brother? What could I say that would convey my sorrow but at the same time save me from being accused of not showing enough hatred against class enemies? Nothing could I say. My right hand on her shoulder, I was letting her know I was there.

Yuanyuan had trouble getting up. Holding on to Hui and me, she brought herself to her feet. Without looking around or saying anything, Yuanyuan quickly retied the white scarf around her neck and walked with Hui and me into a schoolyard that was already lined up with students. Giving Hui and me each a quick glance, Yuanyuan went over to join her class. In a little while, the entire school would leave for the city stadium located just a wall away from the execution site.

I raised my hand when the political counselor called out my

name. Not that he needed to say something to me. He just needed to mark my name on that list of his as being there. He had been doing it class by class, and he had been doing it one *heiwulei* student at a time. It was fine for a non-*heiwulei* student to have an excuse for not participating in an activity like this. There would be serious consequences if a *heiwulei* did the same as the political counselor warned time to time.

It took time to get inside the city stadium and more time to reach the ground designated for schools. No sooner did we sit down on a stretch of sand than shouting slogans started. One school after another joined in before "Down with counterrevolutionaries!" echoed throughout the entire stadium.

After a pause, it was time to study Chairman Mao's quotations. Following the political counselor's instructions and with every red treasure book turned to the first quotation, our school, as one and in one voice, read out loud not only the first quotation but the next four.

I wondered where Yuanyuan was. Her class was behind mine, so I turned around. There she stood with her white scarf fluttering in the breeze. No longer was it a scarf, but a grieving bird ready to take off. Yuanyuan was looking eastward in the direction of an opening in the surrounding wire wall, where four army green trucks were edging along a road into the city stadium.

"Here they come, here they come!" As some screamed, more stood up, bringing about a wave that completely engulfed Yuanyuan. When it ebbed, she wasn't there anymore. Only the four army green trucks were seen crossing the running track toward a wooden platform that had been set up in the middle of the field.

When I saw PLA soldiers each holding a five-*chi* rifle in the back of every army green truck, I closed my eyes. When I heard slogans being shouted ever so loudly, I lowered my head with my knees against my ears. I didn't want to see, and I didn't want to hear. All I could do was to shut myself off. Even though what was going on was for a *heiwulei* like me to see and hear, still what was going on made no sense. It made no sense that a young man was about to die for writing a letter or two. No sense did it make, and it made no sense.

The platform was retreating like a mirage, and so was every sound around as I kept saying to myself "Don't want to see, don't want to hear."

The four army green trucks were moving again, this time westward. A short distance further west, on the other side of the city wall, was where Yuanyuan's brother would be executed. A bullet out of the barrel of a five-*chi* rifle would enter his head and stop his heart. It would be quick, said I to myself. It would have little pain, said I to myself. His spirit would surely go heavenward, said I to myself.

"Look," uttered Hui next to me. I hesitated before slowly opening my eyes. Flying alongside the third army green truck was something white. A kite? No, it wasn't a kite. It was a scarf. Suddenly it dawned on me that it was Yuanyuan, who was trying to catch up with the second army green truck that carried her older brother. Even though he wasn't able to see her, she was there to see him off. Even though she was lagging further behind as all the army green trucks sped up, her goodbye went all the way.

CHAPTER 52

December was cold, and this particular morning seemed colder. In the dark I put on my clothes, grabbed my schoolbag, and groped my way toward the door when Mama told me to eat something first. I pretended not to hear, stepping outside.

Hui wasn't standing outside her door, waiting for me to go to school together yet. It was too early, I said to myself.

Snowflakes, too light to come down, swirled in the air like catkins. As a cluster of thin ice fell on my neck, I shuddered and popped up the collar of my cotton-padded jacket.

Just like I had hoped, I was the first one to arrive. Once inside the empty classroom, I dashed toward my desk in the back and looked in my drawer. But nothing was there. Where was it? My notebook was always in my schoolbag. Last night, when I couldn't find it there, I thought it had slipped out and was left in my drawer at school.

The first class was about to start. Outside the window, the head of the workers propaganda team was seen talking to my class teacher. As they entered, I noticed the green notebook the head of the workers propaganda team was holding. "Mine," shouted I to myself. When the class teacher signaled for me to go to the front, I thought I was going to get back my notebook. But I didn't. The head of the workers propaganda team told me to go to his office with him.

Sitting at a conference table in the office were the director of the revolutionary committee and the political counselor. The head of the workers propaganda team pulled over a chair and sat down next to them, leaving me alone at the other side. Without saying a word, he tossed onto the conference table my notebook, which slid with strips of paper sticking out. They were markers, which meant it had been read. I was horrified. I never kept a diary because I knew how easily it could get me into trouble. Every time I jotted down only a few sentences to get some kind of relief. Of course, no one else was supposed to read them. They were for myself. Myself only.

My notebook teetered on the edge of the conference table right in front of me, and I thought I would pick it up.

"Don't, don't touch it," said the director of the revolutionary committee. "Let me ask you. Is that yours?"

"Yes," answered I.

"Why do you write something like this?" asked the political counselor this time.

"Don't know," answered I.

"Do you love the party and the country?" asked again the director of the revolutionary committee.

"I do," answered I promptly.

"You do? Then why you aren't happy?" asked the political counselor, getting up from the chair.

"I'm not happy? I have never said that," said I to myself in a voice only I myself could hear.

"'Perhaps a maggot in a garbage dumpster lives a better life. Mine is filled with hopelessness,'" read the political counselor, who had come to my side of the conference table to get my notebook and opened it at one of the markers.

"She feels miserable, it means she doesn't like the new society. That's counterrevolutionary," cut in the director of the revolutionary committee, speaking about me in the third person.

It never dawned on me until that moment that I wasn't supposed to feel bad no matter what. If I did, I would be accused of being counterrevolutionary. My heart sank to where it could no longer.

Someone was calling the political counselor, and he hurried out of the door. For a minute or two neither the director of the revolutionary committee nor the head of the workers propaganda team said anything. Only then did I notice a stove in the corner to my left. No wonder it was so warm.

"Having counterrevolutionary thoughts is a serious crime. Because of your age, we'll try to reeducate you," said the head of the workers propaganda team. He had left his seat and was pacing behind the three chairs: the political counselor's empty chair, the chair in which the director of the revolutionary committee was sitting, and his own chair.

Suddenly the school's loudspeaker was on. Like a signal of some kind, the director of the revolutionary committee sprang up and rushed out. Then the head of the workers propaganda team went into a door and came out wearing an army green hat with earflaps. After tucking my notebook in one of his pockets, he told me to follow him.

As I was walking behind the head of the workers propaganda team, a head popped out of an open door in the corridor and asked what was going on. "A struggle session," said the head. Through a side window facing the schoolyard, I could see students coming out of classrooms with stools. The need to sit down meant a longer struggle session.

In the back stage of the school auditorium, the political counselor, surrounded by a group of students, was giving instructions. Hoisted up in the air across the stage was a white banner. I couldn't see its front but was sure my name was on it. While adjusting the PA system, the school electrician didn't seem to mind grating on ears at all.

"A notebook filled with counterrevolutionary thoughts was found in the drawer of a student in our school. It's a very serious matter. To keep our country forever red and get rid of poisonous weeds before they spread, we must condemn her and her thoughts," said the head of the workers propaganda team standing before the microphone.

The political counselor gave me a push forward. I had never been on that stage before, which was the most rugged cliff overlooking a sea. What a sea it was, roaring out loud slogans and rolling up arms and fists!

The students who had been with the political counselor were speakers. The first one marched to the microphone and read from a piece of paper without ever looking up. I didn't catch a word he uttered except my name, which was mentioned several times.

The second speaker was quick. Before I knew it, she finished.

The third one was the most energic. At one point, she stepped closer to me and pointed a finger at my nose.

Among all the speakers, I knew only one, who was a classmate. She was also the one that spat on me. I didn't know why. Even though we were not friends, we were on good terms. Twice I had let her use my pencil eraser.

I wasn't scared, though. What was going on seemed to be just the reenactment of a nightmare I had all the time: The ground gushed out flames, and I tried to run only to be held down by thousands of hands from nowhere. It would be over, I told myself. But before it was over, I would have to go through it.

"*Sheng shi ren*" or "Life is endurance," read a scroll made by Mama. The scroll had long been burned by the Red Guards, but those three words I would always remember.

I found myself staring at my cotton-padded shoes made from scratch by myself. The skill came naturally, due to having seen Wang Nainai and Mama make them. I made *gebei*; I cut the pattern pieces; I stitched the soles using a thimble. They were still in good shape after a long winter the year before and would have no problems to last the current year and the year to come. At that thought my mouth curled up.

"Stop making faces, behave yourself," rebuked the political counselor, who had been watching me from the side.

The shouts of slogans surged again, signaling the end of the struggle session. The students were leaving the auditorium. Through the corners of my eyes, I saw Hui hustling against the crowd around her. She was coming to me. But before she could reach the stage, she got scuffled away.

The electrician was gathering the equipment and winding up cords. As I wondered if I could go back to my class, the political counselor reappeared and tapped me on the shoulder.

"Your problems are very serious. Stay here and think about them," said he before turning around to leave.

I needed to sit. I didn't because I wasn't sure if it was a good idea with the electrician still there. The moment he stepped out of the backdoor, I plopped down. Never had I appreciated sitting so much.

The bell rang, and it was the lunchbreak. The schoolyard was alive for a moment and then became dead. My stomach groaned, reminding me of not having breakfast. Sporadic whines turned into constant growls, and soon a sense of hunger gave way to chills. I shivered in cold sweat. Not knowing what to do, I wrapped my arms as tightly as I could around myself.

The bell rang again and again, each time sounding more and more distant.

An overcast winter day was shorter. As the evening approached, I became worried. A night alone always terrified me even after I had gone through so many of them. The school auditorium sat in a far back corner and was as remote as any wilderness. If someone wanted to kill me, it would be the easiest thing to do. Even if no one had such an intention, I would be frozen to death for sure. It was cold and would be so much colder at night.

The light on the stage was turned on. Before I could see anything, a voice asked me to get up. I tried but couldn't. Then two hands pulled me up. The moment I got to my feet, I felt dizzy. Then I was looking at the head of the workers propaganda team, who still had his army green hat on but with its earflaps down.

For the third time that day I was walking behind him, back to the same office I had been to in the morning. All the way he burped and blew his nose. He had had supper, I thought to myself.

Once in the office the head of the workers propaganda team removed his hat and went into the same door he had in the morning. With the fire in the stove burning, I felt my cold body was melting and whatever was left in me was draining away. I turned lightheaded, trying to grab the nearby conference table

When I came to, I was in an old wicker chair. As I was wondering where I was, the school gatekeeper bumped in, carrying a bamboo-shelled thermos.

"Now your eyes are open," said he in a loud voice before pouring some hot water into a chipped emerald mug.

"Why I'm here?" I asked after taking a sip.

"Two members from the workers propaganda team brought you here. They told me to let you go home," said the school gatekeeper, looking at the clock on the desk.

"Go home, I go home," murmured I, getting up from the chair and stepping toward the door.

"It's cold, use this," said the gatekeeper, bringing over what seemed a blanket from his bed in the corner.

"No, I'm fine," said I with my arms wrapped around myself.

The street outside the school gate was deserted with only a few scurrying along. Next to a flickering kerosene lamp before a door, a man squatted behind a wok. "Hot sweet potatoes," hawked he upon seeing me. I had several smallest coins in my pocket, which would be enough for a small sweet potato. But I looked away and passed him.

"So late, are you ok?" Mama asked, placing a hand on my forehead to check the temperature.

"I'm fine, just tired," said I, sitting down at the table.

"Where is your schoolbag?" asked Mama, handing me a bowl of peppery soup.

"At school," mumbled I, slowly letting my tongue slip into the soup. As numbness was gradually giving way to warmth, I found myself trying as hard as I could to hold back tears.

I pinched myself. I muttered Old Heaven forbad. I ever ordered myself to be like Mama, who seldom cried. The last time she cried, she was telling me that my father had died. She had lost so much weight and was still losing. I was worried about her. If you had seen her, you would have been worried too. Her hair was black the first time it was forcibly cut. Having finally grown back after being forcibly cut the second time, it was almost completely gray. Mama didn't need to know what had happened to me. I would carry on by myself.

"Hui's mother was here. She said Hui had gone to live with her aunt and go to a middle school there," said Mama, flipping a strand of hair off my face.

"I knew, she told me everything," murmured I.

I didn't know, I didn't know Hui was going to live with her aunt. She didn't, she didn't tell me about getting transferred to a different middle school. What I did know was that she had to report on me once a week. What she did tell me was that she had been asked why we were friends. "Neighbors, we are neighbors," replied she.

I still went to school next morning. Past the school entrance, I couldn't help but notice the new big character posters on the bulletin board. They were about me. One had two sentences copied from my notebook with a phrase here underlined and a word there circled. Always in bold and crossed was my name Drawn at the bottom of another big character poster was a maggot with my eyes, complaining about her miserable life in a garbage dumpster.

On the adjacent makeshift wall were more big character posters with two of them just for signatures. There was Hui's name. She had to sign, which for sure was the reason for her to go to another school. If she didn't sign, she would become a traitor.

My class teacher, who had been watching me approach, blocked me at the door. She told me to see the political counselor in his office. When I said I needed to get my schoolbag, she stepped aside to let me in.

Making my way to my seat in the back, I saw faces looking away to avoid any eye contact. I tried a smile, but no one seemed interested in receiving it. Where was the girl sitting at the same desk with me? There she was, having changed to a seat in another row on the other side.

"Your red treasure book?" asked the political counselor next to his desk, behind which a large portrait of Chairman Mao was hung on the wall

"Here," said I, taking out mine from my schoolbag.

"Read it, read it in the morning. Write a self-criticism in the afternoon," instructed the political counselor while going through some papers on his desk, "You must take your problems seriously. If you don't, consequences are..."

He didn't quite finish what he was saying when he got up and hastened out of the open door. Two minutes later he returned.

"I did some investigation. Here's your application form. You lied, lied. Do you know what I'm talking about?" growled he, slapping a sheet of paper on the desk.

I shook my head. It had been more than a year since I filled out my application. I couldn't recall everything I had put in there, but I was sure I had done it to the best of my knowledge. If there was a mistake, it had to be an innocent one.

"Do you know what it means? Lying about your family background is counterrevolutionary too," declared the political counselor in a harsher tone than before. "Your class status is counterrevolutionary, not educator. You lied here, how dare you!"

What was he talking about? As far as I knew, my class status was what my father did as a job that gave him an income to feed his family. To make sure I gave the correct information, I had checked with Xiaoya and Hui. Xiaoya's class status was revolutionary cadre because her father worked as a revolutionary cadre and got paid as a revolutionary cadre. And Hui's class status was worker because her father worked as a worker and got paid as a worker. My father had taught for years, which made my class status educator.

He didn't know what a class status was, I said to myself. But no way was I going to tell him that. As a political counselor, he knew everything and was always correct. If he said whatever was my class status, then whatever was my class status. If he said I had lied, I had lied. He could say or do whatever to me, while I could say or do nothing about it. He reined over me, and over me he reined.

Another struggle session ensued, this time in the classroom below the school auditorium. It wasn't my first time going there, though. My sixth time it was. At both the beginning and the end of each semester, we *heiwulei* students went there for a session by the political counselor, who would read us an editorial or some Chairman Mao's quotations before instructing us to self-examine and self-criticize. This time it was all about me.

I was on my way there. Like every time, as I walked across the schoolyard and along a sidewall to reach that door at the base of the auditorium, I felt I was coming to see them, the three teachers.

Every time I was here, they were here too as if waiting to tell me what had happened to them in the hands of the Red Guards, some of whom were their very students.

How could I forget what had happened to them? One died from his head injuries after being pushed down the concrete stairway to the concrete floor. Another was beaten to death with a stool, which, although wooden, could savage a human body just like an iron rod would. The third was poured enough DDT down his throat to cause seizures to his brain and stop his heart.

The fluorescent tube on the top of the blackboard shimmered. The first time I was here, it looked a cylindrical moon, but each time after, it waned in length as the two ends darkened a little bit more. This time, the sixth time, two thirds in the middle remained moonlike with the rest becoming part of the concrete wall. Already here were my fellow *heiwulei* students. Seated with their arms crossed on the desks, they turned concrete too, each with downcast eyes and a held neck. So did I, but standing.

Were they thinking what I was? How could they not be? They and I all lived in the same neighborhood as the three dead teachers. But they and I would never tell what was on our mind. Besides, we *heiwulei* students didn't say anything to each other. Right there in the second row was a classmate of mine. She and I belonged to the same activity group, but seldom was there a word between us. When two *heiwuleis* talked with each other, nothing good could come out of those *heiwulei* mouths.

While I stood with my head down, the political counselor denounced my wrongs as if they were really wrongs. Because her father was a counterrevolutionary, her family background undeniably was counterrevolutionary too, said he. But she lied about it in her admission application, which itself was a counterrevolutionary act.

While he was talking about me, I was talking to myself. Why did you keep bringing up my father? He was dead, and dead was he. He was no more, and no more was he. He didn't do anything wrong by pointing out that landlords could have played a useful role in the land reform and that beating them to death didn't do the society any good. With their agricultural expertise, landlords could have contributed to better grain productions. My father was correct, and correct was my father.

"We do electroplating," said the worker in charge, who wore an apron so long that it completely covered his feet.

Electroplating? What was that? The political counselor told

me to go to the school workshop, so I came, having no idea what I would be doing. Seeing the puzzled look on my face, the worker in charge led me to a room where two concrete baths lied side by side like sleeping.

"This one for acid solution, that one for zinc solution. Metal parts are cleaned here, and then go there to be deposited," explained he, pointing at the bath before him and then the bath to his left. With wires connecting electrodes to switches and pipes zigzagging the walls, I didn't notice someone else there until he came before me.

"Old Fang, both a rightist and a cow devil," said he to the chuckle of the worker in charge. I couldn't believe my ears. Someone could be so lighthearted about his plights. I took another glance at him. Even though he had a small figure, he exuded confidence.

"The best chemistry teacher. He put this place together," added the worker in charge. Immediately I felt I could breathe a little bit easier. If he could hold in high regard a rightist, he wouldn't be so harsh on someone like me.

I did what I was told to do. As soon as I arrived before seven o'clock in the morning, I started to fill up a basket with metal parts and then carried it to the bath with acid solution. After lowering it to the bottom, I waited for about ten minutes before pulling it out and placing it under a nearby faucet to be rinsed. If it sounded simple and easy, it was. What made it not so simple and easy was the pungent smell of the acid solution. It stung my lungs, itched my skin, and faded my irises, especially when I had to lean over the bath to put in and pull out the basket.

"Take that thing off. Everybody else is fine, why aren't you?" yelled the political counselor through the open door. That thing was the cloth mask Old Fang had given me earlier. I removed it and tucked it in my pocket.

"Behave, otherwise two weeks can turn into four weeks," continued he while turning to wave at someone riding a bicycle.

It was my fifth day there. Everyday about the same time, the political counselor would show up and say something like that to me. Checking on me was like a must-have meal for him.

I was cleaning the eighth basket of metal parts. As I was hauling it up from the bath, I lost my footing and slipped on the step at the base. In my struggle not to fall, my nose hit hard on the concrete edge. Feeling a warm trickle down my lips and chin, I touched and saw blood on the three longer fingers of my right hand.

Old Fang put down what he was doing at the other bath and rushed over. After assisting me to sit on the floor near the door, he looked around for something clean to stop the bleeding. I fumbled out the cloth mask in my pocket and pressed it against my nostrils. It turned red.

"Let me get the school nurse," said Old Fang, running outside.

"Need a permission," hollered the worker in charge, who was smoking under a tree. "Without it, the nurse won't come."

"How about your permission?" Old Fang asked. "You're in charge here, she works here."

"I cannot do that. The political counselor sent her here. Go, go to ask him," urged the worker in charge.

But just a second later, he called Old Fang back, and he himself went.

On the concrete floor I sat with blood dripping down my right hand from the soaked cloth mask into the right sleeve of my cotton padded jacket. But I felt no pain.

Some time had passed before the school nurse came, swinging a first-aid box that had a red cross on the lid. The worker in charge apologized for taking so long because he had to wait for the political counselor to come out of a meeting.

"You aren't being careful," scolded the school nurse like a mother. I held my peace while a swab of cotton was wrung into one nostril and the other.

"Does it hurt?" asked she after noticing a scrape on my forehead. It didn't until she dabbed alcohol on it. When she began to wrap my head with a long bandage, I pleaded for a gauge pad just the size of the scrape. She didn't listen at all.

"Let me walk you home," said Old Fang when it was six o'clock, the time to go home.

"No, no," said I, stretching my arms to show I was fine.

"Let me," insisted he, making a hand gesture for me to go first.

Going home had never been so slow with me stopping several times. When I stopped, Old Fang would stop too somewhere behind me. He was patient just like my father had been that evening on our way to the cinema.

No longer was there a gate to our yard. What was left were rubbles. Luckily it came down around midnight when no one was passing or near it. The implosion woke up all those living in the immediate vicinity, but no one panicked enough to run outside. By that time the neighborhood had gotten used to something like that. The Xingtai earthquake in 1966 cracked every gate in the alley without collapsing a single one at the time. Two years later, however, one gate after another started to tumble down as if being dynamized. Before long the alley had tuned into a site of ruins. Every day I made my way through a ruin. I did.

Hui's mother was seen sewing the last stiches of a sole on her doorstep. So large, it had to be for her husband, Hui's father. The other day she paid a visit to Hui and came back telling me that Hui missed me. I missed her too. We had had each other for about eleven years, which was a lifetime.

Turning around, I asked Old Fang to come in. He shook his head, he waved, and he walked away. In the dimming twilight, he looked a rock from where I stood. He had been a rock to me since I met him. He gave me my father.

CHAPTER 53

June 1970.

"Seven desks in a row multiplied by four rows makes twenty-eight desks all together," shouted I, seating at my desk. No one else was there, and I was in the classroom by myself.

"Today is the last day of your middle school," announced the class teacher during the self-study hour the day before.

"*Wula*," cheered the class in Russian. Not that we all spoke the Russian language, but that all the Soviet movies we had watched in our earlier elementary years had "*wula*" in them.

"Be prepared to go to the countryside," said the class teacher, clapping her hands to emphasize each word.

After mentioning the possibility that some students might stay for high school, she glanced around to see who was interested. I was, but I wasn't going to show I was because I wasn't supposed to have any interest in anything. I was a *heiwulei*.

"So loud, are you upset?" asked Yifang, who walked in through the door in the back.

"Of course not," said I.

"I went to your home, you weren't there. I thought you had to be here," said she with a smile.

"If I go there, I'll die there," said I.

"There? You mean countryside? If you go, you'll never come back? Don't say that. You don't know," said Yifang, sitting down next to me.

"You're going?" asked I.

"My mama is in poor health. She has to work so hard to feed her three children. If I go, it'll be easier for her," said Yifang, whose mother was working at the same postal office as her father before he died of lung cancer several years ago.

"We all have to go," admitted I.

"Let's go to the same brigade, we can be together all the time," hummed Yifang, looking up as if she could see the future. "By day we work in the fields of green crops and wild flowers, at night we sit at the window, looking at the moon and counting stars..."

Yifang always had better dreams. Not to break her heart, I said I would go wherever she was going.

Before we left each other that day, we hooked our little fingers, swearing like lovers that we would stay committed to each other no matter what.

Soon it was announced that those born in the second half of1956 and after could choose going to the countryside or staying for two more years of high school. When the class teacher asked those eligible for and also interested in high school to get up, only I and four others did. Thirteen others could stay for high school but decided not to. At that time, school was considered useless, and education was a waste of time, which was why no one made a fuss about a *heiwulie* like me going to high school

Yifang wanted me to accompany her to her new home. The night before, I was with her, so I wouldn't be late for the long-distance bus the next morning.

We had so much to talk about as though we knew it would be the last time for us to share secrets. Not to be overheard, we went under the grapevines in the backyard, lying on one mat and covered with one bedsheet.

It wasn't the seventh day of lunar July yet, but for a moment we held our breath to listen to the cowherd and the girl weaver, whose whispers echoed among stars, reaching us through tendrils that quivered like question marks.

"Have you thought about getting married?" Yifang asked.

"Hmm," hesitated I. A young man riding a dragon had long stopped crossing my mind. I even doubted if my parents would have gotten married had they foreseen their children would be *heiwulei*.

"Want to marry someone honest and dependable," murmured Yifang. "Do you want children?"

"Hmm," hesitated I again, having never thought that far ahead.

"I want two, a son and a daughter," confided Yifang, uninterested in what my answer was but was eager to give hers.

That night we talked until stars became sparse in the sky and dews came down like a light shower. It was hard to tell if we slept or not. If we did, we just kept talking in our sleep.

It didn't take long before I got a letter from Yifang saying her life there was harder than she had imagined. Day in and day out she left for the fields at dawn and worked for hours before going back to eat something as breakfast. She faced a number of problems: She couldn't tell seedlings from weeds, therefore pulling out what she shouldn't; her shoulders had been swollen from carrying heavy loads; she had no idea how to use a stove that didn't burn coal. The most serious of all was that she became constipated because she dreaded to use the largest manure pit she had ever seen. She was still optimistic, though. "I'm strong, I can survive this," noted she at the end of her letter.

Before the Lunar New Year, I got another letter from Yifang. "All my roommates have gone home, but I cannot until the third day of the Lunar New Year. The brigade head has asked me to feed the mules," she wrote. "Don't go anywhere that afternoon. I'll go to see you, and you're going to tell me what you have learned at school."

It was that afternoon. Mama scrambled two eggs before sitting down with me at the window. A while later when Yifang didn't come, Mama and I guessed why. She didn't get on the bus, which was always packed, not to mention during a holiday; she got confused about the date, mistaking today for tomorrow; she was home, but her family wouldn't let her go out since she was so tired after hours on the bus.

I had to find out. The moment I knocked on the door at the dead end of a narrow alley, Yifang's younger brother answered with her mother and younger sister right behind. I could tell they all were there to welcome Yifang. When they saw me instead, their eyes saddened. The younger brother was too young to hide his disappointment before a guest. He stomped his feet and turned away. It was Yifang's mother who put on a cheerful face and greeted me.

Upon hearing I was there to see Yifang, the mother let go herself and cried. She told me they had been waiting. Since Yifang wasn't home, no one was in a mood to celebrate the Lunar New Year.

Not until a month later did Yifang come home. I went for a visit and found a changed person. It wasn't that her face was tanned somewhat or her hands were rough with callus or her hair turned discolored, but that she had become so withdrawn. Months before, we had been inseparable. Whenever we took a stroll together, an arm of mine was slung on a shoulder of hers. Wherever we sat together, we leaned on each other like one. Now, as I habitually put my right hand on her left shoulder, she quickly shrank away.

She asked about my life in a voice so timid as though she was offending me. When I wanted to know about her life in the brigade, she told me to read the letters she had written me. "Read, read them again," murmured she, a wry smile flashing across her face like a startled bird. After that, she and I simply stared at the opposite wall.

I had spent half a day at that production brigade. Next to the mule shed was where she and six other girls lived. It didn't even have a decent door to protect them from intrusion. Then there was the brigade head, whose eyes wandered.

Yifang asked if I wanted some tea. I nodded, and she got up and went outside. When she returned, she was holding a bowl in which several tealeaves were floating. As I sipped, so bitter was the taste that my tongue went numb.

Once again Yifang faded with me sitting there as if by myself. Yifang didn't trust me anymore. I thought perhaps because we no longer lived the same kind of life. While she toiled in the fields, I tried to learn more knowledge in school, which however, didn't explain at all why we couldn't be friends. Something had happened, and she was afraid to tell me.

It was time for me to go home, said I. Yifang stood up, opened her old army green schoolbag, and took out a pair of black cloth shoes.

"I made, not that good," said she, looking away. "You have big feet, not so easy to get shoes."

I left, struggling to hold back tears.

After being home for three days, Yifang returned to her production brigade. She never wrote me again even though I begged her to in my letters to her. One day I ran into her mother, who told me that

Yifang didn't write home either. "Not the daughter I knew," sobbed she, wiping off tears.

One late afternoon in June, I was on my way home from school when someone grabbed me. It was Yifang's younger sister, who was crying with her eyes red.

"My older sister is in hospital," said she.

"What's wrong?" asked I.

"Don't know, a lot of blood," replied the younger sister, drawing a pool in front of her with her hands, and my heart sank.

Hardly could I believe lying on the concrete floor outside the office of gynecology and obstetrics was Yifang. Murmuring to her at her side was her mother, whose eyes were red too. Her younger brother had gone to call a pedicab.

Tears streamed out her closed eyes down her ashen cheeks when she heard my voice. Kneeling next to her, I leaned over and stroked her hair.

Earlier that day Yifang suddenly arrived home. She had walked several *li* to catch the earliest bus. Not to stain the bus seat, she had wrapped her waist down in the plastic sheet that had been her raincoat.

Yifang had been pregnant for some time. The brigade head, who was supposed to protect her, had forced himself on her on the Lunar New Year's Eve and the days after. It was an easy doing like a vulture devouring its prey because of his position as the brigade head. He scheduled her time such, so she was alone in that remote shed. With her trust in the top official, she let him in when he unexpectedly showed up.

She resisted. Her screams for help hovered above the nearby fields only to scare away a flock of crows resting on the haystacks. Afterward, to stop her crying, he gave a promise that was believable also because of his position as the brigade head. Yifang would be the first to return home in two years.

Seldom did Yifang have her period on time. When she missed two in a row, she didn't think too much of it. Only when her belly started to show did she realize what it was. She had to hide it. At a time when all her roommates were out, she tore her bedsheet into two halves and sewed them into one long strip. With one end tied to the door and the other held to her belly, she slowly rolled. She tugged each time her body turned, and she was breathless when she finished. She uttered a sigh of relief as her hands slid down that part, which was as firm as a wooden board. She had no time to relax, though. Acute pain shot up her spine, and she fainted.

When she told the brigade head about her pregnancy, his face dropped as if she had owed him plenty. Darting glances at her belly through the corners of his eyes, he cursed, "A cheap slut, you got pregnant by yourself."

The brigade head began to bring her tablets he got from the brigade clinic that was like his own. As the brigade head, he simply walked in and emptied every bottle on the shelf. Of course, no question was asked. The barefoot doctor appointed by the brigade head was a grateful one who couldn't thank him enough for being spared of hard labor in the fields. Bleeding started soon after Yifang took a handful of tablets for the second time.

CHAPTER 54

October 1971.

More was going on academically. After one semester of chemistry that introduced Mendeleev's periodic table, we were learning Newton's three laws of motion in physics. First algebraic geometry and then analytical geometry were added to the math curriculum. Several times the math teacher even brought up college entrance exams as an incentive for more attention to whatever he was teaching.

The Youth League had come back. The school had a Youth League committee with the political counselor as its general secretary, and every class had a Youth League branch and its secretary.

Although a recent transfer, Liying was among the first in my class to become a League member and was appointed the League branch secretary at the same time. She often mentioned her father, who was the new director of the revolutionary committee at the Labor Bureau.

As soon as the history teacher finished assigning homework, Liying got up from her seat to announce a meeting to be held after school. It was only for those who were not Youth League members, emphasized she. At that time most of the class were not Youth League members, and only three were

"Everyone must apply. Joining the Youth League is one step further toward being a revolutionary successor," urged she as she kept jerking her head.

I knew that, but I also knew I would never be accepted due to my *heiwulei* family background.

"Turn in your application tomorrow," demanded Liying, blocking my way out after the meeting.

"Tomorrow?" asked I.

"Tomorrow, must be tomorrow. Turn in your application for the Youth League tomorrow," repeated she.

I thought she was new and didn't know I was a *heiwulei.* Had she, she wouldn't have brought up the matter with me. So, I didn't write an application.

It was a Friday afternoon, the time for political study. In the first hour, the class studied an editorial from People's Daily. During the recess, my deskmate and I went behind the classroom to play *pingpong.* As we hastened back to the classroom after the bell rang, Liying, who was in charge of the study, stopped us at the door.

"So late," said she with a frown, telling me to wait there after letting in my deskmate.

"You have a serious attitude problem," said Liying when she returned and shut the classroom door behind her. "A *heiwulei* like you may never be a Youth League member, but you must show your strong desire to become one. That's the attitude you should have."

As soon as I stepped inside the classroom, a struggle session started with Liying saying to the class that I didn't denounce my counterrevolutionary father enough and still lived with my counterrevolutionary mother.

"My father is dead. Isn't that enough? Where do I live if I don't live at home with my mother? How can she keep saying something like that?" retorted I in a voice only I myself could hear.

"I have been doing denunciations for years. I'm tired of denouncing my father, I'm tired of denouncing my mother, and I'm tired of denouncing myself. My father is a good person, my mother is a good person, and I am a good person," I shouted at the top of my lungs in a voice no one but I myself could hear.

CHAPTER 55

The classroom at the other end of the building had turned into an office for teachers teaching our grade. Through the open door, Teacher Gao was seen reading at his desk.

He was my English teacher for that semester, but he was also a *heiwulei* like me. When he was severely beaten in September 1966, he was beaten for being a *heiwulei*, and he was a *heiwulei* because his late father was a landlord.

When a group of Red Guards from his home county found him at a struggle session held by his students, they dragged him to the school basketball court, where he was tied up and thrashed with an iron chain that went for not only his body but also his face. He didn't die, though. His life was spared because ta Red Guard in the group knew his wife was the daughter of a poor peasant in their county. However, about the same time, his wife, a middle school teacher back in his home county, was stomped to death by another group of Red Guards for being married to the son of a landlord.

"Have you read this editorial? It says students should teach," said Teacher Gao, tapping the newspaper on the desk. "How about you teaching an English lesson? You'll do a good job."

I hesitated at first. For a minute all I could think about was

Liying, who had warned me several times that I was paying too much attention to academic studies. But I nodded my head because I wanted to see how Liying would react.

Teacher Gao grinned, squeezing more scars out of the scars covering his face. I always thought one day my face would end up like his. Since both of us were *heiwulei*, we were destined to wear scars on our faces.

For a short lesson, I practiced for hours and hours. For more than a week, the first thing Mama did after getting home from work was to help me. She corrected mispronunciations and pointed out grammatical errors. Mama also told me to stand straight and not to look at the ceiling.

That day came. I wore my best clothes: a white shirt, navy pants, and black cloth shoes. They were not new, but they were newly washed. Mama even ironed the collar of the white shirt with a bottle of really hot water.

As soon as Teacher Gao said my name, I got up but was slow to move my feet, which lasted only a second. The sneer on Liying's face immediately freed me. I strode to the front, feeling as confident as my not so white shirt.

After telling the class which lesson it was, I wrote the new English words and their Chinese equivalents on the blackboard, which I had no problem doing because I had practiced at least a dozen of times on the two doors at home. Then I explained the grammar and translated the text of that lesson. Before my teaching time was over, I called four classmates, girls of course, one after another, to read the text.

On my way back to my seat, I could hear Liying's groans. She was about to explode. She did. Before I could sit down, she jumped up and marched toward Teacher Gao, who was standing near the front classroom door.

"Why you let her teach? Don't you know she is a *heiwulei*? If someone like her teaches, our country's going to change its red color," fired she.

"I'm a *heiwulei* too. If I'm allowed to teach, she is too. I let her do it because of her perfect score on the mid-term exam," said Teacher Gao calmly.

"English is an imperialistic language. We shouldn't learn it, we should denounce it," yelled Liying, raising her right arm.

"Marx says foreign languages are important weapons. Marx is the greatest revolutionary," said I in my teaching voice, which was loud and clear.

I had memorized some quotations from Marx and Chairman Mao, knowing they would be helpful in one way or another.

"Weapons? You aren't allowed to have weapons, you are *heiwulei*," shouted Liying, appearing enraged.

CHAPTER 56

February 1972.

Where the sunshine couldn't reach, snow showed no sign of melting, looking as permanent as the sky above. Whenever the wind blew, dust swirled up and down as if conducted by an invisible wand. It was the first day of the new semester, and I was on my way to school, alone.

The new class teacher had a new idea to seat us. While boys lined up against the wall on one side of the classroom, girls stood together on the other side. Then two, one from each side, were called to sit at the same desk and on the same long stool.

The last time I sat with a boy at the same desk was in elementary school, which lasted for only a week before he dropped out.

This time it was dramatic. The way it was going, the air in the classroom was that at a wedding ceremony for an arranged marriage between a man and a woman who had never met. To be honest, it wasn't so much about meeting someone for the first time since we had been classmates for a semester already. It was more about who it would be. When each pair walked, one from either side, over to their desk, the rest of us laughed hysterically. No one was left out. We all had our turn to make fun of and be made fun of.

When I heard my name after his, I took a glance down the line of the boys on the other side. He was one of those looking the most ordinary and having no feature that would have made a description of him easier. The only thing I could say about him was also the most obvious: he was shorter. Daliang was his name. Like most schoolgirls would do around schoolboys in those days, I made sure he knew he wasn't liked. I slammed my schoolbag into the drawer on my side and then drew a demarcation line in the middle of the desk with a bit of chalk I had picked up somewhere.

We didn't speak at all to each other, but for sure I did my observations. Always on his side of the desk was a pocket dictionary that had Chinese, English, and what looked like Japanese on the cover. I couldn't help marveling that he was learning two foreign languages at the same time. Besides, he never took off his shoes during a class and was better mannered than many other boys.

Sooner than I had expected, the demarcation line faded away. On a rare occasion when my right elbow touched his left one, I found the feel of his elbow so pleasant that I froze mine. After many stealthy glances, I ended up perhaps knowing more about his left ear than himself. He had bigger earlobes, which was a sign for good fate. I thought about saying something to him, but at that time all I knew about speaking with a boy was that the boy had to go first.

It didn't happen until after the midterm. At the end of an English class, a piece of paper slid to my side of the desk. On top of the English word "love" was an arrow pointing to a willow tree in the city park. He was bold. Five thousand years of civilization up to that time had embraced only oblique references and innuendos in expressing that special feeling. There were many ways, but none of them used the word itself. It was a word without any stitch on, a naked word. Somehow a foreign synonym saved him from appearing so shameless. Still, he was bold.

After school and after I wiped clean the blackboard, instead of home, I went straight to the city park, where following the note, I found the largest willow in a row of five with the other four tapering off along one side. Long twigs, almost touching the ground, gently swayed in the breeze, and narrow leaves, so much like the eyebrows of ancient beauties, glittered in the late afternoon sun. I dove in, and he was already there.

On a rock half-buried we sat the way we did at school. But for the first time there were only two of us. Also, for the first time he dared to look me in the eye.

"You like to listen to stories, don't you?" asked he. Only then did I realize he had paid more attention to me than I was aware of. Without waiting for my answer, he went ahead with a story of his own making: A bird was too weak to fly across a river, and a cloud was willing to carry her to the other side.

I liked it. Moving through the air always fascinated me, and riding a cloud was often in my dream even though I doubted it would ever be possible.

Still, we acted it all out before we parted ways that day. As he drudged around the willow tree with a beat in his steps, I was close behind with my hands on his shoulders, a forever scene that showed just how much he and I liked each other.

Two weeks later we had our second date. Perhaps for me to know him better or having nothing else to say, he told me about his family. His father was a regiment commander who was among those having crossed the Yalu River in early fifties to fight the Korean War, his mother a head nurse at an army hospital, and his older sister a telegraphic dispatcher for the army regional headquarters. Besides, his two aunts, three uncles, and five older cousins all worked in the army.

"I'm from a military family," said he with a shy smile perhaps because he wasn't used to talking about his family members.

"Are you going to join the army too?" wondered I, struggling to picture myself arm in arm with a fully-uniformed PLA soldier.

"I'm not the type," said he, rubbing his hands that appeared much softer than mine.

He went on to tell me about the compound his family lived in, which had armed guards at the entrance twenty-four hours a day. Their four-bedroom apartment was inside a building designed by Soviet experts. In addition to high ceilings and fancy motifs, there were screened windows, wooden floors, and wall lamps. The most impressive of all, the apartment had a squat toilet and a bathtub, both ceramic.

"Our bathtub doesn't have hot water. We have to go to the bathhouse in the compound. It opens once a week," added he.

"Does the toilet work?" asked I, remembering Xiaoya from my elementary school had often complained about a toilet that wouldn't flush and having to use a pit outside. Her apartment didn't have a bathtub, though.

"Of course!" He raised his voice, looking surprised at my question.

As that date of ours was drawing to an end, all I could think about was how to let him know I was a *heiwulei*. The last thing I wanted was to disappoint him or break his heart. No matter what, he liked me and meant me no harm.

"My family background isn't good," mumbled I, avoiding using "*heiwulei*."

"I know, everybody knows," said he, looking down.

I didn't say another word, feeling my inside was turning cold fast. Since he knew I was a *heiwulei*, why he still wanted to do something like this with me?

"I don't care," continued he, looking up with a dry grin.

"Your parents do," retorted I, coming to my mind my first-grade class teacher who had threatened to kill herself after finding out her daughter had been dating a *heiwulei*. I didn't blame that teacher at all. She had to think about her family's future generations.

Then I already knew what was ahead of me all the way to the end. For sure I would never get admitted to college. For sure I would never find a full-time job. Who would be crazy enough to show any interest in someone like me? How about never thinking about getting married? How about never having any children? I even seriously thought about becoming a nun although Buddhism had been forbidden for years.

When Liang didn't come to school the next morning, I wasn't surprised at all. I was even amused when three days later the class teacher told the class as good news that he had joined the army.

He told me he wasn't suited for the army, so it couldn't be his idea.

CHAPTER 57

During the long recess in the morning, the entire school gathered in the schoolyard, doing the stretching exercises to the music from the loudspeaker when two PLA navy officers appeared, strolling behind some tall students.

"Who are they?" asked I, tapping Fangfang on her back.

"Recruiters from the North Sea Fleet," said she.

When one recruiter suddenly stood next to me, I somehow felt the need to perform, starting to stretch harder. The moment the music ended, he came before me, asking me to go to the conference room during the self-study hour.

I heard it but couldn't believe it. I couldn't be a Youth League member and date a boy from a PLA family. How could it be possible for me to join the PLA?

"You're tall, look eligible," hummed Fangfang, giving me a nudge. That navy recruiter hadn't done a family background check on me yet, which I knew and Fangfang knew too.

I still went. A group of tall boys including one from my class were already in the conference room with each holding a sheet of paper. While one recruiter was talking to them, the other was turning the pages of a notebook in his hand. I stood close to the door, waiting for a chance to tell them about my bad family background.

There was a knock on the door. It was Liying, who gave me a glance and then went straight to the recruiters.

"PLA comrades, I know something about her. It's important," said she, turning toward me a little bit. "She's a *heiwulei* with counterrevolutionary parents. She herself once was caught for having counterrevolutionary thoughts. She also has relatives in Taiwan and the United States."

"We haven't had time to check family backgrounds yet, we plan to in the afternoon. Your name?" asked the recruiter with the notebook.

"Zhang Liying, my father is a revolutionary cadre," said she with a smile.

"Can I go?" asked I. Before either recruiter responded, I was already outside the door, saying to myself I didn't ask to come.

That afternoon Liying came to school with her father, who was later seen leaving with the two navy recruiters in tow.

The next day Liying didn't show up to lead the morning self-study. Not until the self-study before noon did the class teacher walk in to announce that Liying had joined the North Sea Fleet of the PLA Navy.

Who didn't want to join the PLA? Even a *heiwulei* like me wanted too. Not only was being a PLA soldier glorious, but it offered the best future possible. A student before joining the PLA would certainly have a good job afterward. A rural youth, once a PLA veteran, could be assigned to work in a city as a cadre or a cadre in charge.

Life for a newly-recruited soldier was, however, really tough as we were told by the PLA officer who did our military training earlier in the semester. "Be prepared to suffer," emphasized he. The story he repeated several times was that just like the Red Army during the Long March, after crawling in mud for hours, you would have only grass to eat and only rain water to drink. At night, not on a bed did you sleep but in a trench that teemed with insects.

That PLA officer was from the army. The training for a new Navy soldier was probably different. But as Liying herself said, her life had been easy because of her father. What was in wait for her in the North Sea Fleet could be as comfortable as her father made it to be.

No longer brought up by any of our teachers were college entrance exams. Even though they wouldn't get me into any college no matter how well I could do them, I wanted to take them. I had always looked forward to taking exams since the first grade. Good scores were my salvation by reminding me of the good I could at least do. The moment I received an excellent score was the moment I could feel better about myself. For me, any other moment was under the mountainous weight of a *heiwulei*.

For a while no one seemed to know whether high school would be just two years or go back to three years. As the second semester of our second year drew closer to an end, another year of high school seemed less likely, and more likely we would go to the countryside, which was, in Chairman Mao's view, the best school out there. Those Chairman Mao wanted to go to college were workers, peasants, and soldiers, who would get admitted without taking any entrance exams.

CHAPTER 58

September 1972.

"Come, come, help me do something," said Aunt Shan on her way to the outhouse.

"Do something? Do what?" asked I when she reappeared.

"Make a wedding quilt for Huo. He's getting married you know. I need you do something, let me show you," said Aunt Shan, grabbing me by the left arm.

Stacked on a small mat next to a large one outside her door were a red sheet, a white sheet, and a cotton wadding, each neatly folded up like on a store shelf.

Aunt Shan, holding one side of the white sheet, handed me the other side, and together we spread it out on the large mat. The second layer was the cotton wadding, followed by the red sheet as the top layer. Only then did I notice that the white sheet was larger than the cotton wadding, which was about the same size as the red sheet.

After making sure all the three in their right places, Aunt Shan started to move around, folding the white sheet up around the cotton wadding onto the red sheet.

"When is the wedding?" asked I for the sake of saying something.

"Next Friday," said Aunt Shan. "The bride is a coworker, two years older."

"I forgot to tell you, she wants a new bicycle," said Huo, stepping out of the door with Xiaoer behind him.

"A new bicycle? Yours isn't old. It's hers too after the wedding," hollered Aunt Shan while trying to pull a thread through the eye of the needle in her left hand.

"Mine is two years old. She wants a new one made in Shanghai," mumbled Huo.

"Why didn't you tell me earlier? I say you marry someone else. Who doesn't want to marry into a family like ours? Every member is a worker. Find someone else," said Aunt Shan, staring at her older son.

"She just wants a new bicycle made in Shanghai. Someone else may ask for more, a new wristwatch made in Shanghai, a new radio made in Shanghai, a new sewing machine made in Shanghai," counted Huo by bending his lefthand fingers with his right hand.

"Right, you're right, she asks for just one big item, not two or three big items. I'm going to try," promised Aunt Shan, moving on her knees to another side of the quilt.

"Remember it's a new bicycle made in Shanghai, a new bicycle made in Shanghai," reminded Huo, unlocking his bicycle parked near the pomegranate tree.

"It's too early for your night shift. Where are you going?" asked Aunt Shan.

"My home, my new home, my bride is there," said Huo before getting on the bicycle.

"Your new home, just a tiny room," said Aunt Shan to herself.

"I go to work, go everywhere on foot. I need a bicycle too, a new bicycle," groaned Xiaoer, coming over to squat down next to Aunt Shan.

"Are you getting married too? Who is your bride?" teased Aunt Shan as she was trying to knot the thread before cutting off the needle.

"Just get me a bicycle coupon. I have saved enough money, can pay for a new bicycle, a bicycle made in Shanghai," continued Xiaoer, ignoring what his mother had just said.

"I want to meet your bride first," chuckled Aunt Shan, getting up and rubbing her knees.

"It's for myself. Get me a bicycle coupon, a coupon for a Shanghai-made Forever, not a Pheonix. My brother may want a Pheonix for his bride. I'm a man, want to ride a Forever," said Xiaoer.

"I can't, I have to get a bicycle coupon for your brother first," snored Aunt Shan.

"If you can get a bicycle coupon for my brother, you can get one for me," insisted Xiaoer.

"You think getting a bicycle coupon is easy? I need to bring at least three cartons of *Daqianmen* cigarettes when I go to see the cadre in charge of coupons," croaked Aunt Shan. "Think about it, three cartons of *Daqianmen* cost more than thirty *kuai* in the black market. That's my monthly salary."

"Uncle, can you get a Forever coupon for me?" asked Xiaoer, who had hopped all the way to where Uncle Xu was washing his face outside his door.

"..."

"Cannot," repeated Xiaoer after Uncle Xu, whose voice was hard to hear.

"..."

"Your department store doesn't issue any coupons," repeated again Xiaoer.

"..."

"Doesn't sell any bicycles," repeated Xiaoer one more time before hopping back to where Aunt Shan and I were folding up the just finished wedding quilt.

"Want to learn how to ride a bicycle?" asked Xiaoer, looking at me.

"No," said I without looking at him.

Seldom had Xiaoer and I had a word to each other. He was four years older and looked all right. But in my mind, he was always stomping on whatever was on the ground. Although he had never called me "*heiwulei*," I always thought he would one day when he got upset with me about something. I could end up writhing under his feet like those goldfish.

"Lying, lying, everyone wants to learn riding a bicycle," jeered he.

He was right; I was lying. What I didn't say was that I already could ride a bicycle. It wasn't that I had learned how to ride. I just could ride. Riding a bicycle was one of my basic instincts. When I got on Uncle Xu's bicycle after he got off it the other day, I rode between his doorstep and ours for several minutes with no problems.

When I saw Xiaoer again weeks later, he was on a bicycle that sparkled like being made of stars. He pedaled on until he reached where I was before making a U turn to go back to Aunt Shan.

"A new Forever! Xiaoer, you are something," gushed Aunt Shan, seeing the Forever logo on the head tube. "How did you get it?"

"Someone from work sold me. Not new," said Xiaoer, landing his feet on the ground to stop the bicycle.

"Not new? It looks new. How much?" asked Aunt Shan, touching the back fender with a forefinger.

"Two hundred *kuai, a*ll my savings, not a *fen* left. The guy has a new Forever, sold me this one," said Xiaoer cheerfully.

"How much a new Forever? I know, one hundred seventy *kuai*. For a secondhand, you paid thirty *kuai* more. You make only thirty-two *kuai* a month," complained Aunt Shan, biting her lower lip.

"What could I do? You got a coupon and bought a new Phoenix for my brother, you didn't even try to get me a coupon," said Xiaoer.

"Not for your brother, for his new wife. When you get married, I'll get one for your new wife too," disagreed Aunt Shan.

Xiaoer started to ride around her mother, who laughed, clapping her hands. When Xiaoer finally braked the bicycle to a halt, he got off and steered it inside the door, where he parked it along the backwall. At the same time Aunt Shan hastened over, covering it up with a plastic tablecloth.

Uncle Xu got home from work. After he washed his face, he settled on a short stool, starting to eat from the bowl his wife just handed him. She went on to eat too once she sat down cross-legged on a round straw mat next to him. When weather permitting, Uncle Xu and his wife always ate with their door wide open. Without a window, the door was also their window. Side by side they sat and ate. Behind them was their plank bed, under which was, like a pile of firewood, Uncle Xia's bicycle, which had long lost the leg supposedly for it to stand on.

Uncle Xu could eat every meal at home thanks to his bicycle, which he said he had bought from a pawnshop in the old society. It looked indeed belonging to the past. Beneath rust was more rust. Not only did it show nothing about where it had been made, but also Uncle Xu had no idea where it had been made either, so it had been without an identity for a very long time.

It didn't have a bell. But the moment it was on the move, it clattered like a raspy voice yelping for attention. No matter what shape it was in, Uncle Xu had been riding it two times to work and two times back home every day.

Looking out the window, I wondered where Mama was on her way home. If she had had a bicycle, she would have been home by that time. After the cowshed, Mama was assigned to work at a location of the city museum that was further away from the bus route. She walked to work, and she walked back home. It took her more than an hour one way and about three hours both ways. She had been leaving home much earlier and returning home really late.

Mama needed a bicycle. I knew she could ride one, having seen a photo of a younger her riding a bicycle. As long as it was ridable, she couldn't care less if it was just like the one Uncle Xu had.

I needed a bicycle too when it was time for me to go to the Red Star People's Commune. Its third brigade I was assigned to was a hundred forty *li* away deep in a valley surrounded by hills. It wouldn't take too long by train or bus, but no train went in that direction, and the closest bus station was about forty *li* from the third brigade. I had done some math. I would have to walk at least five hours to reach the third brigade from the bust station, but by bicycle, that distance took only an hour. A passenger on a long-distance bus usually was allowed to bring along a big item like a bicycle, which was good news as far as I was concerned. I could even see myself inside a packed bus with a bicycle similar to Uncle Xu's secured on the bus top.

Initially I had the hope not to go to the countryside. According to the policy announced, those who were the only child or the only child left at home could stay. But when all the *heiwulei* students from the two graduating high school classes attended our last meeting with the political counselor, he made it clear that the one child staying policy didn't apply to us. I almost uttered the word "why" but swallowed it as I had so many times. It was the same doing whatever to a *heiwulei* child.

The need for a bicycle was there, but never did I think I would actually have one. I planned to walk forty *li*, from the bus station to the third brigade, which wouldn't be too hard since I had walked four long days and several hundred *li* when I was younger. I had classmates going there too. I could walk with them.

What had been weighing on my mind was not to end up like Yifang. She was gone, and she was gone for good after her life's worth was taken away just like that. What had remained of her was less than a shadow. Only she knew the pain she had been going through, and she had been keeping it all to herself.

What else could she have done? If she had reported it, she herself could have been blamed for having somehow brought it onto herself or having not fought hard enough. She was alone that night, and she had been alone ever since.

I didn't want any of what had happened to Yifang. I had to take care of myself. How? Even though I wasn't sure, I kicked off my shoes, swung up my arms, and lifted myself up. Instead of my feet, my knees landed on the stool I had moved to the middle of the inner room.

"You still have it," self-congratulated I. Once again I returned to my fight mode. I punched and kicked whenever I could. I no longer sat to eat. While eating, if I wasn't standing on one leg with the other leg on the windowsill, I was doing a split on the floor.

CHAPTER 59

When I walked into the post office, I couldn't really see. Some seconds later I found myself looking at a dark green counter, behind which a middle-aged woman stood.

Where was Yifang? I wondered. There, she was sitting at a dark green table in the back. What was she doing there? Was she sorting mails? Yes, she was. If this woman wasn't here, I would march through that low swinging door at the end of the dark green counter to talk with her.

While standing before a bulletin board against the wall, I could tell that woman was staring at my back. She had to be wondering why I was there or whether I was there for the sole purpose of browsing a People's Daily displayed on the bulletin board.

Fidgeting in my shoes, I guessed who was that woman. Someone in charge here? Yifang said her boss was someone older but had no idea if it was a man or woman. Instead of worrying myself to death, I came to find out.

Besides Yifang, she was the only other person there. She had to be that someone older in charge, but she also appeared very much a mother with children. I was relieved, so I turned around and left. Yifang didn't need to know I was there.

"Uncle Xia is here," said Mama when I walked inside the door. "We've been waiting for you to have supper,"

The word "we" sounded like a curse to my ears. How could it have come from Mama? All of sudden I was a guest in my own home, and he became a member of the family. I retreated to the outside.

The wind rose, blowing all the way from the fallen gate to where I was sitting on our doorstep. Uncle Xia had lived under that gate. The gate was gone, but he was back. What I saw that night many years ago suddenly reappeared: the quiet yard, the approaching figures, their moonlit faces, and murmured goodbyes.

Mama had tried to prepare me for this. Now I knew why she brought up Uncle Xia the other day.

"Remember Uncle Xia? He used to be an art teacher," said she, getting ready to go to bed. "He was sent to a labor camp for keeping an unfinished wood carving of the blue-sky-white-sun flag. After that, he did folk art. Since the Cultural Revolution, he has been doing Chairman Mao's portraits."

Already in bed, I didn't really pay attention to what Mama said about Uncle Xia. What kept me thinking was that a national flag today could be considered as a piece of criminal evidence tomorrow. The blue-sky-white-sun flag had been the national flag for years, but overnight, owning one made Uncle Xia a counterrevolutionary. Why couldn't the nation have a flag representing all its people all the time?

Someone came behind me. It was Uncle Xia, who sat down next to me on the doorstep. Rubbing his hands, he started to tell me not to hurt myself while doing kicks and punches. There was no question that Mama had been filling him in about me.

"I know a *wushu* teacher," said Uncle Xia. "He practices with his students every morning. You just need to get there early."

Uncle Xua took out his glasses from the pocket, wiped them against his shirt, and put them on, while I found myself start to like him.

What was early? I took it as going to the morning self-study at school. I got up when Mama stepped out to go to work and shut the door behind her. By the time I reached the grove near the northern city wall, the eastern horizon was just turning orange red. As I wondered if I was in the right place, banging could be heard nearby. A teenage boy, stripped to his waist, was punching on the trunk of a tree.

"Where is the *wushu* teacher?" asked I when he stopped to retie his cloth belt.

"The *wushu* teacher? Too late," mumbled he through his nose without turning his head toward me.

The next morning, I got up when Mama was still having breakfast at the table. Minutes after Mama left, I raced my way out. Along one side of the grove, under a fish belly white sky, stood a dozen of teenage boys, each in a different pose while doing a different routine.

"Can I join?" asked I, going over to the nearest one.

"You? Talk to our *wushu* teacher," said he, throwing a leg with such force that my hair was flying up.

"Where is he?" asked I, looking around.

"He has left, you're too late," said he in a haughty voice.

"No girls," complained I when Mama returned from work and wanted to know how my morning went.

"They're good boys, students from the opera school. Did you meet the *wushu* teacher," asked Mama.

"No, too late," said I.

"I say, leave home before me tomorrow," urged Mama.

There he was. The *wushu* teacher sat in a cross-legged position with his students lined up behind him in a semicircle. With a roar, he tossed himself up in the air and landed in the same cross-legged position at exactly the same spot as if he hadn't moved at all. As soon as he finished a series of such moves, his students gave him a round of applause. He was really good. He could move as quickly as lighting and sat as still as a rock.

"Want to learn *wushu*?" asked the *wushu* teacher, looking at me.

"Yes," shouted I, keeping my legs together and my back as straight as I could, which I later learned was a legs-together stance.

"What's in your hand? Don't eat before you come and while you are here. It's your will that makes you strong, not food. Eat only what's necessary. Keep your body light."

At his words, I swallowed what was in my mouth and threw away what was in my right hand before showing him a move I had worked on. Standing with my feet apart, I lowered my buttocks like I was trying to sit. Then I froze with my knees bent at a straight angle and my elbows held tight against either side of my torso. It lasted not just seconds but close to two minutes. If the *wushu* teacher hadn't told me to stop, I would have kept going.

"Impressive, you can hold a horse stance for so long," praised the *wushu* teacher.

"A horse stance?" said I, having never heard something like that.

"The move you just did is a horse stance. Need more practice but I see your determination," explained the *wushu* teacher.

"Yes, my determination," said I.

"Join us," declared he while all his students moved closer, clapping their hands. Even though they were already very good at *wushu*, they welcomed me as one of them. I started to bow, not only to the *wushu* teacher but to each of his students.

No way could I do what they were doing. In awe I watched them swinging their arms around in a dazzling speed, jumping up high in the air, and somersaulting faster than I could have imagined. I doubted if I would ever be able to do a move or two of that high quality, but I was determined to try.

"Let's focus on the two stances you did earlier," said the *wushu* teacher who came to me after his students started to practice on their own.

"One is the horse stance. What is the other one?" asked I.

"The other one, a legs-together stance," explained the *wushu* teacher, standing straight with his two legs tightly against each other.

After watching me do the two stances separately several times, he told me to combine the two into one.

"Don't hesitate between the two stances. To be quick and forceful, you must build your strength," said he before doing a combination himself.

"How to build my strength?" asked I again, feeling stupid.

"Do this exercise over and over again to strengthen your legs and core," said he, squatting down before standing back up.

"As many as you can, gradually add more," said the *wushu* teacher, starting to lie down on his back. "Here is another exercise. First lie down, then lift your lower behind."

"Lie down, then lift," repeated I, following his example.

"Bend your knees, place your feet on the ground, then lift," coached the *wushu* teacher.

When Mama came home that evening, I was in a squatting position near the table with my hands holding onto a stool before me. Nor that the *wushu* teacher had told me to use a stool to get up, but that I no longer could after doing it for almost an hour.

"What are you doing? What's in this?" asked Mama, patting on the bulgy bag tied above my right knee.

"Sand, I got from there," panted I, pointing at the shallow crater at the base of the backwall.

The first thing I did when I returned_home after my *wushu* lesson was to cut off the long sleeves of an old overshirt I had. I stitched up the end of one sleeve and patched a hole at its elbow before doing the same with the other sleeve. Then two sleeves were turned into two sandbags. The *wushu* teacher didn't instruct me to use sandbags. I just wanted to after seeing one of his students have at least four sandbags on his legs.

With a sandbag tied below each knee, I did one hour of pushing up my lower back. Once moving this sandbag and that sandbag from below this knee and that knee to above this knee and that knee, I started to squat.

"Only half a *wowotou?* Not enough," mused Mama, seeing me not eat the other half.

"Enough, my *wushu* teacher never eats supper," lied I without blinking.

"Hard to believe," chuckled Mama, coming over with a bowl of soup.

"No soup, I just need some boiled water," said I, getting up and taking the bowl back to the outer room.

"That soup is boiled water with one green leave and one drop of soy sauce," teased Mama to my back.

Even though Mama kept saying it was unnecessary, I still tossed aside every piece of bedding on my bed before lying down that night. I even tucked two broken bricks under my pillow.

CHAPTER 60

"You should stay, the government policy says one child stays," said Mama, sitting down at the table, on which the oil lamp flickered next to a bowl of soup.

"I'm told that policy doesn't apply to a *heiwulei*," said I.

I had no idea why Mama brought it up again. Maybe because not many days were left before I had to leave for the third brigade of the Red Star Commune. But how could I blame Mama for wanting me to stay home? She hadn't seen the other two of her three children for years. A letter from either my brother in Heilongjiang Construction Corps or my sister in Xinjiang Construction Corps before the Lunar New Year was all she got. He or she was always fine as his or her letter would say, and Mama was always fine in her letter to either of them. It had been seven or eight years since my brother and sister left. How had they really been doing? Did they know what Mama had been going through? They didn't. Had Mama told either that our father had died? Of course she hadn't. It didn't do any good to let them know what had been going on at home.

Mama got up and went to the outer room, the oil lamp in one hand and the empty bowl in the other. She returned with only the oil lamp, which she placed on the table again before opening the small table drawer. With a piece of paper and a pen laid before her, Mama said she needed to write a letter. A letter to whom?

"I went to see your class teacher after work, she told me to write a letter to the school," said Mama, twisting off the cap of the pen.

I turned around, went to the back corner, and fell onto my bed. I don't want to think where I was going anymore. I could do nothing and nothing could I do, about where I was going. If I had to go to the Red Star People's Commune, I would go. Not that I was a pessimist, but that I was just being realistic. I didn't want to keep chasing after wind. I had tried, and I had tried hard. Just like I had stopped trying to become a member of the Youth League, I had decided to stop trying not to go to the Red Star People's Commune. I was preparing to go there, live there, and die there.

For a while only a couple of crickets were chirping. Then the table creaked, and Mama came over.

"You've been quiet. Tell me what's on your mind," asked she in a tired voice.

"It's too hard, I see no end to it," mumbled I, lying on my back with my legs raised and extended, which the *wushu* teacher said would strengthen the belly area as well as the thighs.

"True," said Mama, a shadow before my bed.

"I've tried very hard," mumbled I again, dropping my legs to the bed and raising them again.

"I know you have. I cannot explain why it's like this, but keep trying. At the end, you can at lease say you have tried or have tried your best," said Mama, bending over to see my eyes. I could feel her but couldn't see her eyes. Probably she couldn't see mine either. Behind her the oil lamp on the table glimmered as if from a faraway planet. Since a power outage started days ago, nights had turned darker.

Mama asked me to give her letter to someone in charge at school, so I gave it to the political counselor, who was more in charge of me than any other school official and even Chairman Mao as far as I was concerned. Chairman Mao instructed all the youths to go to the countryside but didn't say I had to go even though I was the only child left home.

"You must go. Why didn't you tell your mother that?" scolded the political counselor after taking a glance at the letter.

"I did. My mother doesn't understand. She doesn't understand why the one child stay policy doesn't apply to me," said I.

"Why? Your mother is *heiwulei*, both your parents are *heiwulei*. As a result, you're *heiwulei*. That's why," said the political counselor in a raised voice, flapping the letter in his hand.

"My brother is in Heilongjiang, my sister in Xinjiang. If I go, my mother won't have anyone at home with her," said I, basically repeating what Mama wrote in the letter.

"That's her problem," said the political counselor, dropping the letter on his desk and picking up a newspaper.

For a moment I thought about telling him that my father had died, which might soften his heart a little bit. But I didn't. A *heiwulei* was a class enemy. He was supposed to hate someone like me. The more hostility he showed towards me, the better a revolutionary comrade he was. Besides, I myself never wanted pity. Mama didn't want it either. What we wanted was fairness.

Not only didn't I tell the political counselor about my father's death, but I also hadn't told anyone else since Mama told me. No one else knew. As long as no one else knew, I still had my father. I needed to feel I had both parents.

CHAPTER 61

Off a cracked pavement and alongside a stretch of old houses and low sheds sat *Ganbulou*, an apartment building for municipal cadres. Fangfang lived on the first floor in the section for those working for the Bureau of Education.

"Just one room," she would fire off when she was teased for having moved into a four-story high-rise. "One toilet for the entire floor, it never works."

Through a cluttered entrance on the eastern side, I maneuvered into a cluttered hallway. Following the sound of running water, I came to a washroom where a woman was rinsing clothes before a concrete trough. Nearby was a toilet with an out of use sign hanging on the half-hinged door.

"Fangfang, where Fangfang lives?" shouted I for her to hear me.

"Fangfang? I know, there," she shouted back, throwing her right hand forward.

As I approached a door with beehive briquettes stacked high on either side, Fangfang emerged from another door, swinging an aluminum basin in her hand.

"You, it's you! I just need to get some water," said she.

"Can we go together?" asked I.

"Go together, go where?" asked Fangfang like she had no idea what I was talking about.

"The Red Star People's Commune. We don't have many days left before the deadline," said I.

"That's a poor commune far from home. I'm not going there," said Fangfang, looking aside at a corner where a man was brushing red paint on a wooden wardrobe that was taller than a door.

"You can stay?" asked I, surprised that she didn't have to go in spite of having a younger brother.

"Not that I can stay. I go to a nearby farm," said Fangfang in a lower voice.

"Which nearby farm?" wondered I.

"Don't tell anyone, the farm affiliated with the Bureau of Education," said Fangfang. "The cadre in charge there asked us for a wardrobe. He didn't ask. He just kept telling my father about his daughter who was getting married and wanted a red wardrobe as her dowry. We don't have a wardrobe but are making one for his daughter."

"Is anyone in our class going to the Red Star People's Commune?" asked I, hoping at least a girl classmate would.

"I don't know. I've heard that several have gone to villages where they have relatives. If you have a relative who is a carder in charge in a village, you don't need to worry about anything. You'll be out of there before you know it," declared Fangfang, walking me to the entrance through which I had come. "I don't have a relative like that. My father works at the Bureau of Education, so I'm going to its affiliated farm."

I didn't know how I got home that afternoon. Fangfang had been the only one I thought I could go to the Red Star People's Commune with. "Not an enemy," said she to me when we were assigned to sit at the same desk this last semester. I had been thinking about getting on a long-distance bus together with her and walking all the forty *li* to the third brigade together with her. Together we would eat, sleep, and toil in the fields. Who else would go there with me? Even if a girl classmate was going there, would she be willing to go with someone like me? It was a fact that few were willing to take the risk of hanging out with a *heiwulei*.

Uncle Xia returned. He laid Uncle Xu's bicycle down at the base of the sidewall and slowly made his way across the yard to our door, with his canvas bag still strapped to his back but empty. Mama handed him a washcloth she just wrung out of the washbasin. With it he rubbed his face and neck until they turned red.

Uncle Xia's canvas bag was full when he came in the morning. After he took everything out, on the table were three bottles of Zhuyieqing liquor, two cartons of Zhonghua cigarettes, and two mounted ink paintings.

"My own paintings, I didn't buy them," said Uncle Xia to Mama

"Here," said Mama, adding another carton of cigarettes to the table.

"Peony cigarettes, they're harder to get," murmured Uncle Xia, picking up the carton.

"Did I give you enough money?" asked Mama, to which Uncle Xia nodded.

Through the open window Mama asked to borrow Uncle Xu's bicycle. No sooner did Uncle Xu bring it outside than Uncle Xia got on and rode away with a bulging canvas bag strapped to his back

He was on his way to the first brigade of the East Suburb People's Commune, where he had done a Chairman Mao's portrait and knew its accountant as he said. Twenty-five *li* away, the brigade was further than the farm affiliated with the Bureau of Education but much closer than the third brigade of the Red Star People's Commune, which was one hundred forty *li* away

"Didn't go well?" asked Mama, pulling over a stool and sitting down next to Uncle Xia at the table.

"... at first he said no problems," mumbled Uncle Xia after a long sigh.

"He changed his mind?" asked a surprised Mama.

"Not that. He asked for more information," explained Uncle Xia. "I told him she had the best grades in her class. He said he didn't care about grades, he just had to know the family background. He said it couldn't be good. He asked if she was the child of someone like myself, someone who was a *heiwulei* and once was or still is in prison or a labor camp. What did I say to that? I had no words."

"Did he take the gifts?" asked Mama.

"He did. He said he liked them. He even smoked a Zhonghua cigarette while I was there. But he said he just couldn't let a *heiwulei* join his brigade," continued Uncle Xia. "He said he would be in big trouble if he did. Their brigade has only *hongwulei* students."

"A child is a child, what *heiwulei*? She is a good child," cried Mama.

"Agree," said Uncle Xia.

"Who's the brigade head? How can an accountant make all the decisions?" asked Mama.

"He has the ear of the brigade head. When you are illiterate, you have to rely on someone who isn't, like an accountant," explained Uncle Xia.

"It's bribery, not right," said I, punching into the air with one fist at a time.

"Not right, I know it's not right, but that's the way it has been. Even gifts don't help us," complained Mama.

"Agree," said Uncle Xia again, staring at the wall next to the window, where a poster showed Chairman Mao in a green army uniform waving against the backdrop of a rising sun.

Just the other day, two cadres from the residential committee came. While one of them put up the poster, the other read me several quotations from the red treasure book he brought with himself.

"My work," said Uncle Xia, stepping closer to the poster. "It's my work. Let me see, the forty-ninth."

"The forty-ninth? Remember so well," said Mama, coming over.

"Here," said Uncle Xia, pointing to the lower right corner of the poster, where hardly visible was a number.

"How many have you done so far?" asked Mama, patting him on the shoulder.

"One hundred fifty-two, far from forty-six thousand," said Uncle Xia.

Forty-six thousand was a huge number, I thought to myself even without knowing what that number actually meant. I would find out.

After supper, Mama and Uncle Xia followed each other outside, where they sat on the doorstep and talked. I couldn't hear them, but I knew they were talking about me. Mama was worried. She wasn't just worried about me leaving home; she was also worried sick about me being a *heiwulei* away from home.

Near my bed, I was working on my *wushu* again, the fourth time that day. Since I would leave for the Red Star People's Commune soon, I had stopped seeing the *wushu* teacher in the morning. But I continued with practicing what I had learned from him four times a day even though I knew *wushu* wouldn't really help me much in defending myself. But it was at least something I could do. If I could, I would. Everything else wasn't up to me.

How bad could the third brigade of the Red Star People's Commune be? Would the peasants there hate me as they did Liu Wencai, the evilest landlord from Sichuan. The exhibition about him was an educational site on class enemies, which showed how he had enriched himself by exploiting poor peasants. Liu Wencai had been long dead. It wasn't clear though, whether he had been beaten to death or executed. If he had had children, were they still alive or had been beaten to death or executed? If they still lived, they were *heiwulei* too, like me. Also, would the peasants in the third brigade hate me as they did Huang Shiren, another evilest landlord, but in the movie, *the White-Haired Girl*? Even though having seen that movie many times, I still wasn't sure how Huang Shiren died. Probably he was beaten to death because at the end of the movie he was surrounded by an angry crowd of poor peasants. If he had surviving children, they got to be *heiwulei* too.

Hopefully the third brigade of the Red Star People's Commune would be like the brigades I had been to during my middle to high school years. I was just one of the many students sent there to do farmwork. Not one brigade cadre did I get to meet, and nothing did any of the families I was assigned to know about me, which was probably the reason I was still alive.

After Uncle Xia left, Mama came inside and latched the front door.

"I'm worried, really worried," moaned Mama, switching on the light.

"Don't worry," hummed I.

"Your Uncle Xia was telling me about his two cousins. It happened a couple of years ago, but who knows? With so much hatred and violence, it can happen anytime," continued Mama.

"What happened to them?" asked I.

"They were beaten to death before dumped in a river. They didn't do anything, they were class enemies because of their father," cried Mama with her hands covering her face.

It could happen to me too. If someone wanted me dead, I would be dead. There wouldn't be a murderous criminal. Instead, there would be a hero for getting rid of a *heiwulei* or a class enemy. I was lucky that it hadn't happened to me so far.

I had no way of knowing if the Red Star People's Commune had a cadre who wanted me dead. I just hoped it didn't.

"I'll be fine," said I to Mama when she came over to me.

"I have something to tell you, Uncle Xia is going with you," said Mama, patting me on the back.

"He's going to the Red Star People's Commune with me?" asked I, not sure what Mama was saying.

"He paints the best Chairman Mao's portraits," said Mama, turning to look at the poster next to the window. "He's asking to go to the Red Star People's Commune to paint Chairman Mao, you two can go there together."

"He plans to paint forty-six thousand," remembered I.

"That's what he says. He thinks about that number all the time," said Mama. "Impossible to paint that many. Maybe just four hundred sixty."

"What do these numbers mean? What's going on?" asked I, curious about how one number was related to the other.

"Chairman Mao once said it was no big deal for the First Emperor Qin to have buried alive four hundred sixty scholars. Why? Because he himself had buried alive one hundred times as many," explained Mama.

"One hundred times as many? When did he say that?" asked I.

"...1958," said Mama after a pause.

"Since 1958 many more have been killed," said I, feeling certain about what I just said.

"Many more, your Uncle Xia says that too," said Mama with her eyes turning tearful again. "He paints Chairman Mao to remember them. He says it's the only way."

I stepped closer to the poster on the wall. A smiling Chairman Mao was still waving but this time like having just won a killing contest over the First Emperor Qin. That mole on his chin appeared no longer benign.

CHAPTER 62

"See that, we are here," said Uncle Xia, pointing at the gate ahead, on top of which a newly-painted red star shone against an overcast sky.

The closer we got to the gate, the stronger a foul odor became. Uncles Xia looked around and even stepped to the roadside to see if there was a manure pit.

Not until we almost reached the gate did I notice an on-going struggle session in a nearby corner. It wasn't really a struggle session since it was so quiet. It was indeed a struggle session, for there were those on their knees, each holding a placard. They were covered in manure. What had been in the buckets next to them had been emptied onto them, turning them into manure.

"Who are they?" asked Uncle Xia, handing a Daqianmen cigarette to the man sitting at the gate.

"Who are they? *Heiwulei*, we just had a struggle session. It lasted only two hours, so they were ordered to stay here for another two hours." said the man, the cigarette in his mouth.

"Parents and their children?" asked Uncle Xia, noticing some youngsters among the adults.

"They're children and grandchildren. Parents died long time ago. You must know, few landlords lived through the land reform.

Here are their children and grandchildren," chatted the man after lighting up the cigarette. "To be honest, many landlords weren't that bad. My father was a poor peasant. His landlord, he says, treated him well. He has refused to come to any struggle session so far. Are you looking for someone? I'm the gatekeeper here, ask me."

"The cadre in charge of propaganda," said Uncle Xia.

"He went home after the struggle session. The cadre in charge of the Revolutionary Committee is still here. There, his office," said the gatekeep, aiming the cigarette at an open door inside the gate.

"My letter of introduction," said Uncle Xia, handing over the envelope he had taken out of his canvas bag.

"My surname is Zhao, call me Old Zhao. Let me see, from the county propaganda department," said Old Zhao, looking at the letterhead.

"I'm here to paint Chairman Mao for your commune. This new campaign is for Chairman Mao to be everywhere," explained Uncle Xia.

"I knew, I knew. Chairman Mao is our great leader, his great images must be everywhere," enthused Old Zhao.

"How about tomorrow? I can start tomorrow," suggested Uncle Xia, patting on the aluminum water bottle he had brought with him

"We want large murals that can be seen in distance. Large murals, you do them, don't you?" asked Old Zhao, his eyes fixated on Uncles Xia.

"I do," replied Uncle Xia without any hesitation.

"We want two here, one on that gable wall and one outside the gate. Our commune has twelve brigades, we want one for every brigade. Our commune is to have fourteen murals all together," said Old Zhao, rubbing his hands in excitement.

"All together fourteen murals, no problem. Here my…daughter," introduced Uncle Xia, looking at me.

"Your daughter? Taller than you," said Old Zhao, stepping back in surprise.

"Not my biological daughter," added Uncle Xia with a shy grin. "She just graduated from high school and is assigned to the third brigade of your commune."

"The third brigade, let me see," said Old Zhao, turning to the table behind him and starting to look through some papers. "Here, forty-eight students from this one class. Forty-eight students, every brigade gets four students. Noone else has arrived, she is the first one. What's her name?"

My heart started to beat fast. On that paper Lao Zhao was looking at, right after my name, age, and gender was my *heiwulei* family background. Sooner did he see my name than he would know I was a *heiwulei.* What was he going to do? Although he didn't appear hateful, I held my fists and adjusted the way I stood.

"Here, her name… family background counterrevolutionary, *heiwulei,*" read Old Zhao.

"Her father is not a counterrevolutionary, she is not a *heiwulei,* just a child. She doesn't even know what counterrevolutionary means. Who knows what that word means? Do you know? Her father didn't do anything. he just said something, he said that landlords could have helped with the land reform," went off Uncle Xia, defending my father and me like no one else had.

"I know, but it's the policy. I don't decide policies, I just follow them. If I didn't, I wouldn't be here," explained Old Zhao.

"A child needs something to live for," continued Uncle Xia. "No one shouldn't take that away from a child."

"I know, I know, let her stay with you. Helping you paint

Chairman Mao is also work, the most important work. I'll tell the third brigade about it," said Old Zhao, staring at Uncle Xia again. "You resemble someone."

"Resemble someone? I've heard that many times," chuckled Uncle Xia, scratching his chin.

"Here is a question, your introduction letter says you were in a labor camp. Why were you there?" asked Old Zhao, tilting his head a little bit.

"Why? I didn't throw away an old national flag I had made as an art student," said Uncle Xia.

"The blue-sky-white-sun flag," added Old Zhao wryly.

"The national flag today, criminal evidence tomorrow," said Uncle Xiao,

"Well, you can always paint our great leader Chairman Mao. As long as you keep painting Chairman Mao, you're fine," assured Old Zhao, signaling for Uncle Xia and me to follow him.

On the other side of the yard was a building that had three doors. Old Zhao pushed the middle one open and led Uncle Xia and me into a small empty room with a dirt floor. To the side was another door, which creaked ajar by itself as Uncle Xia turned toward it, showing a smaller empty room also with a dirt floor.

"When it's too late after a meeting, some brigade cadres sleep here," said Old Zhao, giving a lump of straw on the floor a kick. "Our commune is the poorest in the county, we don't have what you have in a city."

"Don't say that, everywhere is the same," said Uncle Xia while helping me get my quilt pack off my back.

"Well, you two do what you need to do. I'll be back later with something to eat," said Old Zhao before hastening out.

"Where is my flashlight? It's for you," mumbled Uncle Xia,

turning his two canvas bags upside down and inside out. Only when he unrolled his quilt pack, did he find his flashlight wrapped up in an oilcloth together with two candles. He switched it on and off twice before handing it to me.

"Your room, let me fix this door first. Are you ok with sleeping on the floor?" asked Uncle Xia, fiddling with the latch on the door to the smaller room.

"Of course," said I as dry straw on the dirt floor crackled under my feet.

"I want you to feel safe," said Uncle Xia, tightening the latch with a screwdriver.

A young boy came running, carrying a small basket. Steps behind was Old Zhao with an old kettle in one hand and two bowls in the other.

"My son," said he as the boy dropped the basked and bounced away.

Uncle Xia lit one of the two candles he had brought with him. It flickered, casting shadows just like the sun during the day and the moon at night. Three of us sat around, forming what seemed to be a small crowd on the walls.

"My, my older brother, you look like," said Old Zhao, touching the sweet potatoes in the basket to see if they were still warm.

"I'm almost fifty, how old is he?" asked Uncle Xia.

"Forty-five if alive," said Old Zhao.

"He died? When he died?" asked Uncle Xia

"More than twenty years ago, soon after he graduated from college. He and my father were thrown down a well that was then filled up with rocks. Later that day my mother hanged herself. At the time I was away in high school. Our family cook found me and brought me here, his home village. Days later I joined the PLA by using his last name," said Old Zhao before dropping two tea leaves into the kettle.

"How long were you in the army," asked Uncle Xia.

"Eleven years," said Old Zhao

"Your family cook still lives?" asked Uncle Xia.

"No, he died six years ago. The last thing he said to me was to remember my own father, a good man who didn't mistreat anyone. Sometimes I think about going back to give my father and brother a proper burial, but I know it will never happen. It isn't only about myself anymore. I have a wife and two children. I don't want them to be *heiwulei*. I know I'm not a filial son," said Old Zhao, looking up only to shut tight his welled-up eyes.

"My parents and my younger sister went to Taiwan. They moved there with the university where my father was a professor. Today I don't know anything about them. The university where I was teaching at that time decided to stay. After some years in a labor camp, here I'm," Uncle Xia, looking aside only to shut tight his welled-up eyes.

I wasn't sure why I started to think about him, a brother of mine who was the closest in age to me and who Mama miscarried the same day when my father was taken to a thought-reform camp right after the 1949 liberation. Even though it had been years since Mama told me about him, I wondered about him all the time. He could have been the same height as me and resembled our father like me. I missed him the most when I was alone and afraid. Needless to say, we could have been going through being *heiwulei* together. Before I could utter a word about him, I felt a lump in my throat. The only thing I could do was to look down and shut tight my welled-up eyes.

For a moment, none of us said anything. It was so quiet that the candle was heard breathing. Why did a manmade change have to be like this? It made no sense at all. At all it made no sense.

"Why manure is all over them? You know what I'm talking about, right?" asked Uncle Xia as if he had just woken up.

"Yes, I know. I have to do it. I'm told Chairman Mao has called for it. The cadre in charge before me was fired because he wouldn't do it," said Old Zhao, wiping his eyes.

"Does Chairman Mao say to pour manure on landlords and their kids?" asked Uncle Xia.

"Yes, in one of his poems," sputtered Old Zhao.

"Which poem? Let me think… he does, now I remember," said Uncle Xia, nodding his head.

CHAPTER 63

Old Zhao came out of his office and walked up to the mural again. Sidestepping from one end to the other, he stopped only to squat down and look at a sanguine Chairman Mao from a lower angle. Even though he had been doing it several times a day for several days since its completion, the great leader never seemed to be bothered, keeping on smiling. Instead of a green army uniform, he wore a white shirt this time.

"Chairman Mao is always looking at me," said Old Zhao, coming over to Uncle Xia, who was cleaning his paintbrushes one at a time.

"Always? You're so handsome," teased Uncle Xia.

"Serious, what's your trick?" demanded Old Zhao.

"The trick is called Mona Lisa's eyes," explained Uncle Xia.

"Whose eyes?" asked Old Zhao in disbelief.

"Mona Lisa according to my college professor," said Uncle Xia.

"Sounds like a foreign name, I don't know who that is. Just tell me how to do it," said Old Zhao.

"No problem, let's start now," said Uncle Xia, turning around to get his tool bag.

"Now? Not now. Remember the new wall I told you about? After that wall is built, do two murals, one on each side," said Old Zhao. "How about both have the same kind of eyes?"

"Sure, I'll do as you say. When is the new wall ready? I haven't had anything to do for days," said Uncle Xia.

"You'll have a lot to do. Listen, teachers, you both are going to be teachers. We don't have anyone who can teach right now. I have asked the county to let you two teach. They say it's fine as long as you don't say or do anything against the revolution. You taught before, she just graduated from high school, you two are good teachers, I'm so excited," said Old Zhao.

"Tell me more," asked Uncle Xia.

"We plan to have four classes, one class for one grade. I'm told first and sixth grades aren't necessary, so we start from second grade up to fifth grade. You two, one teaches second and third grades, the other fourth and fifth grades. Our students are older than normal elementary students, a second grader can be eight or nine years old.

"Teach two grades at the same time? How to do that?" asked Uncle Xia.

"Not sure how many are coming. Some parents don't want their kids to go to school. If one grade can get ten to fifteen students, that's a lot. How to teach two different grades at the same time? One grade here, the other grade there. You teach this grade for twenty minutes and then that grade for twenty minutes," explained Old Zhao with his right hand pointing here and there.

"Are there textbooks for arithmetic and language?" asked Uncle Xia.

"Yes, here the arithmetic textbook for fourth grade, this one for fifth grade," said Lao Zhao, handing over two crumbled textbooks. "We don't have new textbooks. These're from 1964."

"Language textbooks?" asked Uncle Xia.

"I'm told not to use old language textbooks. They're either feudal or bourgeois. Just teach Chairman Mao's quotations. You have a red treasure book, don't you?" said Old Zhao, waving for me to come closer to get the arithmetic textbooks for the second and third grades.

"Where is the school" asked I, eager to see where I would be teaching.

"Over there, follow me," said Old Zhao, leading the way to the gate.

On a stretch of lower ground off the dusty road stood a mud building with its thatched roof flapping in the wind like an oversized straw hat. Hardly did it look a school. Uncle Xia and I had passed it the day we came and then everyday afterwards. Not once did I realize it was a school.

"Come in," said Old Zhao, stepping inside before Uncle Xia and me.

Near my feet on the dirt floor lay a long stool with only two legs, and next to it was the part of the other two legs held together by a rung. I picked it up only to see the tenon of each leg had completely broken off

"Stools are used as desks here. We don't even have enough of them. Students just sit on the dirt floor with three or four of them sharing one stool as a desk," said Old Zhao.

"We need to cover up these two windows. Two windows here, two windows in the other room? Yes? I think I have enough plastic sheets to cover four windows," said Uncle Xia.

"Where is the blackboard?" asked I, not seeing one on the front wall.

"We don't have large blackboards, but there are two small

blackboards in my office. One for this room and one for that room," said Old Zhao, pushing the door in the front right corner.

"Do students have paper and pencil," asked Uncle Xia. "They have to take notes since they don't have textbooks."

"Some have, some don't. Some have been trying to learn something by themselves," said Old Zhao. "To be honest, they all belong to the first grade since there hasn't been any school for six years. I just hope they all can catch up."

"What time the school starts in the morning?" asked Uncle Xia.

"Some of them live hours away. Be flexible, start when most of them have arrived. Let them leave early in the afternoon. Some of them eat only once a day, it's when they get home after school," said Old Zhao.

"This room for second and third grades, that room for fourth and fifth grades?" asked Uncle Xia, walking toward the right corner.

As they followed each other into that room, I checked out this room that would be my classroom, not with me as a student but with me as a teacher.

I was looking around for stools when I saw a bare foot under a pile of straw. The moment I bent to touch it, a girl sat up, staring at me like no one else had.

"Cold, isn't it? Why don't you wear shoes," said I.

"No shoes," murmured she, taking a glance at my cotton-padded shoes, which, patched as they were, made me feel uneasy for the first time.

What's your name," asked I, squatting down next to her.

"*Heiwulei*," said she, removing a straw from her hair.

"It's not a name," said I, shocked that she could be so as a matter of fact.

"It is," muttered she.

"It cannot be a name," persisted I.

"I'm called that," said she, her right hand scratching the back of her right foot.

Frostbites, she had frostbites on her feet. I knew because I had them too. Not only did they itch, but they also hurt. Blisters always broke, incurring a running mess. Night after night, taking off my socks was like peeling off skin for me. I had frostbites even though I wore socks and shoes, and she wore nothing.

"Why are you here?" asked I.

"It's my classroom," said she.

"Are you a student?" asked I.

"Yes, I'm eight years old," said she, her eyes having not blinked once.

"You're my teacher."

I felt relieved that she overheard everything because it would have been so hard to say I was your teacher for the first time.

"You're here by yourself?" asked I, getting up.

"No," said she, getting up too.

"She's here with her uncle," said Old Zhao, coming out of the other room.

"Her uncle?" asked I.

"Her uncle, he makes bricks and lays bricks. We need a new wall for Chairman Mao's murals, his uncle is here to build that wall. Come with me, our kiln is over there."

Along a flattened ridge that stretched straight ahead like an arm, Old Zhao and Uncle Xiao strode up dust with the girl trotting aside me. Already she was like the younger sister I had always wanted to have.

"Your feet hurt, don't they?" asked I, holding her very cold right hand.

"No," said she, shaking her head.

"It hasn't snowed this winter. Hope it does soon" said Old Zhao, stepping off the ridge and grasping a handful of loose soil from the field.

"It's as dry as the loess plateau," said Uncle Xia, glancing around.

Right there wedged between two slopes was the commune's only kiln, more like a disheveled head with dead weeds sticking out of every crack. It was the first time I saw a kiln. Uncle Xia, who had once made a statue of Chairman Mao by using a kiln built by himself, was telling me that the opening at the base was where mud bricks went in and fired ones came out. Then I saw a man and a boy digging clay in a low-lying area to the left.

"Old Hu, come to meet the artist who does the best Chairman Mao portraits in the world! I wasn't sure if you would be here today or tomorrow until I saw your niece. What time did you get here?" asked Old Zhao as the man dropped his spade and hurried over.

"What time? It's hard to say. I have to start as early as possible, this kiln hasn't been used for years, needs some repair," said Old Hu, bending to pick up a broken brick only to throw it away.

"I know, our school starts next week. The artist teaches fourth and fifth grades, his daughter second and third grades," said Old Zhao.

"Dalong, come, come, your teacher," yelled Old Hu at the boy, who darted over to stand before Uncle Xia.

"How old?" asked Uncle Xia.

"Twelve, he should be in fifth grade. He knows many words, he has been learning them by himself," said Old Hu.

"His name is Dalong. What's her name?" asked I, patting the girl on the back.

"Her name? Xiaofeng, she knows words too," said Old Hu. "I've been worried about them. Now they can go to school."

"You brought some potatoes," said Old Zhao, seeing a basket behind a pile of broken bricks, and next to that basketful of potatoes was an old quilt tied into a bundle with a frayed straw rope.

"Our food for half a month. We got them from our brigade yesterday," said Old Hu.

CHAPTER 64

Uncle Xia stirred the aluminum pot with the ladle and then stepped outside. When he returned, he was peeling off the outmost layer of a green onion. He tore it up over the pot before adding several drops of hot pepper oil. The aroma rose, so was the warmth that gradually turned a mud-made place homey, especially on a freezing cold evening.

Spread over the dirt floor where Uncle Xia slept at night was a plastic sheet that had been our dining table. Two steps away, the fire inside the mud stove glowed like a lantern festival. Uncle Xia built that stove three days after we got here and one day after Old Zhao promised a supply of some firewood. It was smokeless. Not that it didn't have any, but that smoke went away through a hidden passage in the backwall.

Through the door to the smaller room, Xiaofeng was seen writing words on the small blackboard she had brought back from the school. She would keep writing until both sides were covered with words. Then she would wipe clean both sides and put it behind the door. Not once had she forgotten to take it with her when she left for school in the morning.

She was wearing shoes now, my old shoes. The shoes I had

inherited from my older sister but didn't get to wear for long. At Xiaofeng's age, I was already wearing the shoes my sister wore when she was eleven. For this reason, my old shoes, in spite of also my sister's old shoes, weren't that terribly old. Mama sent three pairs of my old shoes for Xiaofeng and another three pairs of my brother's old shoes for Dalong, all of them washed clean and repaired.

My room was also Xiaofeng's room now, and my straw mattress was next to her straw mattress. Not only was I her teacher, I was also her much older sister. For the first time in my life, I felt I was lucky. Even though I didn't have my father, I always had Mama. And there was Uncle Xia, who had been more than a father and more than a teacher to me.

"Back, they are back!" yelled Uncle Xia the moment he heard footsteps going to the next door. "Come here, noodles for supper."

"We have been eating your food for some time," said Old Hu, squeezing through the slightly opened door, followed by Dalong, who always went to help his uncle at the kiln after school.

"Don't say that. It's so cold, let's have some noodles," said Uncle Xia, using a ladle and a pair of chopsticks to get noodles into two dented aluminum bowls and two chipped enamel mugs. Without another bowl or mug, he would eat from the ladle as he had been ever since there were three new members in the family.

"City residents don't have much to eat either. How many *jin* of grains do you get a month?" asked Old Hu.

"How many *jin*? Twenty-nine *jin* of grains, actually grain coupons," said Uncle Xia. "With them, I get all kinds of stuff, not always flours, sometimes beans or dried sweet potatoes."

"We don't have grain coupons here. I usually get points, nine points a day by doing what the brigade asks me to do. I'm told I can get ten points a day by firing bricks for the commune," said Old Hu.

"Nine points a day, what do you get from nine points a day?" asked Uncle Xia.

"Hard to say. Sometimes I get about half a *jin* of grains with husks. For the past two months, get a *jin* of potatoes or sweet potatoes," said Old Hu.

"That's not enough," sighed Uncle Xia.

"Well, better than nothing. I like eating together like a family," said Old Hu. "I used to eat with their family, their mother is my older sister."

"Your older sister? What happened to her?" asked Uncle Xia. sitting up with his back against the wall.

"She and her husband died in a fire," said Old Hu.

"Died in a fire, an accident?" asked Uncle Xia."

"No, it's not an accident. Their father set on fire the house he had built. He chose to die with his own house, my older sister chose to die with him," said Old Hu.

"Why? Why did they choose to die?" asked Uncle Xia.

"Too much to bear. I don't know if I would be here if not for Dalong and Xiaofeng. On that day I wanted to die too," said Old Hu.

"Why? What happened?" Uncle Xia asked again.

"Their paternal grandpa didn't own any land and was given the class status of middle peasant during the land reform. When he died, he left behind only an old mud house. His only son, Dalong and Xiaofeng's father, wanted to marry my older sister in a brick house. More than four years, it took more than four years for him to build a brick house. Why it took him so long? He didn't have time, and he had to work for the brigade first. It was a small house, twice the size of this room, but it was the only brick house in our brigade."

"Which brigade?" asked Uncle Xia.

"Third brigade," said Old Hu.

"I have heard it's the poorest brigade," said Uncle Xia without mentioning me as a new brigade member there.

"It is. When you have a little more, no matter how hard you have worked for it, you become a class enemy. At a struggle session for someone else, he was suddenly declared a landlord by some Red Guards. They said he was a missed landlord," said Old Hu.

"A missed landlord? Any evidence, evidence like land deeds?" asked Uncle Xia.

"They said his brick house was their evidence. Day after day they came by his house, shouting condemnations. I lived just down the road. For the safety of his wife and children, he let them stay with me. One night, he came very distraught, saying the Red Guards had the plan to confiscate his house the next day. He said he wouldn't allow that to happen, he said he would rather burn it down. Then he asked my older sister to divorce him as soon as possible. 'You're my good wife, do it for our kids, I don't want them to be *heiwulei*. It ends with me,' cried he. I think he died for his kids, that house was only a house. He just couldn't bear his kids being *heiwulei*. Xiaofeng was only two at the time," said Old Hu while sobbing.

"Made to die," sighed Uncle Xia, wiping his eyes several times.

"The Red Guards did come. While they were trying to knock the door down, a big fire broke out inside the house. It was a big fire made of two fires, one in each room. When my older sister saw the fire, she told me to take good care of their two kids before bolting outside. The Red Guards that had gathered in front of their house were running away, but my older sister was running directly into it," said Old Hu, his face buried in his shaking hands.

Dalong put down the aluminum bowl he was holding and cried,

while Xiaofeng quietly got up and went to the smaller room, shutting the door behind her. Still, she could be heard crying.

"I never told her, it's the first time, Dalong knows a little more. Their parents are gone, but they're still called *heiwulei* and treated as *heiwulei*. A child should get twelve *jin* of grains a month but they each get only nine *jin*. After husks are removed, only seven or eight *jin* is left. How can that be enough for a growing child?" said Old Hu, who turned to give Dalong a hug.

That night I didn't sleep. I just couldn't. I had had many sleepless nights, but that night was the longest. My heart was bleeding. It hurt, and it hurt so much that I felt hardly able to breathe. What did Xiaofeng's father do wrong? He was just a middle peasant who wanted his new family to live a better life. He didn't exploit anyone. He had built that small house by himself with the bricks he had made by himself, which was why it took him more than four years. What pained me the most was that he died to save his children from being *heiwulei*. My eyes were wide-open but didn't catch a glimmer of anything in that dark windowless room. I tried my uttermost not to cry. If I did, I would certainly wake up Xiaofeng, who had been crying until she fell asleep.

Xiaofeng was eight years old, and I was sixteen on that cold winter night in the first month of 1973. We had been *heiwulei*, and we still were. But we had been getting up morning after morning. Later that morning, we would get up again the moment Uncle Xia was heard getting up. We would have a full day ahead of us, doing what we could.

Printed in the United States
by Baker & Taylor Publisher Services